THE
Best
OF THEM

MORE FROM KELLY

The Surfside Beach Series

The Tentative Knock (Book 1)

Another at the Table (Christmas Novella)

Run This Way (Book 2)

Practically Family (Book 3)

Another Fifth of July (4th of July Novella)

Non-fiction

Swerve: When Life Throws Curves, But God Said Live

Anthology:

Riptide: Stormy Stories of the Grand Strand

KELLY CAPRIOTTI BURTON

THE Best of THEM

SURFSIDE BEACH BOOK 4

First Edition, 2026

This is a work of fiction. Names, characters, organizations, places, events, and incidents are either products of the author's imagination or are used fictitiously.

Published by Green Ferns Publishing House
Myrtle Beach, South Carolina
www.greenfernspress.com

Cover and author photos by Anna Williams | 963&Co

Interior design by Nora Smith

ISBN: 979-8-9996047-5-0

For proof that we are never done meeting all the people we are going to love,

and in soul-level appreciation of Saturday Nights,

this is dedicated to my age gap besties, Betty Jane and Gregory Batthew.

PROLOGUE

*L*eave it to Julie to become a bridezilla on the day of her actual wedding.

Paul tried to be amused rather than irritated. He looked around his daughter Julie's apartment, which seemed eerily quiet. Julie was in the bedroom with her older sister Danielle and her twin Katy. No one else was invited or allowed, which was probably why Paul felt particularly alone. He realized as he was scanning the room that he was not only wishing Jessie was there, but perhaps even more so, wishing for Leah.

Yes. It was Leah, his first wife, mother of his three girls, who should have been there. She shared Julie's calmness, bordering on stoicism during occasions that sent the other females in his life all aflutter, bordering on insanity.

Danielle's wedding day had been the stuff of *Southern Living*, with seven bridesmaids, two flower girls, two preachers, an event tent, a horse, and a catering bill he had paid off around the time the first grandbaby was born. Neither Danielle or her mama had responded kindly when he suggested naming the new baby Shenandoah after the wedding palomino.

1

Katy, the youngest and the wildest, would probably get married while jumping out of an airplane, if she ever settled down long enough to fall for someone.

Julie had fallen for Robin, who was unafraid of her. He handled Julie's tough questions, occasionally harsh criticisms, and sometimes impossibly high standards, and he did so with a wry, adoring smile on his face. Julie's long list of former loves had either turned mean or gotten swatted away by her. Robin was stalwart enough to handle her energy without matching it or squashing it. *Godspeed, Robin.*

But that energy was off that day. His middle daughter, the elder twin by minutes and emotional lightyears, had been for the first time in her life almost giddy, during all the weeks leading up to the wedding. Paul should have known she would crash, that she would have to muddle through the muck of their family's now eternal complication: everything was wonderful, except that Leah wasn't there.

Two and a half years before, he had stood by his best friend's side in a hospital office, one of those glorified cubicles in the emergency department where they brought a person to tell her that her life as she knew it – and someone else's life in totality – was over.

Paul had been thinking absurd thoughts as the scene unfolded. Did Jessie know she was his best friend? They'd worked together for years, planning, writing, publishing curriculum. It was work that swung between creative and tedious. Jessie never seemed to mind, so even when he was bored of it, he kept going, to see her.

At the time, he had one grandson. That was the other joy in his life. Their daughters were adults, independent. Danielle was a married mother, and the twins were doing their things. Leah was embracing some sort of scripted Southern woman life: easily lording over their property management business, running thirty miles a week, lunching with friends, and appointing herself director of their grandson Christian's cultural development. She took him to the library, to plays, to Charleston, and cooked with him, painted with him, dressed him up. Being a grandmother seemed to awaken some sort of sparkle in her that hadn't existed before.

Probably because she was too busy making sure the girls were fine and he didn't relapse. Who had time to be sparkly?

Paul enjoyed her post-menopausal coming of age. She had more patience for him then. He hadn't always been a good husband, but he tried to be a good friend, a reliable partner.

The contrast was stark. Jessie and her sister Maggie constantly told him he was a Good Man– emphasis theirs– and practically nominated him for sainthood on the husband front.

But Leah hadn't gotten that version of him. And then she died.

The evening it happened, two and a half years ago, Jessie had gotten the news first. Randall had had what appeared to be a massive heart attack while driving his car. At that time, they didn't know if that or the ensuing accident had killed him. He had veered off the road, hitting an embankment, and the car turned over.

Like a typical scene in the movies, Jessie had almost collapsed at the realization of it. She had initially refused to sit, as if doing so would seal her husband's fate. Paul was ready to catch her. In the moment, it hadn't mattered how his instinct was always to treasure the short embraces they would share as friends, how he resisted the temptation to kiss the top of her head and smell her hair. It only mattered that he caught her and held on, as long as she needed him to, not as long as he wanted to.

He couldn't remember, how long that embrace had lasted. He could recall that she'd settled into a chair while he stood behind her, that his intent had been to be her rock and process all the administrative things that would bog her down and probably escape her in the midst of the worst, most surreal, most nightmarish moments of her life. But then his own phone rang, and it was the hospital's number, and his instinct to protect Jessie had been replaced by another instinct he couldn't name.

So he stepped away without a word, and his own worst moments began. There was no one to catch him, so he didn't sway. He didn't cry. He didn't even tell Jessie at first, and he couldn't remember now how she found out or what they said to each other, whether he sat next to her; he couldn't remember who escorted the two of them to a whole separate room, where their kids would converge and what was actually the worst part would begin: watching his daughters realize their mama was gone.

That was the real nightmare. He grieved his wife, of course. They'd made a life, a better life than he could have ever imagined as a kid whose dad knocked him around, whose mom let it go on, whose brother abandoned him, as a man who fought his way out of that tidal wave but only by using a bottle as his oar and anchor for decades.

But the prevailing panic, underneath the shockwaves that coursed through him all that night and for a blurry period after, was that his daughters were getting robbed of the life they should have had with their mom, of girls' weekends and weddings and delivery rooms and babysitting and advice. What good would he be to them without Leah? He didn't know how to be a family man without her.

It felt like a lifetime later as he sat on Julie's beloved couch, purchased in Arizona when she'd lived there for a while out of pure spite, and pretended to flip through the current issue of *Running World*. He wondered how Robin was doing over at his parents' house, if his mama was fussing, if his sisters were teasing, and very likely, if he and his dad were having a beer and trying to subdue them all. He wondered if Jessie was distracting herself while helping Danielle's husband Matt with the kids. Christian would be fine, even if a tux was a big order for a six-year-old. Vivi was a toddler and would probably be a handful, but she loved her off-white flower girl dress, a miniature version of her Aunt Julie's.

Paul smiled to himself, thinking of her. He wondered if she would scatter her pedals down the aisle of the church, if she would fling them at her brother or if she would simply run to the back row, where she knew that Mr. Bohannon kept his basket of lollipops every Sunday. He wondered if Jessie had managed to get some curls in Vivi's hair or maybe settled for two of those plain little braids he loved so much. And he thanked God that Danielle had opened her heart to his second wife— giving her kids the gift of a grandma because Leah had sure loved being one —and he didn't want them to miss out on having that role fulfilled, that love given.

He almost felt guilty for how much he loved Jessie.

He also felt guilty today, for how much he missed Leah.

That was just how life was for them, and that was probably why Julie was locked in her room, where he could hear Katy yelling a little, where Danielle was probably crying out of frustration, where Julie likely looked perfectly stunning but was repainting her face entirely rather than admitting she missed her mama. He wasn't sure what would happen if he walked down the short hallway and insisted they let him in. He wasn't going to try. One thing that life had constantly reminded him of—whether he was hiding from his father or hiding his Crown in his desk in the principal's office, or hiding his truth from Leah or Jess—was that he had a place, and he was better off staying in it. He wouldn't force his way in with Julie. He would wait and observe, and then—

"Daddy!" Katy appeared at the living room end of the hallway, her tanned legs sticking out from a huge, fuzzy pink robe that he recognized at Leah's. Her hair was curled and piled on top of her head, *Goddess-like*. Her eyes were outlined in striking dark blue, but there had been tears. He could see it. "Julie needs you."

He smiled at his youngest. Even with her bleached-blonde hair, she looked the most like him. She was filled with a fire that he didn't recognize, but he wasn't scared of it anymore. She was grown, and the world needed fire.

She waited for him. He stood in a seamless motion, walked to her, took her hand, headed down the hall to his second daughter, his and Leah's second bride, feeling less alone, relieved to be needed.

Jessie

1

Two and a Half Years Later

I married another man.

Thinking about it that way still surprised me at times. It wasn't that Paul and I weren't living some kind of dream; it's just that a second marriage, a marriage after living a great one for over thirty-five years, love after love, love after loss, a full life after a devastating death, doesn't always compute as something that is really happening, as something that is allowed to happen.

I was standing in front of a group of around twenty women, widows and divorcees and singletons traumatized by their own bad choices or those of idiots. This was new; I had been invited by a community church in Georgetown, one where people weren't quite so legalistic on the exact type of Upstanding Christian Woman they invited to speak. *If you know, you know.* I could read their minds. A few were looking for answers as to why their lives had gone a certain way. Some were hoping I would tell them how to get where I was, because as far as they knew, I was completely happy, and life was simple and magical in every way. But most were just seeking validation that however they were attempting to move forward toward that damn new normal, it wasn't crazy, sinful, or doomed.

I couldn't promise them that. I could only give them mostly-unfiltered honesty.

"Are there complications?" I asked, a wry smile on my face. "Seems like a new one rises weekly. Second thoughts? Constantly! And third, and fourth, and so on. But doubts? Now, that's a different story."

I paused for a moment and thought of my new husband, still new though we were over two years in love. I did not once doubt my commitment to the second man I had married. Not once did I doubt that he was my best friend, a man I admired and adored and wanted completely, utterly, sometimes a bit lavishly.

"I don't doubt that choosing to live life with someone different, someone new, is not only *okay* but a great choice for me. It's a great choice for anyone who chooses it with your eyes wide open, that there will still be every part of Ecclesiastes three, a time to mourn and *all the things* (Jessie Standard Version). The doubts that creep into me are not about living this new life, but about my own ability to navigate all those complicated thoughts and circumstances because quite honestly, I doubt those will *ever* cease."

Paul was so very different than Randall, the jovial and open-hearted man I'd said "yes" to as a nineteen-year-old with a shaky sense of herself and a baby boy. He also had greatly differed from me, that unwed teen mother who grew up to be that southern mama with a big front porch, a never-ending capacity for sleepovers, and a tendency to grandly celebrate most real and made-up holidays, often with a theme dessert and a signature cocktail.

"One of the biggest doubts I navigate in my own new normal is whether our blend is sustainable," I admitted. Dear God, I barely had admitted that to myself or to my sister-friend Maggie, and here I was telling strangers. "My new husband is quiet a lot of the time. Now, I have known and worked with him for fifteen years prior to our current chapter, but I didn't realize how quiet he was, nor how quiet I am not, until we began occupying the same space outside of working hours." I allowed a moment for some knowing giggles in the room. "I am used to music and TV, the din of conversation and back-and-forth of plan synchronization, group errands, unplanned visits that turn into spontaneous meals. Paul was used to informative exchanges, solitary agendas, and stillness. I've taken time to notice and greatly appreciate the effort he's given to get used to my lifestyle, usually without complaint or mention, and this has forced me to admit just how different we are."

I thought of Paul sitting at the kitchen island sipping his tea while various members of our family fluttered and buzzed around the house, never at a low volume. Truth was, I used to apologize, to him or myself, for being *a lot*, but I didn't feel bad about it anymore. He knew what he was getting into.

"Sometimes," I told the group, "he retreats. Because we are new together, that used to make me panic, but now I just accept it. We all have different coping mechanisms for stress, and make no mistake, starting a new life with someone is *stressful*, even if it's also delightful. So, I have to remind myself that it's not me, it's him, when he retreats into solitude. While I might find relief in cooking for my family or even planning a party, he does in hitting golf balls alone or putting a few hours in at the community garden. Rather than meeting his people for coffee, he prefers it alone at Benjamin's Bakery with a book or by running a bit through our eclectic Surfside Beach streets or, thanks to me, walking on the shore. He would not have dreamed of that before we were together. I inspired him to care about the beach. I take great pride in it."

There was another amused murmur. I decided to wrap it up with another anecdote about Paul and Jacob, my youngest grandson. They'd nicknamed each other Mario and Luigi, and when things got particularly chaotic at a family event, one of them would declare, "Time to save the princess," and they'd retreat to the "cousin nook," an odd-sorta-bedroom in the middle of our house, and play video games together, silently.

It was heartwarming and hopefully, just how I liked to leave people — be it a formal gathering like this one or a few of my own family members. I wanted everyone to believe that a "new normal," though a somewhat hateful phrase in my opinion, could be just as sweet as it was hard.

As I took my place at the little table set for me to sign books (*Grace in the New Normal*. I sounded so all-knowing), I was ticking off the sweet vs. the hard. Sweet was the way Paul's eyes lit up when I suggested a dinner out at a place like Neal and Pam's, where he could keep it simple and eat a hot dog. Hard was the way he was finding excuses more often lately to miss the hustle of those family get togethers. Sweet was the way Paul read my facial expressions, body language, and silences, and always responded to me in a way to be helpful and supportive and loving. Hard was not knowing what he was thinking in his quiet moments, wherein Randall had rarely even had quiet moments.

Sweet was learning something new about each other almost every day. And hard was realizing all the things we didn't know about each other, almost every day.

A woman with a silver pixie cut and tired brown eyes sat in the chair across from me. She picked up one of my books and said, "I would love for you to sign it. I'm going to read it, but then I'll give it to my daughter."

"Oh, that's sweet," I said. "Do you want me to write her name in it, or yours?"

"Hers, I think," she replied thoughtfully. "Her name is Emma."

"Is she living the new normal, or you?" I asked it gently, but people usually wanted to talk at this point.

"Both," she said, not missing a beat.

"Oh." I was dumbfounded. I had not heard that answer before.

"My husband – her father – and her husband were in a boating accident together last year. They both died. And now she is a single mama of a three-year-old, and I . . . well, I'm getting remarried on New Year's Eve. The sweet and the hard are at odds pretty much all the time right now."

"Wow," I said. "What's *your* name?"

"Molly," she answered. "I don't expect to find a bunch of answers in your little book, but it is nice knowing I am not the only widowed woman who is crazy enough to believe in a little bit of happiness."

"Oh, Molly. One of the hardest things is reconciling what makes your heart happy and what hurts your kids, especially when it's the same thing!" I started personalizing a second book for her.

"See? That's what I mean. I appreciate that you *get* that."

"It's nice to be understood," I said. "Here. Keep one for yourself. I'm so sorry for your losses – and I hope your courage helps Emma take all the steps she needs to take to move forward. And . . . to understand you *and* herself."

A tear escaped Molly's eye and traveled down her cheek. There was a palpable heaviness between us, two strangers who understood the sweet and the hard, all the things about it that even the best writer, which I was far from, could not put into words.

"Thank you," was all she said. I met her eyes and nodded, almost grateful when she walked away.

A dozen signings and a delectable piece of ten-layer chocolate cake later, I was on my way home. Sometimes I brought Maggie with me to these events, but this night, I was grateful for the time to myself. My own words felt a little haunting to me, and I needed to listen to my songs and think my thoughts. The somber mood of Simon and Garfunkel's "The Boxer" and Zac Brown's "Colder Weather" did nothing but stoke the ick I was feeling. *Turn on Elevation Worship.* Whether that was Randall's voice or that of Jesus Himself, I wasn't sure, but I obeyed.

The music switched to raising hallelujahs and a personal favorite, turning graves into gardens. That's all we were trying to do, right? Live those ecclesiastical promises. Dance, mourn, weep, laugh, win, lose, uproot, plant. And the pair I struggled with most: speak, be silent. Paul was more silent than ever since our accident back in the summer, and I was trying to give him all the space he needed.

But sometimes, when he retreated into brevity, he stopped looking at me, which was his default, and looked past me. He would answer with terse phrases, no embellishments offered. He would stiffen at my touch. And I knew those times were not about me, but oh, did they challenge every need and inclination I had.

Paul retreated from everyone, including his kids, and might be content to stay there if someone didn't pull him out. It was a vast contrast to how I lived. I *needed* companionship and noise and physical contact, and if I ever retreated, it was either with the goal of a brief recharge, like my current ride home, or with the hopes that someone or everyone would notice and come get me.

I wasn't sure Paul believed anyone would notice his retreat.

But I always did. And unless something immovable stopped me, I planned to always chase after him.

2

"**I** cannot let anyone else see me with my pants down."

Robin walked to the doorway of the bathroom, his rinsed toothbrush still in his hand, his eyes widened at Julie's proclamation.

"I know we aren't each other's first loves, baby cakes, but I really do prefer it that way. Just so you know."

Julie shook her head at him. She was sitting against the bamboo headboard, wrapped in a huge white towel while braiding her damp hair. They had run together that morning, the usual 10K loop around Market Common, starting on Farrow, turning up 17 Biz, and going through the bike path until they were back at his store. (It was theirs now; he made her a partner a few months after they got married, but still). He noticed her stamina was taking a hit, but he knew better than to say anything. She was a bit more than three months pregnant, and he figured that eventually, the running would have to stop.

"I mean the appointment, obviously," she said. Her fingers had reached the end of her long, golden-brown hair, and she immediately unraveled all the plaits she had completed and started shaking out her locks. Robin had told her once just the week prior that she was always a thing of wonder

14

in her restlessness, but that in her current state, she was also a force that nearly scared him. Hmmm. Well, whether she was sparkling or seething, her energy crackled at an all-time high, and he could either go with it or get zapped by it. She was relieved that he stuck to the former.

"I'm sorry I can't be there," he said. She hadn't been so vocal about missing her mom since the night before their wedding, when they'd come home after the rehearsal dinner and she had a complete meltdown, wondering out loud if she should really tie the knot with someone when her parents' marriage had been such a sham. She didn't explain and hadn't mentioned it since then. And the one observation that he'd dared to utter — that her that her dad seemed more like a remarried divorcee than a widower — was also the one time thus far that she'd slept on the couch during their marriage.

"It's okay," she said softly, withholding her signature shrug. It wasn't really okay. She wanted him there, of course. But they had no backup at the store that day, and it seemed silly to close for a routine visit with no ultrasound or anything. "This is the only one. And I'm sure Dr. Masselli is just going to give me the stink-eye for the running and then send me on my way."

Robin put his hand on her shoulder. "Personally, I wouldn't mind if we both cut back a little."

She poked him in the midsection, giggling. "I don't think we should, yet. Unless we're also going to cut down on the pierogis."

He patted his hint of a belly in response and said in faux-lecture mode. "Food is not a reward for exercise, Julie."

"Maybe not, but potato dumplings fried in butter aren't necessarily fuel, either, punk."

She gave him just a hint of a smile then, and he leaned in, brushing her lips with his. He tasted like cinnamon toothpaste – the kind without fluoride and flavored with essential oils that he pretended not to like—and she found herself parting her lips and welcoming more from him than she had in days.

Robin folded himself into the sliver of bed that was next to her and kissed her again, pressing himself against as much of her as he could reach. Truth was, she had been self-conscious about the ripening of her body. She had already gained five pounds, but it looked like ten, and every bit of it was in her waistline, which she knew was the expected and proper thing; she just didn't think it would happen so fast.

What surprised her most about it, though, was that Robin couldn't seem to keep his eyes or his hands or, in the appropriate circumstances, his mouth, off of her.

She enjoyed it in this moment more than she had lately. The circumstances were perfect; they had forty-five minutes until either one of them had to leave; they both smelled good, the blinds were closed, the sheets were relatively clean, and Mellow '90s Gold was playing on the Echo.

Julie relaxed into his kisses. She exhaled as his hand ran up her bare and freshly shaved leg. And then, the song changed, and Duran Duran was singing about a rainy Thursday and a lost, ordinary world.

Immediately, the mood darkened for her. Her legs stiffened, her knees closed together, and she struggled to sit up under Robin's weight.

"Jules, what's wrong?" He had already jumped up from the bed and was studying her, not in disappointment or even bewilderment, but worry. "Did I hurt you?"

Julie darted across the room to the dresser. "Echo!" she snapped. "Stop music!" It kept playing. "Echo! Echo! Stop this God-forsaken song."

Before the Echo could respond, she had unplugged it and threw it across the room. Her face was red, and there were tears coursing down her face.

"Jules!" Robin hurried toward her, and she tried to push him away, but *damn*. His arms had now long-been the safe place she didn't know she was searching for her entire life. She let herself melt into him, but just a little. The melody of the song, that stupid, stupid song, was still bouncing around her head.

"Are you okay?" he asked, a bit feebly. Of course, he was hesitant. His second wife had turned into a pregnant whack job.

You were wacky when he married you, that ever-present voice in her head said.

Shut up, *Mama*, she silently answered.

"Yeah." She answered her husband out loud. "I just really, really hate that song."

Robin, completely unphased, hugged her and laughed. "I hate every song on this playlist," he said. She formed a scowl right into his shoulder. He was right. She should find a new default station.

Julie had no intention of explaining why she hated the song, so she pretended to be in much more of a hurry than she was. She gently but swiftly kissed his neck; they would not be picking up where they had just left off.

"I better get ready," she said. "Do you want me to bring you lunch later?"

Robin raised an eyebrow. "Just call me when you're done, and we'll see where we are. I want to know everything, anyway."

After a few more kisses, she sauntered off to the closet to don her pregnant-runner-entrepreneur uniform of black leggings, a fitted gray tank, and a lightweight half-zip, unzipped. They had reached the time of year when they would shiver in the morning and be sweating by two in the afternoon.

She slipped bare feet into her all-white On Clouds and walked to the mirror to re-braid her hair.

Robin liked two kinds of music: classic rock —the vinyl kind from the seventies — and classic country, the CD kind a la Garth Brooks and Alan Jackson. She had never been a fan of either, but she needed that nineties music — the kind her mama would blast in the car, while baking her fall pumpkin breads, and any time they ran together — out of her head.

3

"**I** saw the attorney's letter."

Leah met him in the doorway of the kitchen. She had one of those steel tumblers in her hand that was as big as she was. She was dressed in gray leggings with a matching tank, and perspiration was glistening on her neck and forehead. He guessed she was fresh from spin or Zumba, but she still smelled like her signature Marc Jacobs Daisy and not one hair was out of place.

"Oh yeah?" he answered, not really asking. When she filled a door that way, magazine glossy, statuesquely perfect, he found himself at a loss for words. She'd already figured out how he felt. She didn't need his answers any more than he needed her questions.

"What are you going to do?"

"Ignore it."

"Paul—"

"Leah."

"I know you don't want anything from them."

That was the catch. If she knew that, if she *really* knew that, why was she going to attempt to persuade him to do otherwise?

"Maybe you do," he snapped. "But I don't think you know how *much* I don't want anything from them. Not a single thing. I don't want to talk to a lawyer. I don't want to fill out a form. I don't want to hear their names, and I wish no one connected to them had our address and managed to get a letter to me."

"I understand," Leah answered, in the slow, deliberate tone that made him feel like he was on the student side of his principal's desk, being scolded for chewing gum in PE or whatever rule seemed completely non-sensical to him back in the day. "But Paul, it could mean a lot of money. We have three girls heading to college . . . "

He scoffed. They had just attended a conference with Katy's health teacher after she'd been caught in the back of the classroom blowing condoms into balloons and making salacious drawings on them.

"Well . . . " Leah rolled her eyes. "At least two."

"Darling," he said, just as deliberate in his tone, hoping he sounded more composed than he felt. "I would rather work twenty hours a day, seven days a week, to give the girls everything they could possibly think of wanting, than accept a single penny connected to my father. I need you to accept *that* . . . and move on."

At that point, Walter Jameson appeared at Leah's shoulder. His piercing, dark brown eyes bore virtual holes into his son. Paul was seven years old again, his heart accelerating as Dad finished with Charlie and headed toward him, fists clenched, muttering "worthless bastards" or some iteration.

"I don't want you to have it anyway," he seethed.

And Paul woke up.

He was sitting in the armchair by the window, a reading corner in their bedroom that they never used. It was always the back porch, the front porch, or the kitchen table, or sometimes, it was the built-in desk between the kitchen and the living room. If Paul really needed quiet, he would retreat to his desk in their shared office, and that is where he graded essays for the solitary War and Memory course he kept teaching at Coastal. But he never read in their bedroom, and though Jessie never used the chair either, she didn't let him pile any clothes or books on it. It was aesthetic. He let her get away with that nonsense even though Leah was never off the hook with it. Maybe because Leah had been ninety-percent aesthetic and ten-percent everything else. *Damn, boy.* He knew better than to tread that ground. Leah had been fine. She had every right to be who she was. Jessie was different, and that was one reason why this relationship was different, and if he hadn't liked living in a museum where he couldn't even leave a pair of shoes by the door or a magazine on the coffee table, he should have handled it then. Leah was gone now, and Jessie had her corner chair and her artisan quilts, but he could put his stuff wherever he wanted, *and* he was happy, and there was no sense or worth to compare his two marriages.

Actually, his life seemed to mostly boil down to before and after Jessie, and that was simple and also sad. He'd married her well into his sixties. His daughters were still devastated by their mother's death. Living six and a half decades with just a modicum of joy did not feel like a victorious testimony. He felt ungrateful, like his whole life he'd been waiting for Jessie and maybe didn't see the good things he'd had before then.

He was waiting for her now, while she was in the bathroom, doing all her bathroom things. One of the only ways she was similar to Leah was how she woke up and immediately got herself just a little bit together. Teeth brushed. Deodorant on. Leah would put on a full face of makeup while still in her nightgown; Jessie slept in random tank tops and tiny shorts, but she always came out of the bathroom a little glowy, her eyes framed in mascara. The only time Jessie ever lapsed in the practice was during her radiation, when her energy got so low that Paul lived in fear for weeks.

She grew more comfortable with him then. She had to. He smiled at the thought. All of their leveling up through the years had happened as a result of some kind of trauma. Their foray into a romantic relationship was kickstarted when he stepped in a hole and ended up in the ER. Their reconciliation after a brief—and horrible—time apart had happened after he had surgery and her beloved dog died. And a few weeks after their honeymoon, Jessie had been diagnosed with uterine cancer, with thankfully clean margins and relatively straightforward treatment. It had catapulted their somewhat tentative beginning to "you and me against the world" level devotion. And the previous month, when they were in a car accident together—

Well, they might still be getting over that. It had been more than a bit traumatic, getting T-boned at an intersection in Georgia, on the Fourth of July, while they were helping Sam's family prepare for their move there. Jacob and Summer, Sam's. younger two kids, had been in the backseat, and Paul had been bleeding profoundly.

Paul was trying really hard not to fixate on it. Jessie had recovered like a champ from bruised ribs, a feat she attributed to being in hot-yoga-and-boot-camp-five-days-a-week shape. He agreed but also gave credit to her pure refusal to rest for more than a day or two. She powered through and likely mended herself from sheer will. His own healing from a concussion had been frustratingly harder, which he tried to keep from Jessie, but she noticed anyway; she blamed their chaotic schedule right after the accident and not enough rest for Paul. All he could do was shake his sixty-five-year-old head, which apparently didn't bounce back as quickly as it once did.

He had headaches just about every day. His stamina was half of what it usually was, and that made his patience less than half of what it had been. He tried not to show Jessie or his girls, or her girls (including Maggie), because they were all meshed together like a lovely, very supportive but very loud sorority, and no one was safe from their helpful suggestions, sharing of Instagram reels, or margarita-infused rants.

Just the week before, it had only been Jessie and Maggie in the kitchen, and Paul, for the first time in over ten years, had been tempted by the smell of tequila. It was never his drink; he'd preferred the stiff and efficient burn of whiskey. But on that particular Taco Tuesday, the fajitas and Coke Zero weren't cutting it. His head hurt. His heart inexplicably ached. And he wanted something to lower the volume on his whole life.

So he'd gone for a late-night run, about three miles through Surfside, managing to narrowly avoid tree roots and texting drivers. Running helped, most of the time.

At the very least, it helped him hide his woes from Jessie, so he thought.

The bathroom door opened. Jessie took one step out, her tank top askew, her hair in the messiest of messy buns, but her face a little glittery. She took one look at him, cocked her head, and asked, "What in the world is wrong with you?"

Jessie

4

"What are you talking about?" Paul asked. His tone was innocent.

"Don't. Something happened. You look . . . " I didn't want to say "stricken," but that was the word, and it was not a typical expression for him, even of late when he'd been concussed and stressed and exhausted. I couldn't expect him to be transparent while I was holding back, so I shrugged and as gently as I could, said, "Honestly, love, you look a little spooked. Are you okay?"

Okay was relative. At our later stage in life, with enough offspring that something was almost always wrong with someone, I rarely even knew how to answer that question myself.

I walked over to him, in his out-of-place position in a chair we never used for sitting. He immediately took my hand while still looking into the distance, seeing something I couldn't.

"I'm fine," he said with a nod.

I knelt deftly—thank you Yoga with Emily—right next to him. He was wearing a non-descript pair of gray gym shorts, the kind he slept and did yard work in. I rested my chin on his knee, my hands automatically moving to his calf, giving him a little caress along the firm muscles.

"Conversation or cookie?" It had become code for us. I wouldn't make him talk, but I would always offer.

Paul reached down to cup my face with one hand and sighed deeply, his eyes brimming with emotions I couldn't label. "Sometimes, it sucks that you know me so well."

"Tell me about it," I answered. We agreed in honest communication before anything and then space when we needed it. Hence the safe phrase.

He shrugged. "Been having a lot of dreams about the past lately." Then he smirked. "Seems like such an old man thing."

I felt a pin-prick of understanding at his words. "We are getting . . . older. There's a lot of past."

Paul was six years older than me. It didn't matter much; Randall had been even older. But it also meant he was that much closer to mortality, save for the odds of disaster striking me first. Hopefully, we had seen our share of disasters already and would pass away peacefully while sleeping, on a hammock, on a private beach, in thirty years or so.

I stood and moved myself to the chair facing his. Our room was so pretty and cozy. There were no little kids to come in and move our stuff around, no big piles of laundry because we weren't too busy to actually keep up with our household chores, and no work overflowing from our tidy office spaces. Even our corgi, Dolly, was peaceful and orderly. Sometimes, the lack of chaos made me feel uneasy; I was so used to it that the calm and quiet actually set me on edge. Paul thrived in it, though; that is, he usually did.

"Anything in particular?" I asked.

He appeared to be studying the slate gray wall above my head. There was a canvas hanging there of my four children during a golden sunset in one of the craziest eras of my life. Sam was eighteen, Mikayla and Brittney were eleven and ten, and David was two. That season had been a polar opposite to my current one. Someone had always been needy, in trouble, sick, breaking something, fighting, crying, hungry, messing in a diaper, having a birthday, or going somewhere. Randall had always been traveling. Sam had been too busy with basketball and his job at Twister's to be much help at home, and anyway, he had been a boy. Mikayla had always tried to help, which had always made me feel guilty and inadequate. Mostly, I had been in the kinda-single-mom trenches with Maggie, who had actually been single. She'd lived a five-minute drive from me, so we would retreat to my porch a few nights a week, once her girls were home from whatever extracurriculars they attended, and David was finally asleep in my bed. We would down a bottle of cheap wine and talk nonsense until we couldn't stay awake anymore.

I never imagined I would miss those days, but the truth was, sometimes it almost physically hurt to look at that picture from one magical summer evening. Randall had been somewhere in Florida, and the kids were some-what easily wrangled for a few shots. David got absolutely covered in sand by the time we were done; he had always been my beach-loving baby. Alicia, our longsuffering photographer, had insisted I get in a few of the shots, and the best one shows David in just his diaper, Sam smiling sweetly, Brittney nearly rolling her eyes in exasperation, Mikayla looking at her baby brother in horror, and disheveled me, in some random old shirt that didn't match anyone else's, laughing my fool head off. That picture, that *outtake*, was framed in a smaller version and had stood on my bathroom counter across three houses now. It always served as a reminder that there was joy in chaos, that I could be the anchor in a mess of waves.

All that nostalgia, and Paul still hadn't answered me. I tried harder to keep my focus while I waited. It was a challenging task.

Finally, he rescued me. "Might be the head injury," he finally said. "Can't do all the stuff I normally do, so my mind wanders, my calm is disturbed. I mean, you know how this goes." Ah, yes. Physical vulnerability always brings out the best in men.

"I do," I said, still willing myself to be patient.

"So it's . . . Leah stuff. And Walter stuff. Not the best combination for me, you know?"

Since my first marriage hadn't been tense and ceremonial, nor was I abused as a child, I definitely did *not* know. But my overwhelming level of empathy served me, at least in this instance. Still, I just nodded.

"A long time after he died, I got a letter from an attorney." *Oh, boy.* This did not seem like the start of a short story. I mentally rearranged my whole morning and relaxed myself into the chair. "Through a series of escrow events and other dead relatives, I was bequeathed what turned out to be a pretty valuable piece of land just outside of Florence. I mean, it was just a few acres of fields when my great-grandfather bought it, and all that was left was a delipidated barn and an uninhabitable house. My grandfather had bought it with his active-duty money, meaning for it to be family land forever, and Walter just left it sitting there. No one could reach Charlie," (Paul's now-deceased only sibling), "and one of the cell tower companies wanted the land."

Boy howdy, did that clarify some things. My friend April had a piece of land out in Andrews that two cell companies got into a bidding war over. Let's just say that ended with a paid-off mortgage for her *and* her mama, and then some.

I kept willing myself not to ask questions. He was telling the story at his pace. And I *hated* when anyone asked me clarifying questions in the middle of a story. *I . . . am . . . getting there!*

"The thing was, Jess," Paul finally looked into my eyes instead of everywhere else. "I had thrown the letter in the trash. Read it once, saw Walter's name, and almost lit it on fire. But one of the girls had called me or something, and I just pitched it into the can under my desk. At home. Well, Leah cleaned in there, and she saw it, and she confronted me."

I let that dangle in the air for a minute. Paul's recollections of Leah to me were few and far between, and to be honest, I took them with a grain of salt. What else could I do? His late wife had been my dear friend. We hadn't been as close as Maggie and I were, or even as Paul and I were because we worked together almost every day, but I had adored Leah. Yes, she was different, truly a southern belle, more formal, more put together, and yes, less warm than I. But the more Paul characterized their marriage as cold, as businesslike, as a tad bit loveless, I checked myself not to turn her into any kind of villain. One, it was not necessary. If Randall hadn't died, I would have never fallen in love with Paul. And two, the Paul who Leah married and the one I married were two different people. My Paul was settled, mostly healed, and at peace. Her Paul had been waging a war against himself and the son-of-a-bitch father he'd emancipated himself from. He had been an alcoholic for half of their daughters' childhoods. And he had definitely kept Leah at a distance, even when she stayed with him and helped him battle a few of his demons. *Nah.* I would not paint Leah in a shady light. I absolutely would have read the letter, too, and Paul likely knew that.

As if reading my mind, which he did often, Paul continued, "I am not saying it was a big deal that she fished the damn thing out and read it. We're human. But she was relentless in her pursuit. She wanted me to call the attorney and accept the land and sell it for every penny it was worth, because we had daughters and financial obligations, and at least I would get something of value out of my shitty start in life besides moxie and alcoholism."

"Whew!" I said, not bothering to edit myself. "That is a lot, darlin'." I had no prior inkling of this story, but it sounded like it had happened early in my friendship with the Jamesons. We didn't share those types of storms from the onset. Not like the present, when we always seemed to be a few feet from the eye of a hurricane.

Paul leaned forward in his chair, an indicator of being done. "It was. And now it's nothing. So, I just need to get it all back out of my head." He stood.

And I . . . resumed my default position on all things that involved tension and my loved ones. I stood close to him, looked at him carefully, and said, "Do you? Because maybe it's there for a reason. Something unresolved, perhaps?"

"Jess," he said softly, not missing a beat and staring back with his pervading way. "It's resolved."

Did he contact the lawyer? Did he accept the land? Sell it? Put it in a trust for his daughters? Let Leah handle it? Donate it to some charity?

"You're vibrating," he murmured. He usually said that to tease me when my brain was in overdrive. There was only solemnity in his voice just then.

"I am who I am," I answered.

He rose and started to walk away. It gave me that urgent sensation that I tried so hard to quell, be it with prayer, a dram of whiskey in my tea, or the latest, a CBD seltzer—thank you to all my thirtysomething daughters for that. I wasn't ready for the conversation to be over. He didn't seem okay, and I was not okay with that. I wanted to hug him. And also, I really, really wanted to know what had happened.

"Paul . . . "

It was unfair of me. One of his conceded weaknesses was my voice saying his name. He turned.

"You don't have to tell me, but I wish you would."

He mouth turned up just a bit at the corners, though the smile didn't reach his eyes. He shrugged. "Ask Julie." And then he kept walking.

Not so many months ago, that would have been a call to arms. But Julie, Paul's middle daughter, the oldest of his twins, had gone from being my detractor to being my biggest ally in the Taking Care of (Paul) Business.

I was not going to ask her, though. She was pregnant, and that didn't make her weak or incapable (God forbid and many eyerolls), but I didn't want to bother her. And sometimes, most times, I wanted my new husband's stories firsthand.

I would wait. What happened to the property was likely inconsequential to Paul's current life. But there was a reason for a brewing storm and his disturbing dreams, and it was my self-appointed task to bring him to peace whenever I could.

5

"Mama, I was listening to Tara-Leigh Cobble, and now I'm almost to my meeting. I'll see you tonight. I've got the . . . chips and salsa."

It was the easiest and cheapest without her bringing a predictable carton of ice cream or a few two-liters of something. Brittney had been faithful to her mama's Tuesday nights now that the golden child, her oldest brother, Sam, had moved his precious youngins almost seven hours away to the north Georgia mountains. Actually, it was impressive how much Mama was holding it together since she had spent most every Tuesday of Summer's and Jacob's lives feeding them tacos and desserts, playing Uno, watching movies, and having summer sleepovers. Brittney had decided on her own to pick up the slack, and most of the time, her nephew Travis, Sam's oldest son who stayed behind to finish college at Coastal, joined them, too. She had lost touch with Travis in his latter teen years, so catching up was good, though the mind of a twenty-year-old man-child was a thing of utter *wonder* to her. Things had sure changed a lot since she was that age.

Everything is changing a lot, she reminded herself, throwing her Crosstrek into a space that wasn't flanked by other cars. Parking had never been her strong suit.

Neither is having hard conversations. *There were several on* her list that felt pretty immediate, but first, she had an easy one to tackle. Her little social media marketing company was starting to thrive, and she was very thankful that Mama and Daddy had instilled loyalty to local businesses in her early on. All those years of owners knowing their family by their name, all the extra dollars here and there for tacos that weren't from Taco Bell or coffees that weren't Dunkin' were paying off. Those proprietors were willing to take a chance on a fellow entrepreneur, someone who also loved where she lived. And if Brittney could score this account, potentially with a one-year contract, her roster would be just about full; she wouldn't need extra shifts at the Fishwalk like she thought she might, and she could potentially save herself a little nest egg for next year when she was really going to need it.

"Get it, girl," she said aloud, checking on her purposely messy topknot in the visor mirror. She grabbed the tote carrying her iPad and her emotional-support water bottle and headed into her favorite café for hopefully the most important meeting of her new career so far.

Sixteen and a half minutes later, the owner Lee had signed Brittney's document, served her a decaf cold brew, and gave her a hug goodbye as he hurried toward another meeting. Brittney now had a six-month agreement to do social media for Benjamin's Bakery, where she had grown up getting bagels and donut holes with her family, and if they met the growth and engagement goals, the business would be hers for another eighteen months. Between that news and the s'mores syrup in her coffee, she could have floated out of the café. Instead, she took her giant smile down the street into Los Gordibuenos, where she ordered doubles of chips, salsa, and guacamole, and kept it on her face all the way to Mama's house, where Travis was pulling in at the same time.

"Hey Goober," she called. He carried an overstuffed laundry basket under his left arm, and he side-hugged her with the other, unphased by the nickname.

"What up, Oops?" He was unphased because her nickname, inspired by the Britney Spears song he used to sing when he was a preschooler and she was teenager, was worse.

"Just got another Insta-gig," she said, a little more proudly than she planned to announce it. Travis was attending Coastal for Cyber Threat Intelligence, whatever that meant. Even though he was her nephew and younger, he probably thought social media was not even a real job.

Why do you care? And why do you still think like that? And it's not even true.

"Big one?" he asked, opening the door for her.

"Benjamin's!" she practically squealed.

"You got it!" Mama's ecstatic voice bellowed from across the house, where she was likely cooking the Tex-Mex version of a fatted calf in the kitchen.

"Yep!" Brittany didn't even feel like editing her glee. It was a huge win, and she had plenty of other things to fret about. This was a moment to shine.

Travis had headed to the laundry room, and Mama had darted toward her. She hugged Brittney in her own unedited way, with total passion, like Brittney was four and had brought her a dandelion. Unbridled Mama could sometimes be too much, but in times like this, she was exactly who and what Brittney needed.

"Thanks, Mama," she said, barely able to breathe through the force of the embrace. Mama laughed as she released her.

"Sorry," Mama answered, bounding back to the kitchen. Brittney followed her, throwing her bag down on a dining room chair and inhaling the smell of baked . . . something.

"What did you make?"

"Taco salads!" Mama was already opening the oven door to display the source of the amazing smell: giant, baked tortilla shells.

"Please tell me you made those from scratch," Brittney said.

Paul breezed into the room then. He stopped in the doorway and shook his head knowingly, peering at the oven. "Don't encourage her, Brit. Of course, she did."

"It was just an experiment!" Mama said, setting her baking sheet full of wonder on the stovetop. "I can't believe I lived sixty years as a Mexican food lover and never made my own tortillas."

"Yes," Paul teased. "What have you even done with your life until now?"

"Shut *up*," Mama said, studying her creations. "You won't think it's so funny when you're eating this masterpiece."

"Actually, I'm on my way to meet Carter," Paul said. "I thought I told you."

Mama turned around and scrunched her face up at him. "Of course, you didn't tell me. Look. One, two, three, *four* carefully crafted tortilla bowls. And—" She paused and pointed to the slow cooker. "Chimichurri steak has been cooking all afternoon."

"I'm sorry—" Paul started.

"You should be, Pablo," Travis said, clapping a hand on Paul's shoulder. "But I'll happily eat your share."

Travis was no bigger around than a string bean, but he could eat like a *rassler*, which Daddy used to tease him about. He was the first grandchild, raised right alongside David, the youngest child, and he was the only one to call Paul "Pablo." His younger siblings, and likely Josie before long, called him "Poppy Paul," but often shortened that to Poppy these days. Brittney, like her siblings, called him Paul. That didn't seem quite adequate for whom he had become to their mother, but there was no viable alternative. There was only one Daddy, and any iteration of that word was simply unacceptable.

Paul gave Travis a thankful smile and walked to Mama's side. "I really am sorry. I really thought I told you." He broke the tiniest piece of tortilla off one of the shells and popped it into his mouth. "Aw, Jess. You are a wonder." He looked over at Travis. "You may not eat mine."

Travis pretended to be disappointed, and Brittney kept focused on him while Paul kissed Mama goodbye. It was fine, absolutely fine. Except it stung a little and maybe always would.

"See y'all. Enjoy!" Paul smiled brightly at both of them and left through the side door.

"Mama, you two should use that Time Tree app I sent you," Brittney said, opening her bag of tortilla chips.

Mama shrugged in her direction. "You know I have four more of these ready to bake anyway, right? And Brit, honestly, one more app won't help. My head spins all the time, and Paul still isn't used to communicating simple things like where he's eating dinner."

"Really? I mean, I'm hardly an expert, but 'dinner' seems like a very husband-ly thing to talk about before actual dinnertime." She shoved another chip in her mouth. Her tummy was rumbling even though she'd had a huge peanut butter cookie at Benjamin's. Maybe the baby just liked chips.

Good gravy. If she thought about the baby too much while she was here, Mama would surely see right through her and guess what was happening.

Instead, she looked a little miffed. "We eat together most nights." Was that defensiveness in Mama's voice? "I think he just likes to let me have my Tuesdays with my own offspring. Or something."

Well, that was a whole pile of hogwash. Paul was almost always there when Jacob and Summer still lived in town. And he was there plenty of times since Brittney had been pinch hitting.

Was there some kind of drama? And more to the point, did she want to get involved in Mama's relationship drama?

Absolutely not.

The atmosphere had already shifted, though. They let Travis steer the conversation while they put their taco bowls together. Brittney heaped on shredded lettuce—what was it about shredded lettuce that made it more palatable than an actual salad? She added plenty of steak and skipped the beans; Baby did *not* like. A big handful of cheese and huge scoops of salsa and guac were next. If Paul was up to anything stupid or even just less than attentive, he was an idiot. No one could cook like Jessie Oakley.

Unrelated, Brittney was so glad Mama hadn't changed her name.

Travis, who seemed a bit tuned in to the weirdness in the air, was struggling to tell them about his Digital Forensics class. Brittney felt her head swim and glanced over to see Mama's eyes glazing over. They were decidedly *not* computer people or science people or technical people or in any way interested.

But Trav was their baby, so they'd fake it.

We fake too much, Brittney thought. *I want to ask Mama what is up with Paul.*

Around the time her nephew was scraping the bottom of his tortilla shell, Mama's phone rang. It was David, making his weekly appearance at Taco Tuesday. Mama beamed brightly at the screen, greeted her youngest child, and then handed the phone to Travis, who made a beeline for the laundry room, probably to talk about some nonsense in private more so than to change out his clothes for his sheets.

"Everything okay, Mama?" she finally asked, breaking off a piece of chimichurri-soaked tortilla and relishing the taste.

Mama raised one eyebrow. "Yes. Why?"

"You got mighty out of sorts about Paul and dinner." Perhaps that was an exaggeration, but she wanted to keep the attention off of herself and on to anything else anyway.

"You just meet me, Brit? I'm not even dialed halfway up tonight."

She shrugged. "Believe it or not, Mama, I know you've mellowed considerably in the past few months. I mean, you kinda had your hand forced, what with the golden child moving away."

Mama's face betrayed her instantly.

"What do you want me to say, Brit? That I'm fine? I am. I don't like any of it. I hate that David and now Sam and Abby and the kids are not right around the corner, but they have a right to live wherever they want. It's not like Horry County is a hotbed of opportunity. Anyway," she paused and sipped from her sangria with a sardonic upturn of her lips, "At least I still have you and Mikayla here."

Haha. Of course, she was teasing, and that set Brittney at ease. The truth was, she missed her brothers, too. "It's jarring to have all three of them just . . . gone from here."

"All three?" Mama said.

"Daddy, then David, then Sam. The men in our lives. Altan isn't blood and he's the one left." Would Mama add Paul's name to the mix?

"Altan is stalwart," Mama said of Mikayla's husband, "and your sister will never leave me." The tone stayed light because they both knew that to be very probable. "But you're right," she agreed. "The picture of our family has been rearranged like a jigsaw puzzle that doesn't quite fit together anymore. Maybe your brothers will move back one day. Maybe you or Mikaya and Altan will decide to move away. I mean, things are still new with Harrison, but . . . "

"I'm not moving to D.C., Mama." *Yuck.* Of all the places she could think of to start a new life, there wasn't one big city on the list, and certainly not one that included a real winter or an ex-wife. Of course, nothing with The Harrison Situation was that simple, but Mama didn't know that yet, and best to keep it that way. "But maybe you could go visit more often, you know? You aren't tied to the tea room, an office, or babysitting much." That might change once Mikayla had *two* babies. And Brittney one. And Julie one. Would she welcome Mama into that part of her life?

Suddenly, what should have felt happy—the joy of three kind-of sisters being pregnant at the same time—felt like a cloud. Mama hadn't answered about taking those trips, and Brittney couldn't help herself. "I love everyone," she said, sincerely. "But I wish things could just go back to being the way they were."

Mama reached her hand over to cover Brittney's and said very quietly, "Don't you think I understand that?" She paused. "I know what it looks like, that I am living my hopefully-ever-after with nary a care for what's been lost sometimes, but it's never true. Yes, I am hopeful. Yes, I love Paul deeply and his kids, too. But I mourn Daddy and the loss of *our* life every single day, Brit. Sometimes, every single minute. Sometimes, even in a moment that is happy and should be carefree, I think, *this isn't how it's supposed to be.* Maybe it is, and maybe it isn't. It's better than what a lot of people get after losing a husband. It's simply not what I imagined."

She took a breath and nearly whispered, "And Paul knows it."

Brittney decided that was an opening. "Are you two okay? I don't mean to beat a dead horse, but him leaving right at dinner and you not knowing about it seemed . . . off."

Mama got real breezy and started clearing their plates. Brittney was sad that her tortilla was all gone, because it was so delicious and because it was likely 2000 calories and she'd practically inhaled it.

"Everything's fine, Brit." She walked the dishes to the sink as though the Dish Police were knocking down the door. "My brain just doesn't hold information like it used to. I'm sure he told me, and I forgot, and it's not like I don't cook for twelve anyway, even if . . . "

Whether she didn't finish the sentence because it wasn't necessary or because she was sad, Brittney filled in the blanks. Mama had always thrived on hustle, bustle, crowds, chaos, and her kids. Tonight, the kitchen was quiet, and it felt lonely, even to Brittney.

Brittney stood. "We should go get ice cream. Drippy's will be shutting down for the season before you know it."

"What about Travis?"

She shook her head. Mama either needed more sangria or a vacation. "He can come, too, Mama!"

"Original or pier?"

"Let's go to the pier," Brittney said. Their favorite ice cream place had opened a new location once the Surfside Pier had finally been rebuilt post-Hurricane Matthew. "I will even walk on the beach with you if you want."

"You're too good to me," Mama said, drying her hands. Brittney thought she saw the glisten of an unshed tear or two, but if Mama was keen on ignoring it for the moment, she'd let her. Harrison would be there for a blink-and-we'll-miss-it-visit in just a few days. God knew Brittney would not be able to ignore her own problems much longer.

40

Brittney

6

Harrison could only stay for one real night this time. It was absurd, really. He left DC—well, Alexandria, the suburb where he lived—as soon as he got off work on Friday. With the rush hour traffic, the campers getting to the beach and all the high school football fans clogging the roads, he didn't pull into Brittney's driveway until almost two in the morning. She was in bed with "Pearl Jam Unplugged" on YouTube, dozing on and off fitfully, wanting to be awake and pretty for him, but caving in to her own unprecedented exhaustion. She saw the headlights on her wall as he maneuvered his big truck into her tiny driveway. Rather than getting up to fix herself, she burrowed deeper into her bed cave, with its untold blankets underneath her on-high ceiling fan. She heard him unlock the door and felt the butterflies in her stomach as he made his way to her. The only light was from the TV. In a fluid motion, he'd kicked off his shoes and slid his jeans to the floor. Then he was in the bed with his limbs wrapped around her, inhaling her hair, sighing softly. She let his presence buoy her. It had been two weeks since she'd visited him, and every day without him made her that much more certain of how much she wanted him.

They slept in; she realized that his definition, as a dad of school-aged kids, meant more like eight in the morning instead of her close-to-noon Saturday wake-up. After a quick run to the store for provisions, they spent the afternoon at the beach, went home to make dinner, and now they were back for the sunset. She'd spread out a blanket, and he'd dusted off and brought her acoustic guitar. They sat caddy-cornered to each other, so they could talk and see the ocean at the same time.

"Aren't you hot?" she asked, eyeing him in his t-shirt and jeans. Though her favorite season, Locals' Summer, had begun, the humidity of September was as stifling as August, and sometimes more so, because everything she saw on social media was about PSLs and sweaters, tricking her mind into believing the weather should be thirty degrees cooler.

"Nah, but you are," he said with a shrug and a twinkle in his eye. She was still wearing her emerald-green bikini top and cut-off jean shorts, her hair piled on her head, full of sand and salt and all the effects of said humidity. She was already sad the day was ending.

"Thank you," she replied, her voice flirty and much lighter than she felt.

He didn't notice her apprehension. He had picked up the guitar and started strumming in that absent-minded musician way that could mean he was playing a song he remembered from fifth grade choir or randomly composing a symphony. She'd always loved that about El, her best friend since freshman year and Harrison's younger brother. Musicians in general seemed to be her favorite people. Everyone has an outlet for their crazy. Music was a much better one than most.

As soon as he started softly singing the words, she recognized the song *and* had to tamp down her stomach flutters. Harrison was a bass player by default. He rarely sang, but when he did . . . *oy*. Tonight, he was singing that she was the sweetest sunflower and his sun, and it made her insides melty.

Her cheeks got hot. His eyes were closed, but she beamed at him.

A few passersby smiled at them as they walked. His long hair fell in a loose ponytail down his back, and the sunset was reflecting just a little bit off the wooden guitar; Brittney could admit that they probably looked like something off a Hallmark movie or even a music video.

Snap the ^%#$^ out of it, Brittney! Dang it. More and more, Katy's voice was in her head. Katy, the stepsister she gained as a thirty-year-old. Katy, who played a similar role in her family of origin that Brittney played in hers: youngest daughter, hothead, outlier. Normally, Katy's choices made Brittney's look pretty sane, but Brittney was about to take everyone's cake. Even her older brother Sam's, whose cake had been getting his college girlfriend pregnant, but they'd gotten married and lived happily ever after ever since. Even her younger brother David's, whose cake had been dropping out of college and running off to Arizona with Julie, Katy's twin sister, a few months after their dad and Katy's mom had died in a car accident together. They were the hot mess express.

And Brittney was about to trump them all. She'd already done it, technically, but now, once the words were out, her reign of ridiculousness would begin, never to be trumped.

Harrison finished his little ditty but kept picking. She kept her eyes closed, half to relish the moment, half to pray.

I know I am going to lose him, God. Thank you for the time we had. Thank you for what is to come. Thank you for the promise that I will not be alone in this.

She sighed. Looked at Harrison, who was staring at her, not in the hungry way he did sometimes (which she loved), but in a contemplative one. As soon as she met his eyes, he dropped the guitar on his lap.

"It's been great to be near Ruthie and Dakota. I know it's the right thing," he said quietly. "But I wish things could be different."

It had only been two months since he moved away, and not quite four months since they met at all, starting as reluctant and hostile roommates before (kinda quickly, in retrospect) falling for each other. Their feelings intensified once they knew Harrison was moving away, back to the DC area to be with his kids. Of course, it was the right thing; Brittney wouldn't argue that for a second. And she was single and unattached and even working for herself in a job that could be anywhere, but she felt so tied to her roots that moving to be near him seemed frivolous, too risky, too soon.

It wasn't as simple as all that.

"I do, too," she finally answered, biting on her lip, looking at her hands in her lap, particularly at the left one, void of any tangible promises. She might not have lived the traditional last decade that her mama wished for her, that her sister Mikayla had had, but she did yearn for those things: a ring, a wedding, fully belonging to someone.

"I have to tell you something," she blurted. She'd rehearsed a big build-up. Now that seemed frivolous, too.

"Okay." He didn't seem a bit rattled by her proclamation. In fact, he reached over and stroked her hair, sending fresh tremors through her stomach. She had to get this over with.

"I'm pregnant, Harrison."

In her opinion, everything should have stopped then. She had told no one since that first positive test a week before. Normally, her M.O. was to tell her people everything: Mama. Mikayla. El. Katy. This time, she didn't even tell the voice of Daddy in her head. This was too big. This was too eternal. Once she stopped keeping it to herself, it became the big tick mark in the before and after of her lifeline. What would be the first scene in her *after*?

Well, the ocean waves kept rolling. The two men fishing not twenty feet away from them kept talking and laughing. A seagull ate from a trail of potato chips. A family with an errant toddler chased him right past them.

A very happy black Labrador tried to give Harrison his frisbee. Harrison patted the dog on its head and sent the disc flying. She was amazed at the strength in his arm at that moment. She felt like all the energy had left her body. All she could do was tense herself, waiting for his response.

Anchored with one hand, Harrison reached toward her with the other, then stopped, and covered his mouth for a moment, staring at her or into some future she wished she could see.

"Oh," he said. "Brittney. My God."

Was he happy? Angry? Amused? Panicked? Did he even believe her? They were so new together. So new . . .

"I . . . I know . . . " she said, feebly.

"Anything I say is going to sound stupid," he said. "But are you okay? Do you know how far along? Do you know what you need?"

She exhaled from her actual soul. He didn't ask the Big Question, the one she was braced for and desperately hoped he would not say.

Because, of course, the baby was his.

She might have been dumb as hell and pretty unlucky at times, but she was faithful.

She reached her hand out to his face, feeling the stubble prickle against her, feeling him press his cheek to her hand while never breaking his direct, searching gaze.

"It's about nine weeks," she said softly. "I haven't had an appointment yet. I just . . . I kinda waited to even take a test. You know me, overwhelm leads to inertia. And I wanted to tell you first, but I also wanted to wait a minute, because Mama and Mikayla have both lost babies, and I didn't want to turn the whole world upside down for something that maybe wouldn't even happen."

Without thinking about it, she lay her other hand across her belly. Without ado, the thought of the little life inside there made her feel protective in a way she never had before. "But I think it's happening, so you need to know. And I'm sorry, Harrison. I really am."

"Brit . . . " He put his hand over hers and lowered it from his cheek to his lips, kissing it with a gentleness she hadn't seen him display and wasn't sure she'd ever experienced. "Don't be sorry. We both made . . . him. Her. We both did this."

Her stomach gave another, more intense flutter. He didn't sound upset, thank God, but he didn't sound sure, either.

She could use some reassurance just then.

"It's pretty complicated," he finished. He waited a beat, and then, to her surprise, he embraced her, laughing.

"What's so funny?" she asked, her face against his shoulder, where she wanted to stay.

"Buttercup, this is a mess, but for a minute, let's just be happy." He kept one arm around her and stayed close, and he looked out over the water. Brittney matched him, breathing in sync with the waves. She marveled again that the world seemed to keep spinning. She hadn't knocked it off its axis with her announcement. People got pregnant every day. Women become single moms, women far younger than she, with much fewer resources, with much more challenging relationships statuses. Whatever happened with Harrison—

— and *oh God,* her hopes were impossibly, absurdly high—

—she was going to be a mama. And it hadn't been until the first (four) positive tests that she realized she really, really wanted to be one.

"They started playing a half hour ago," Brittney said. She was sitting between Harrison's legs, leaning against his chest, pretending everything was fine, that they had no worries.

"Of course, we're not going," he said, tightening his arms around her.

"Really?" She craned her neck to look at them. The Salty Lips—their favorite band, the one for which Harrison had recently been the bass player for, *El's* band—was playing. Brittney had rarely missed a gig. "It feels weird not to."

"I know," Harrison said, speaking right into her hair, where he was nuzzled. "But I'm leaving in fourteen hours. I don't want to be around 200 other people."

She didn't want to share any more than he did. Fourteen hours might as well have been one. Still . . .

"You don't want to see El?" When Harrison had first arrived in town, the relationship between them had been tenuous at best. Now, it was more brotherly than it had been since they were kids.

"Yeah. I should. I mean, I do. You wanna see if they'll be at the house after the show? We can stop by. Less crazy there."

Brittney sent a quick text off to Katy, who was probably playing the bass at that very moment but would have a chance to answer before El, the lead vocalist, would. Sure enough, less than a minute later she got a

How she managed to stay in tune with the show and text an answer with random Spanglish followed by four different emojis escaped Brittney. She always had to work really hard to focus on any given act, a staunch practitioner of mindfulness in a multitasking world. She tapped back a heart and flung her phone back to the blanket, wishing she was on the set of a Netflix romance, and she and Harrison could just spend the night, undisturbed, right there on the beach.

"Done," she murmured. "But it will still be hours before the show is over."

Harrison lifted his chin, speaking right into her ear. "What do you want to do? See a movie? Go get ice cream? Stop by Jessie's house and tell her the news?"

His teasing sent a jolt through her. *He is teasing, right?* "Um . . . yeah. I'm planning to tell her sometime in the third trimester. That should give her enough time to be mad and then forgive me enough to make a month of dinners for my freezer. And hold the baby while I shower."

She stopped abruptly at that, hearing the undertones of her words. She scooted away from Harrison and started banging the sand off her flip-flops.

"Brit . . ."

She had already glossed over her facial expression—*You're getting nothing from me*– and refused to meet his eyes. The reverie of him holding her on the beach, pretending everything would work out just fine, was over.

"It's fine," she said. "I don't know if you know, but Mama had a one-night stand and then Sam when she was nineteen, and then Sam knocked Abby up with Travis in college, so this situation is kind of a thing in my family . . ." There. All lighthearted. Like Daddy wasn't looking down from Heaven shaking his head with one eyebrow raised. Like Mama wasn't going to freak the fu—

"I don't know if you know," Harrison replied. "But you aren't nineteen, or in college, or alone in this."

"But—"

"You're a grown woman who owns a home and a business, and this baby will be loved by a mom and a dad."

"Harrison, I see what a great dad you are. But you live six hours away to be a great dad to two kids you already have. And we are . . . " She searched for the right word and gave it her best shot. "Really new."

He nodded slowly. They both stood and silently folded the blanket together. He held the guitar, like suddenly it was made of glass, and he looked at her like she was, too.

"Just because we can't figure everything out tonight doesn't mean we *won't* figure it out," he said.

His sweetness pierced Brittney's tender, pregnant heart. She held back a sob and nodded silently.

"So, what should we do now, like right now tonight?"

She turned toward the Surfside Pier, absolutely sure of herself.

"Drippy's Peanut Butter Oreo. Then home for a while."

Ice cream and lovemaking couldn't solve everything, but at the moment, it was the best course of action.

Two of El and Katy's bandmates were leaving El's when Brittney and Harrison got there. Geno—the guitar player who ironically resembled the Pillsbury Dough Boy in stature and was a bread baker by trade—was coming down the stairs trailed by Ringo—the stoic, dreadlocked drummer. Since Brittney's short stint being El's housemate and some Katy-led hijinks over the summer, Brittney felt even more kindred with the members of The

Salty Lips, and usually, Ringo did more than grunt at her like he used to. This was not to be one of those times.

Geno, a boisterous forty-something who played the role of Chosen Big Cousin and had, in fact, sold Brittney her mobile home, gave her a bear hug and a loud smooch on the cheek; all the while, he told Harrison that "No offense to El's Missus, but we miss you, bro. And those little biker groupies who ride in from Johnsonville sure do, too."

Harrison pretended he cared and traded barbs with Geno, while Ringo rolled his eyes at Brittney—yay for a sign of camaraderie! — and then looked away. They both pretended to be patient until Geno's phone dinged and, "It's Emily!" he said. Everyone even remotely connected to Geno knew that when his formerly estranged wife was looking for him, via text, phone call, or Facebook post—or storming to the edge of the stage and throwing a not-quite-empty can of Twisted Tea at his face—he was going to stop whatever he was rambling on about and reply to her. She'd taken the cheating lout back, and he had no more chances.

He was halfway to Ringo's truck before they could even say "Adios." Ringo tipped his Braves hat at Brittney and Harrison and then followed him.

"That's a lot," Harrison grunted. He put his hand on the small of Brittney's back and guided her up the stairs.

She inwardly swooned at the gesture. It was small, but the security emanating from that hand to her shaky innards was huge. "He's harmless."

"Not if you're Emily," Harrison said. "I think you're just used to chaos. That guy is the walking definition of it."

"Says the single father of two kids," she quipped. And then she shut her mouth as the flashing neon light in her head read, *You're an idiot.*

But Harrison had the tiniest smile on his face, and he shook his head as he opened the door without knocking.

"What uuuuuuuuup?" Katy jumped from the couch and pounced on Brittney. Harrison widened his eyes at her as Katy swayed back and forth while embracing her. Brit shook her head; this was Katy's normal sort of greeting. This was Katy at like a level five. And she didn't know a thing about what Brittney had going on.

"How was the show?" Brittney asked. Harrison had already walked past them, with a bemused nod at Katy, toward the kitchen, where El was standing at the counter constructing peanut butter and jellies in between shoving handfuls of Fritos in his mouth. Post-show meals were as predictable as Katy's hugs.

Katy shrugged. "It was fine. Dave," (the other guitar player) "was mad because El changed the end of the first set and didn't tell us until tonight. I mean, I live with him, and I didn't even know. And it was literally changing from 'Call Me' to 'Symptom of Being Human.' They're practically the same song."

"He's only happy when he's not," El said with a shrug. He passed Katy a paper plate with her sandwich, Fritos, a sprig of grapes, and a brownie. Brittney's smile came from the inside. Two of her favorite people in the world were turning out to be a pretty adorable little couple.

"I don't know how you put up with all that BS," Harrison said, and the two of them launched into bandspeak. Brittney understood it, but at the moment, she just wanted the perfunctory visit to hurry so she could be alone with him again, for the small balance of their time that remained.

Katy started up her own monologue about her fumbles on their newest set addition, which was "all gas, no brakes"; they'd started covering Shinedown, whom Brittney happened to love. Also, two of Atalaya's orbiters had shown up but left at intermission when El wouldn't look at them despite their cat-calling him during the last song of the set.

"I really kinda wanted them to come for me," Katy continued. Brittney shook her head, because their last encounter with El's ex and her clan had sent a truckful of them on a toilet papering, house-egging bender back on the third of July, which now seemed like an entire lifetime ago.

Katy didn't get it yet, how life could make you grow up so much in the blink of an eye. Brittney kinda didn't either, but she knew she was about to live it. Her hand found her stomach again without her even thinking about it. She covered it with her other one; Katy might be high octane, but she also noticed every dang thing.

"You don't really mean that," Brittney said, meaning it but careful to sound like she was joking. They were in their thirties. An occasional catfight or house-egging was one thing, but a lifestyle of it seemed tiresome and very, very stupid.

Katy was unphased. She shrugged, taking a big, globby bite of her sandwich. "I guess. I have other things to worry about anyway. Steven wants to make me some kind of manager at the store, and I might need to go back to faking incompetence."

"Why would you want to do that? Isn't it a good thing?" Brittney knew better than to take anything at surface level with Katy, who had been working at a music store in the mall that was more successful than most specialty stores could dream about in their day and age. They'd brought her on mostly to give guitar lessons, but—

"I guess selling the shit out of the guitars and everything else has gotten me some attention," she shrugged, pushing a sweaty strand of long blonde hair behind her ear. Brittney figured it was the hair, the long legs often highlighted by the short shorts, and the hard to label but couldn't be missed *magical thing* she exuded that made people naturally enchanted by her and gravitate toward her, that aided her success there as well.

"You're a charmer," Brittney told her, wincing because she sounded just like Mama. "The kids love you. You actually act like you're patient with them. And you sold a freaking accordion last week. To a guy with one arm! Who bought you drinks."

They both laughed hard at that. The guy in question had been an Irish tourist named Finbar who had actually had his arm in a sling from a broken elbow. He was gray-haired, red-bearded, and after purchasing the accordion in question for fifteen-hundred dollars, he'd asked Katy for a drink and bottomless fries at the Red Robin. She had found this too funny to resist and came home from a chaste hour with him filled with Tito's Blue Chills and enough Irish-tale-fodder to last for a week. Thankfully, El had been a good sport, even if he was not quite as amused as they were.

"You know me," Katy shrugged. "I know I would kick ass at it, but it isn't that much more money than what they're paying me now, because it's music. And . . . *Myrtle Beach*. Plus . . . me and responsibility? I'm not afraid of it. I just don't know if I want to yet."

Brittney smirked at her. She understood. Up until just a few weeks ago, she kinda felt the same.

"We probably aren't always gonna have a choice, Katy."

"Well *you* certainly don't anymore!"

An indecipherable sound escaped Brittney. Something like, "Gaaaaaah." Because *how* did Katy *know*?

"How is your little castle, anyway? We need to stay in and watch movies one night, or something. I should give El a break from me before he realizes what he's done and *I'm* homeless, again."

Ah. Okay . . . Brittney was safe, for another little bit anyway. And Katy was right; she had a home that was paid for, but she had lot rental and insurance and utilities and all the things, even without accounting for a whole other human.

Holy shit.

She felt the heat rise from her belly up her neck and straight to her ears. El and Harrison were in the middle of a beer and an analysis of Ringo's vocals on "Kryptonite" (the crowd *loooooooved* their singing, dreadlocked drummer). She wanted to wait before she asked Harrison to take her home, but suddenly, the world felt a little too crazy and hot to handle.

"Hey babe, I'm so sorry to interrupt, but . . . I don't think those tacos agreed with me . . . "

"Ugh. Did you get *fish* again? Brit . . . "

"Shut up, El," she snapped automatically. They hadn't even had tacos.

Harrison was at her side in a second, wrapping his arm around her shoulders and chiding, "Yeah. Shut up, El."

"When we gonna see you again?" El asked his brother.

"Four weeks, so long as Denise keeps the visitation status quo and nothing stupid happens." Everyone knew what a loaded statement that was, so everyone just nodded kinda vapidly.

"Well, be safe!" Katy finally called out, sunshine in her voice. In her signature style, she gave Harrison a grandiose hug. "We miss you 'round these parts. I would even share my bassin' duties with you if you ever decide to come back."

Ooph. Brittney tried not to visibly cringe. Katy had no idea how much was loaded into that sentence. Come to think of it, Brittney didn't even know . . . did Harrison *like* living there? It had been such a short stint, and his job was remote. All he did was play music, go to his boot camp classes, and make Brittney fall in love with him.

But her dark, broody boyfriend flashed an easy smile at Katy. "You don't have to share. You're way better than I am."

"Looks way better, too," El added, wrapping his arm around Katy's waist.

Brittney sighed. The moment was warm and sweet, and she wanted to freeze it. Her best friend, her boyfriend, her stepsister . . . what a formidable and free little tribe they could be, if Harrison didn't live so far away and her life wasn't about to be completely upended.

She narrowed her eyes and looked back and forth between Katy and Harrison. "I don't know," she said playfully. "Harrison's just as pretty as Katy is, bestie."

She beamed as Harrison squeezed her shoulders from behind, planting a kiss on her neck with its own private signal to her, even while he said, "I think that's our cue. See you guys soon. Be good."

Katy caught her eye as El slapped a hug on his older brother. It hadn't been so long ago when there wasn't much beyond hostile silence between the brothers. Here they were, proof that sometimes complicated things just took a while to work out.

Harrison walked her to the passenger door, and before she climbed in, she stood on her tiptoes and threw her arms around his neck, burying her face there. Sometimes, she was still a bit tentative to show him how much she wanted him, how close she wanted him, but there couldn't be much separation now. They made a life together, and she needed him.

"Mmmmm," he whispered. "You good?"

"I am," she said, not moving her lips from his skin, pulling her arms tighter around him.

He followed suit, and she felt him take an exaggerated inhale from his spot against her cheek.

"Whatcha doing?" she asked.

"I just want to savor the smell of you being the air I breathe," he murmured, quite deftly taking her breath away. "And how you hold me."

The drive back to her place was less than five minutes, even if they stayed on Ocean Boulevard, on which the speed limit was a ludicrous ten miles per hour. Brittney loved going that way, though. Somehow, it reminded her how close she lived to the beach, in her own little home, that was just perfect for her own little life.

And maybe it would be perfect for two of them.

And, if she dared to hope beyond reason, it could be perfect for more of them . . .

7

"Danielle, I'll call you back. Daddy's here."

She'd been right in the middle of a riveting story about six-year-old Christian tormenting both his little sisters with the carcass of a, thankfully dead, Palmetto bug. Mama had always taught them, *We never call them roaches here, and the Yankees who think that's funny can go back and sit in the traffic jam where they came from.* Danielle stopped short and said, "Give him my love! Talk later!" and hung up before Julie could say a word. Maybe Christian was whipping some other disgusting thing around the house. Julie kicked the dishwasher door shut, set down her phone, wiped her hands on a flour sack dishtowel, and headed for the door.

"You know you can just come in, right?"

"You know I hate greetings like that, right?"

"Sorry!" She rolled her eyes as she hugged him, grateful he couldn't see. "Hi Daddy! Thanks for bringing this by."

"Well," Paul started as he set an industrial blue Rubbermaid tote on the floor next to the door. "I know better than to leave you waiting, Jules."

"And you're sure this is the one?"

"Open it," he said, walking toward the kitchen, most assuredly foraging for coffee.

Julie propped open one corner of the battered lid. She saw an approximately twenty-nine-year-old quilt, its yellow and white daisies, pink daffodils, and inexplicable lavender kittens a familiar site, and she smelled her mama's signature Mrs. Meyer's Honeysuckle laundry detergent. She took one deep breath, closing her eyes and remembering being eleven years old, fighting with Katy over her brand-new Hollister hoodie, dealing with the first day of school on which she had ever been *menstruating*, and totally breaking form and crying into her mama's lap.

Honeysuckle.

Mama.

It was definitely the one.

"Are you hungry?" she asked, catching up with him as he pumped honey into his mug. It was the only sweetener she kept in the house, which usually drove him crazy. He picked less since she was carrying his fourth grandchild.

She would never catch up with Danielle. Babies were probably going to be a one and done thing for her.

Well. She might have to check on Robin's feelings about that.

"I'm good," Daddy answered. He was at her table, one foot across his knee, one hand around his mug, one hand drumming his fingers on the bamboo table.

Julie ignored that. She placed a slice of banana bread—allergen-free from You Eat, I Bake—and a few strawberries on a plate and set it before him. He almost smiled, and he immediately took a bite. Daddy was a 100 percent sweet tooth, no matter what kind of mood he was in, and she sensed there was a storm brewin'.

"Robin said you're gonna cover the store next Thursday morning. Thank you," she started.

"I don't want him to miss your appointments anymore."

She exhaled softly. This was tricky ground she was about to tread on. *She* certainly didn't want Robin to miss another OB appointment, either. And she hadn't told anyone but her friend Hazel, who was miles away in Raleigh and didn't know any of her family, about the mild-to-moderate panic attack she'd had after the nurse took longer than ten seconds finding the baby's heartbeat. Dr. Masselli had offered her a low dose of Zoloft, which she had refused out of principle as well as pride. Robin probably would have encouraged her to take it.

She was certain he thought she was a little nuts, anyway. But she didn't want *any* unnecessary drugs, and as long as she could run most days, she kept her crazy contained. Yes, the store was steady all the time, thank God. But they usually could handle it.

And . . . she just . . . wasn't . . . sure . . . that Daddy could.

"I appreciate it, Daddy," she answered. "Chicago Dave has an appointment, but he should be there to help you by 10:30 at the latest." The store opened at ten, and she had Tracy Ann on standby just in case.

In case of what, Julie? For Heaven's sake!

Mama's impatience for her worst-case-scenario-preparedness extended beyond the grave. The constant voice of descent in her head was Mama's. The narration of what to worry about, what to do about it, and what she should have done in the past, that was all Julie's.

Daddy raised an eyebrow at her. "Store hoppin' these days?" During his months of actual employment, from the time she and Robin fell in love until shortly after their wedding, Daddy had been a regular part-timer.

They were, in fact, busier these days; they tried not to have anyone working there on his or her own if it could be avoided.

"Oh, well, yes." She shrugged to communicate an air of breeziness. "We try to have two people there all the time."

"And?"

If Mama was her conscience, Daddy was her reality check. Not only that, but he could see right through her pretty much always.

"I mean, you're filling in. There's some stuff you might not know about. Products and stuff."

Products and stuff. That wasn't how she talked. She had just backed herself into a corner.

"Julie, I was just there last week when you got the Gylcerin Max. I checked in the Feetures so you and Robin could have lunch together. I think I can check people out for two hours, unless . . . "

There it was.

" . . . you don't think I can?"

Julie chewed her bottom lip, putting off the inevitable conversation. She watched him, as he was not looking back at her. He was looking at the plate of half-eaten banana bread. He was drumming his fingers in a faster rhythm. He already knew.

"I just worry about you," she said, softly, like he would admonish her.

"Julie? I am fine." His tone was of the *I am mad, but I don't want to admit it* variety.

"You have a concussion."

"*Had.* Weeks ago."

"And sometimes it takes at least that long to recover fully."

"Sometimes. That doesn't mean that's what's happening."

She let the silence fill the room. She was her father's daughter and did not require small talk to feel comfortable. She also didn't intend to back down. Something was going on with him, and if he wasn't ready to tell her, she wasn't going to pretend like that was okay with her.

"Did Jessie speak to you?" he finally asked.

Julie had to keep her jaw from dropping. This was a concession in a variety she did *not* expect.

"About you? C'mon, Daddy. I know we're practically besties now, but that's a little much, don't you think?"

He deadpanned, "There are seven adult females in this family, Julie, and one not far behind. *That* is a bit much. You ganging up on me is not far-fetched at all."

"Gang up on you for what? To tell you to take it easy? To let your brain get over the big shaking it took not three months ago?"

"Three *months*, Jules."

She looked past him, out the window where mostly she could see the townhouse next door. It was painted a vibrant turquoise. She didn't want their own place to be painted that color, but she always liked seeing it. She took a deep breath. It didn't used to be this hard to say things to her father.

"Post-concussion syndrome is a thing, Daddy."

Without missing a beat, he answered, "You always think the worst is happening, Julie. It's probably my fault for being such a mess when you were young. But it isn't true."

Ooh. Was it the smell of Mama mixed with the simple phrase "when you were young?" She felt a fire start to form in her. She uncharacteristically put a protective hand on her abdomen. She hadn't felt the baby move yet, and she didn't wish to be melodramatic about this whole pregnancy thing, but the instinct to protect was as real as the table in front of her. Confused by it, she tried to shake her head as if to shake the uneasiness off.

"Daddy, that wouldn't be the worst. It would just explain your . . . lack of stamina, maybe your lack of cheerfulness lately?"

He just stared at her, but she would not be unnerved.

"Danielle said you forgot to pick up Christian twice. That is completely unlike you."

He blew out a breath. "I'm getting older, Julie. That doesn't—"

"Why is it so hard for you to accept an actual explanation for things? 'Getting older' isn't one. It's a guess. A huge knock on the head that hasn't healed yet; that's an actual reason."

Another silence followed. Daddy broke it again. "I feel terrible about forgetting Christian at school. I hope your sister believes that."

"Danielle pretty much believes the best about everybody and everything, but she is *worried*, and she doesn't need to worry about anything else. Three kids are enough."

"And so is one pregnancy and a business, Jules. So drop it and let me take care of myself."

She gave a solitary nod. "So, you're going to force me to talk to Jessie about this, then? Because at least she seems to have a fighting chance of making you listen."

He stood up, walked toward her, and kissed the top of her head. "I have to go, Jules. I am actually meeting Jessie and Maggie and Don at one of those wood studios. We're going to make a 'welcome' sign. Like we need one."

Julie smiled in spite of herself.

"See? My humor and personality, all intact, as is my ability to remember where I am supposed to be. I'm just not perfect, Jules. Please extend some grace and patience, whether I deserve it or not."

She stood and met her father's eyes.

"Daddy, none of us expect you to be perfect. We love you."

They hugged and said nothing more of it. As soon as he closed the door, she did something she never thought she'd do: she started a group text with her stepmom and her sisters. It was time they collaborated to make Daddy listen.

8

"Thanks for coming."

The fact that her mother-of-three older sister dropped everything (except for Baby Lexie, who was still a champion nursling) to go through her baby box with her was no small thing. Danielle stayed cloaked in her maternal responsibilities, and even though Julie mostly liked and even loved her brother-in-law Matt, she sometimes thought he needed to fun Danielle up more. She was young and used to be so active, and these days, all she did was talk about nervous system regulation parenting and embracing a crunchy-lite lifestyle.

Julie was actually into both those things, but still.

"You want me to hold her while you eat that?" Julie had served her vanilla bean ice cream and a slice of bona fide pound cake—the real Paula Deen recipe she had made for Robin to make up for being psychotic half the time. She had some self-awareness, for crying out loud.

"Sure." Julie scooped Lexie from her sister's arms. Lexie was dream-sleeping, in that mystical state where she still moved her sweet little lips as though she was nursing. Julie imagined that her own baby girl (She *knew* it had to be a girl. She only knew girls!) would be just as peaceful, beautiful, perfect. She had missed out on her niece Vivi's babyhood just a little; she'd been career-driven and then grief-stricken and then across the country acting out in Arizona. She relished Lexie and tried often to make up for it with Vivi.

As Danielle methodically devoured her dessert, Julie told her about her doctor's appointment, her strange as all get out cravings for buffalo wings, which thrilled Robin, and Toaster Strudel, which mortified her. After her run the prior day, she had eaten *three* of them along with her protein shake with banana and PB2. She was going to gain 100 pounds carrying this baby.

Thank goodness, she could start running longer miles post-partum, and the baby would be totally worth it.

"What are you trying to find, anyway?" Danielle asked. She had already finished the ice cream and was methodically attacking the cake, dipping each bite in the melted remnants before popping it into her mouth. Julie wasn't an amazing chef or anything, but like their mama, she had a few recipes she could absolutely crush, and this was one of them.

"I am pretty sure there is a collection of Little Golden Books in there. And I definitely want the overalls." Mama had dressed all of them in Old Navy denim overalls when they were toddlers. "And anything girlie as long as this is a" —she shifted Lexie to one arm and patted her own small, rounded belly dramatically— "Tiny queen."

Danielle raised an eyebrow. "And what if it's a tiny king?"

Julie shrugged. It wasn't like she hadn't thought of the possibility, but considering what a girl-heavy family they already were, with Mama having three sisters, then three daughters, and now two granddaughters, a girl seemed more than likely. At least, she kept telling herself that.

"Want me to take her back so you can dig in?"

As much as Sweet Auntie Julie wanted to say no, Control Freak Pregnant Julie won. She handed Lexie back and kneeled on the floor by the tote, peeling the lid off without any further ado. She and Danielle both inhaled deeply and took a moment of silence.

"I haven't used any Mrs. Meyer's since she died," Danielle finally said. "This makes me think maybe I should again."

"Smells like her . . . and home," Julie agreed. Then she looked down.

Oddly, the quilt she saw when Daddy had dropped by was only covering half of the contents. A see-through plastic bag was on top of the other half. Julie stared at it as if it was a relic from another planet. Then its identity became clear.

"Oh, my God," she breathed.

"What? Julie, what?" Danielle carefully kneeled on the floor next to her, still patting the sleeping Lexie's back.

"It's Mama's stuff!"

"What do you mean? Stuff from when she was pregnant with you?"

"No!" Julie's heart and head raced. He must have shoved it in here when he was packing up the house. Why would he? Why would he not have remembered? "From the hospital! It's her . . . her . . ."

Mama rarely carried a purse, and unless she was on an outing with Christian, Danielle's oldest, she packed super light. The plastic bag contained a slim, mulberry-colored phone wallet. Her driver's license has been removed and was visible as well. That was it. But undeniably, that was all that had been with her, and as far as Julie could recall, she had never asked about it.

Their mother had been thrown from the car, and her ID was found yards away from her.

Jesus. She hated to think about it.

As if the bag would burst into flames or maybe bite her, Julie removed it from the tote. She pulled on the little drawstring and removed the lovely case. Mama was a big fan of lovely things, artisan crafts, one-of-a-kind accessories. They could have opened a secondhand boutique with the belongings she'd left behind. At the time of her death, her two youngest daughters had been like vagabonds, not yet ready to hold onto too much. Danielle had one of her bed quilts, many of her jackets and shoes, and some jewelry. Most of the rest was probably in a storage locker, unless Daddy had been careless with that, too.

"I cannot believe this is here, and he didn't tell you. *Warn* you," Danielle said. She typically had less grace for Daddy than her younger sisters did, probably because she remembered him at his worst much more clearly than they did.

"Do you think he knew?" Julie asked. "I mean, it's not okay either way. He either disregarded something that was super important and forgot about it, or he just left it here for me to haphazardly deal with."

Danielle busied herself setting Lexie in her little vibrating bouncy chair. The tinny lullaby sounded a little soothing. She exhaled. "My guess is that he didn't know. Look at how manically he moved around: into Jessie's, fricken couch diving, my house after his surgery, then to the new house. Emptying out and combining the storage units after the old house sold. I am surprised he even knew this was the box of your baby stuff. Obviously, I've had mine for years, but I have Katy's, too. I have Mama's box of high school stuff. I have Granny's cookbooks, which I am sure Aunt Sherron doesn't know. Daddy has no idea what heirlooms are where. But he should have known about the phone."

They sat in the quiet of Lexie's baby version of "Three Little Birds," staring at the bejeweled phone as if trying to decipher what it was.

Julie picked it up and asked the inevitable question: "What should we do with it?"

The answer, at least for the time being, was nothing.

Danielle wanted to give the phone to Daddy. Julie refused. She wanted to talk to him about it, but didn't want him to have it, however bratty that might be. She promised Danielle she wouldn't confront him right away, as long as Danielle promised not to tell Katy, who would drive them both insane about it.

After that, going through Julie's sought-after baby box didn't seem as exciting. They unearthed the overalls, two handmade blankets besides the quilt, her first Christmas hat and bib, the Little Golden books, and dozens of other tiny dresses, hats, and her very first shoes. Thankfully, there were no photos; Julie didn't think she could take that. Mama had not been a scrapbook person or a baby book person. Julie already had all the photographs of her Mama and her younger self that she would ever have, and finding more would have been more of an emotional surprise than she could handle at the moment.

Danielle and Lexi left. Julie, though it was three in the afternoon and no one had told South Carolina that it was fall and didn't need to be ninety degrees in the shade, changed her shoes and socks for a run. She was supposed to meet Robin at the store for run club at six, but she *really* didn't want to be around people, and he would refuse to let her run twice in a day. She scrolled through her phone to find a playlist for her mood, but nothing seemed to be in sync with *Love My Father and Appreciate His*

Happy New Marriage But Damn, Could He Be More Sensitive About How His Children Are Still Grieving. So she chose Paramore, hit "shuffle," and stretched for ten perfunctory seconds before she took off down the street, trying to outrun how truly crappy the phone revelation felt.

The worst part is, she told the voice in her head, *I don't know whom to talk to about this. Danielle, yes. But Katy will just unhinge. Robin has two happy, living parents and he doesn't understand. I want to talk to Daddy. Or Mama. And I can't. I have no one.*

That is stupid. Mama's voice never had any patience for her absurdity.

But Julie had learned through her own poor choices and a bigger-than-healthy dose of self-reflection that when it came to matters of her parents' marriage, her mother's death, and her dad's new life, she was alone. No one saw things the same way she did.

She plugged Mama's phone in to its charger and took off running.

Five Years Before

"Mama, I thought we were running together?"

Julie had come home from work and changed in a flash so she could get her two miles in *and* meet her co-op from Acute and Chronic Illnesses to start their final project. But Mama was standing in the kitchen with a glass of water in one hand and her phone in the other, glistening with sweat and smiling down at her screen.

"Mama!"

"Oh! Jules." Leah set everything down on the counter and blinked a few times, like she was trying to focus. "I have a possible showing in about an hour, so I thought I should go ahead and get it done."

Julie frowned. There was something off in this scenario. They'd been running together every Wednesday, 5:30 PM, two "speedy" miles, for months. It was part of their plan to stay "5K ready" all the time, no matter what. It had been *Mama's* plan. Julie tried to stray a time or two, and Mama had practically lost her ever-loving mind about commitment and lactate thresholds.

"A possible showing?" Even that seemed unlikely. Some realtors jumped at every phone call. Leah Jameson was not one of those.

"Yes, Jules. It's a repeat client, and she wasn't sure what time she would get here from Cherry Grove. I'm sorry. Do you want to try for tomorrow night?"

"No. I want to know what you did with my mother who never breaks plans. And what are you *listening* to?"

"What?"

"What. Are. You. Listening. To?" She raised her voice. It felt more like a conversation she'd have with Nana than whoever this person was, acting all weird and twirly.

Leah scrunched her face up and listened for a few beats. "Honey, that's from my running playlist. It's Vertical Horizon."

"I know who it is, Mama. It's just not what you listen to."

"It is for speedwork, Julie. For crying out loud."

"Okay, Mama." *Whatever*, she added in her brain, because no matter that she was twenty-four-years old and a professional health-care worker, no matter how irritated she was with her, Julie would rarely if ever sass her mama.

Leah was already staring back at her phone with a rueful smile on her face. Her thumbs tapped rapidly as she fired off a response to something.

"Well," Julie said, feeling confused and, a rarity for her, awkward. "Hope things go well with your client. I'm going to change and get this run in."

"'kay, darlin'." Leah looked up briefly and smiled at Julie. Julie smiled back and hurried out of the kitchen.

Her mother was not breezy. She was not easily distracted. And she did not sparkle. But that day, in that moment, she was inexplicably all three.

A few weeks later, apparently, Leah closed on the house in question. Julie watched her put together a gift basket of Duplin wine, Benjamin's coffee beans, and Lord knows what other lovely, local, fussy offerings. She always put extra thought into her client thank you gifts, but that one seemed like a lot even for her. When Julie made a comment about it, Mama answered, "It's Alex, my favorite appraiser. I just want to take good care of him; he always takes good care of my clients. That's how you get just a little ahead, Jules. Personal connections. You know that."

Of course she knew that. Her mama had preached *and* modeled that her whole life. So Julie left the questions she had unasked . . . Why had Mama included a wine called Midnight Magnolia instead of her customary Muscadine Moscato? Why was there a Kelly Clarkson CD in there? Why shad she rewritten the thank you note *three times* while Julie was standing there? She just let it go because Mama did seem a little lighter, and maybe even happier right then, than she had been any time lately. She seemed not to like Daddy being home as much as he was; his curriculum creation second career seemed to be drawing nearer to its end, and even when he was working, he worked from his office they'd set up in their garage.

And Mama had always cherished her alone time, autonomy, space, whatever she was calling it these days. Having someone underfoot all the time, for the first time since the girls had been little, was not a welcome change for her. Even if the someone was her life partner.

"Are you going to seek out more listings once this one closes, or are you starting to slow it down, too?" Julie asked.

That got Mama's attention. Her head snapped up and she looked in Julie's eyes fully for the first time since she'd gotten there. "Why would I do that?"

Was she mad? Why would that make her mad? "Oh, I just thought . . . with Daddy's schedule changing . . . Y'all can do some of the things you want to do, that you can do, because you don't have to worry about us. You have money. You'd have time . . . "

"Oh, well." She started shifting things around in the basket again, essentially lifting each item out and replacing it exactly as it had been. "I am sure we will do some things. You know, Daddy is pretty content to stick around here and golf or . . . whatever."

"You guys talked about that Alaskan cruise. That could be a thing. And it's not like you'd have to stop being a realtor to take a vacation."

Mama scoffed. "You know Daddy isn't going to go that far. He just . . . "

Julie wrinkled her nose. Mama made him sound like a scared old codger. Julie always assumed they hadn't traveled more because of all the obstacles that were now being lifted.

"Mama, I bet he would. Why don't you just . . . book something? Surprise him? I can help you if you want."

Julie heard the hint of something like desperation in her voice, and she couldn't pinpoint why. Mama heard it, too.

"Julie, what in the world? Why are you concerning yourself with this? If I want to take time off or away, I can. If your father and I want to take a vacation, we will. It's not a *thing*, so let's not make it one."

She went back to fake-rearranging the basket, and Julie decided at that point to leave it. She knew there were things Mama wasn't saying, but she seemed happy, so Julie decided to leave her in peace, even if she didn't feel it herself.

Julie stopped at two miles in, right near the traffic circle in front of Publix. She'd already finished her water, and she was already questioning her choices. It was hardly dire straits; she was close to home and the shop, and she could just waltz into the grocery store and cool off, get water, call for a ride (*no way—how embarrassing*). She leaned over to catch her breath and felt herself sway the slightest bit. *Shit.* Her center of gravity wasn't what it used to be, and the humidity was bananas.

You have no business running this time of day right now.

"It's your fault," she said aloud. So now she talked back to the voice in her head, to the imagined admonishment from her dead mother. Fantastic. Was this pregnancy brain or some other abnormality? She should borrow the hoodie she'd gotten Katy on their last birthday. It said, "Undiagnosed, But Somethin' Ain't Right."

She didn't continue the conversation out loud, but she was wrong. This was her fault. She had no idea what was on that phone, whether Mama had secrets in her life. But she did know that it was hotter than hell outside, that her body's resources were going to her baby, and that she had to come up with a safer way to deal with stress. She took a few deep breaths and started walking toward Publix.

The air conditioning blasted in her face, a welcome relief from the outside air that very much resembled a convection oven, baking everything with the sun while it batted around heavy, hot air. She walked to one of the coolers by the check-out lanes and snatched the first Gatorade she saw and, in spite of its questionable ingredients and startling neon blue color, opened it and chugged it. Then she took a water and sipped before running everything through the scanner and paying with her Garmin watch.

She stood in the vestibule between the doors contemplating going back outside. Her heart was still a little racy, but she didn't feel lightheaded anymore. She could easily walk back home and be there in thirty minutes. She was obviously done running for the day.

Ask him.

Mama's voice was a bit more tentative than usual. It was softer. And Julie knew this was all in her imagination, but she believed in it anyway, because she knew the truth behind it: Her parents never asked each other for help. They didn't admit to weakness or moments of ridiculousness. They didn't want to need each other. And it had cost them. And it had cost their three daughters, who each took some sort of long, twisted road toward intimacy in their lives.

Ask him. This time, the voice was Julie's own. She took her phone out of her pocket and tapped her husband's name. There was a flood of emotion threatening her, catching in her throat. When he answered, all she could muster the voice to say was, "Come pick me up."

"Don't you have to go?"

An hour later, Julie's cheek was resting on Robin's bare knee, and both were sweating. It would have been uncomfortable if she hadn't felt so safe, reassured, peaceful.

His hands were braiding and unbraiding the end of her hair. He hadn't stopped since they got home. "Jenna is handling run club tonight. We're staying home. Eating bread. Drinking salty things."

Julie smiled, her mouth brushing his skin, and she tasted salt. Probably not what he had in mind. "I don't think margaritas are allowed, even in the second trimester."

"You're hilarious," he said, unraveling her hair again. One of the wisest decisions she'd ever made was marrying a man who had sisters. The braiding was intoxicating all on its own, one of many surprises he had saved until after they were married. "Get up. I'll get you an LMNT and then we can order dinner. Or—"

"I would love one. Thank you."

Robin had been making her (crunchy, and all-natural of course) peanut butter and (raspberry) jam sandwiches on Toffino's amazing bread since week thirteen, when her morning sickness went away and her 24/7 ravenousness began. At first, that was her only craving, but it had steadily been joined by pierogis at Atmosphera, quesabirria tacos at Tu Taco, the bianca pizza at Fratelli's, and, God help her, the Detroit fries at Grumpy Mustache, ever since Katy had convinced her to get *hot dog chunks* on top. She tried to ration most of it, kind of disgusted with herself, but the daily PBJ was a non-negotiable.

And Robin was a little sardonic at times, but he was also an absolute saint. He shifted to stand and fetch her order, but she stopped him.

"Just one second," she said, her hands pressing down on his leg. "Just . . . stay? For a minute?"

"Yeah. Yeah, of course." His hands went immediately back to her hair, and before she could stop herself, a satisfied little whimper escaped her. She tightened her hands around him.

"Babe, are you okay?" he asked. It was inevitable that he would.

"Yeah, I just . . . " It was one thing to admit physical weakness to him, but it felt disloyal to Mama to admit out loud what was growing inside. Because as sure as the baby was developing, the doubt about her mother and the foundation of their family was fully burgeoning as well.

"Daddy brought my baby stuff here earlier," she finally said.

"Good. I mean, you wanted it, right? You weren't sure he'd be able to find it?"

"Oh, he found it." Julie felt her face get warm. "He just didn't bother to go through it first."

"Oh jeez. What else was in there? Not some naughty magazines or something?"

"God, I wish." She savored the vibration of his skin against her.

"What's worse than that?"

She could think of a lot of things, probably because *Playboy* was about as far out of her father's wheelhouse as anything could get.

"Mama's effects were in there. The bag. From . . . from the hospital."

It was the second time she'd said it out loud that day, and she vowed at that moment that she wasn't going to repeat it again.

Robin, like always, hung on her every word. She was getting better at not being disarmed by the way he cocked his head and looked right at her, maybe into her, when she was speaking. "Baby cakes, are you afraid of something on that phone?"

How did he know?

Julie swallowed against the lump in her throat and the butterflies in her tummy. When she opened her mouth, no words came out, but the nodding of her head was his invitation to move closer and hold her. And she let him.

Brittney

9

Her jeans would not button, and even though she preferred maxi skirts and flowy linen pants anyway, that was as sure a sign as any that it was *time*. If nothing else, Mama needed to know, and then everyone else could just fall in line. She was going to make it clear to the familial masses that how she proceeded to raise *her* baby from here was not up for debate. How she proceeded with Harrison was also off the table, unless someone happened to have a brilliant idea that she hadn't thought of during her many insomniac hours of late.

She stopped at The Grumpy Mustache on the way for a double order of inexplicably great queso. Had Brittney thought ahead, she would have had Mama meet here there for Taco Tuesday, as there was slightly less chance of a scene in public places.

Slightly.

She made small talk with Betty and Greg for as long as she could justify before taking her container of liquid gold and heading down the street to her potential doom. They were down a cook and a bartender, and she felt a little tug inside of her. Their hours there were way better than The Fishwalk; they closed the kitchen at eight, and people cleared the bar by nine. Maybe she'd go back for lunch the next day she had open and . . .

"Holy. Shit."

The words escaped her from down the street. Mama had already told her Paul would not be there, that it would be "just the girls." Well, Mikayla's car was there. Aunt Maggie's car was there. Freaking *Julie's* car was there. Had there not been Salty Lips practice that night, Katy would have been there, too, but at least she probably could have counted on her to be an ally.

Holy shit.

She wanted to take her cheese dip, turn around, and shove it all in her face from the comfort of her couch while rewatching season three of *New Girl*. At the very least, she wanted to text Harrison and ask him what to do. But it was so immature. He had to figure out how to tell his *children*. The least she could do was tell her mother. She was an adult.

No. Really.

She parked and walked into the house like she was going to face a firing squad, which wasn't that far off. The raucous conversation was crystal clear as soon as she opened the front door. Mikayla was sitting on a swivel chair at one end of the dining table that could be pointed toward the kitchen or the living room. It was pointed toward their mother and Aunt Maggie at the island, apparently debating which farmstand had the better tomatoes at this precarious time of year. *Good. Get nice and worked up before we even start.*

As Brittney gave cheek-kisses and started unpacking her bag, Julie emerged from the bathroom. Her baby bump was sprouting and even though they still held each other a bit distantly, she couldn't help but admire it. "Oh my God," she said, stopping just short of giving Julie a belly-rub. "You are adorable. Sorry. But you are."

Julie flashed a self-conscious smile. "Please do not apologize for calling me anything remotely nice right now," she said. "This cute little key lime is messing with my center of gravity already. I had a dizzy spell at work yesterday, and now Robin is watching me like a hawk."

Who was this person? Julie was the stepsister Brittney knew the least. The few times they had hung out, Katy had been there narrating, navigating, and filling all available spaces so nothing would be too awkward.

Luckily, Aunt Maggie had the same gift, because Brittney was concerned as to whether this chatty, open version of Julie would stay all night or morph into scary, probably judgy Julie.

"Tell Robin to look the other way," Aunt Maggie stated, rhythmically chopping a jalapeño. "You're smart, and you've taken care of your body this far."

"Yeah, but all bets are off with pregnancy," Mama cut in, dicing up tomatoes with her own special tomato knife. "He's just looking out for you, I'm sure."

Brittney shook her head. The whole night was going to go like this. Mama used to be all kinds of tentative with Julie, because they used to be all kinds of enemies with each other. But since they made peace and Julie gave her Dolly, the displaced dog of one of her co-workers, they'd continually mellowed out. There were bumps along the way—especially around Julie's wedding, which Brittney had put out of her head for all the secondhand awkwardness—so she was surprised Mama was going to dole out the Jessie Oakley wisdom here.

Julie surprised her again, first by rolling her eyes directly at Brittney, where no one else could see, and then by saying sort of brightly, "I'm sure, too. Just doesn't make it any less annoying to have every move I make be analyzed. We're still newlyweds; I'd rather every move I make be admired. Adored, even."

"Oh, pregnancy changes everything. Everything," Mikayla chimed in from her chair. "But now in your second trimester when everything starts rounding out just right and you *glow*? He will conveniently forget how delicate you are, at least some of the time."

Were they in bizarro world? Was her refined and reserved big sister actually referring to *sex* around the rest of them?

Julie launched into full-on banter with Mikayla, and Brittney just wasn't in the mood to hear about their gorgeous husbands who basically worshiped them. So, she stayed at the counter, longingly eyeing her mother and aunt's sangria glasses and wondering how long until the food would be ready. They seemed to be chopping a whole lot of *things*.

"What exactly are we having for *Taco* Tuesday, Mama?"

"Oh. You hungry, baby? Start in on the queso. We're just having street tacos, but with pico de gallo."

Of course. Chop away. It could not be as easy as opening a damn jar of salsa. She tore into the queso, conveniently topped with Grumpy's delicious, homemade *pico de gallo!*

"Brit, you should have some wine," Aunt Maggie said, passing her glass over. "You seem a little somethin'-somethin'."

Oh, she was somethin' alright. "Thanks, but . . . my stomach is doing a thing. I'm just gonna grab a Bubly." Her stomach was doing *so many* things.

"Rough day?" Mama asked. Finally, she was putting all the things in a bowl and stirring. This was a good sign.

"Not really. I just . . . " Brittney looked over to Aunt Maggie, who was now talking animatedly to the other two. "I was kinda of looking forward to a low-key evening."

"Oops. I'm sorry . . . you should have said something."

"No. It's your house and your . . . Tuesday."

"Do you want to go outside and talk? Or to my room?"

"No, Mama. Don't make a fuss—"

Too late.

"What's up, Miss Brittney?" Aunt Maggie asked.

"Nothing. I—nothing. Is the food ready yet?" She looked at her aunt and put on her best hangdog expression. "I'm so hungryyyyyyy."

"Oh, sweet Lord, *you're* hungry? *We* are eating for two!" Mikayla called, looking to Julie in a sisterly way that did not sit well with Brittney. *Not at all.*

"I didn't know I needed special status to want to *eat food*, Mother Earth." Brittney snatched Aunt Maggie's sangria glass and took one slow, fortifying sip. It would maybe calm her nerves and also throw them off her scent. There was no way she could have the conversation with Mama with the rest of them there.

Mikayla started to snap back, but Mama cut in. "It's ready. It's ready!"

Brittney *almost* laughed at that, because in that moment, it was like Mama had PTSD from when they were all kids, and she was frantic all the time. The exchange with Mikayla was mild. If Brittney was being honest, she was also annoyed that they couldn't just eat freaking generic ground beef tacos like normal people. It always had to be a new recipe or some grand homemade mango-habanero-whatever.

"Good. I just want to eat and go home."

She didn't mean to say it out loud, but there it was. And whatever. The silence was awkward, but she grabbed a plate and filled it with tortilla chips, the salsa and queso, and finally, the carnitas that Mama had probably spent all day cooking to perfection.

Once everyone was seated, she muttered, "Sorry. Just a bad day."

Aunt Maggie responded with, "Well Brit, being a big, titty baby won't get the food to your mouth any faster," just as Julie said, "You're allowed." Mama and Kayla were just eating their tacos. Clearly, Brittney had pissed them off, too.

Brittney rolled her eyes at her aunt, pointedly saying, "The carnitas are great, Mama."

"I could drink this queso," Julie said. "Where did you get it?"

Brittney started to tell her, but Mama cut her off. "The point of Taco Tuesday, Brittney Jane, is *gathering*. Not just eating junk food. You can have Taco Bell any night of the week you want. Eat Tostitos dip out of the damn can. But one day a week, I still get to cook for some of the people I brought into this earth. And if you don't like that, I am sure one of your brothers can help you find a place to live near them, since living *here* is clearly passé."

"Wow," Julie said. Mama glared at her, and Aunt Maggie smirked. "Sorry," she added. "But Jessie, that was an impressive escalation."

"I have to agree," Aunt Maggie added.

The two of them tucked back into her food. Mama turned her glare toward Brittney, who returned it for a moment, and then looked away, wishing she could start the night all over again.

"If there is enough left, can I take some to Altan?" Mikayla asked. "I can't even stand the thought of cooking meat right now. It's been a lot of beans and rice and scrambled eggs at our house."

"Ew," Julie said. "I can't do raw eggs either. Or sour cream. The smell of it . . . "

Brittney suddenly felt her stomach lurch. Whether it was the strong smell of the seasoned pork on her plate or the imagery of egg yolks and sour cream jiggling around, she was catapulted out of her seat and ran straight for the hall bathroom, where, as if on cue, she proceeded to empty the entire contents of her stomach.

It's just the flu, she told herself. *I can convince them it's just the flu.*

She splashed water on her face and squirted some emergency toothpaste from the cabinet into her mouth, even though Mama only bought hippie stuff that tasted like baking soda and sadness. Then she sauntered back to her seat as though nothing had happened.

All four women around the table literally stared at her with either one or two raised eyebrows, depending on their genetic abilities.

"What?" she said, looking at her plate. There was no way she could eat any more of it.

The reply was a mingled chorus of "Are you sick?" and "Are you okay?" and "What the hell, Brit?"

"I'm fine. I just . . . I guess an empty stomach and then all the strong smells and . . . talking about raw stuff." She threw her own glare Mikayla's way, but Kayla didn't notice. She was staring at the ceiling, apparently in her own deep thoughts.

"That never bothered you before," Mama pointed out. "You have a stomach of iron."

"Oh!"

As soon as the exclamation escaped Mikayla's mouth, Brittney knew she was done for. Surrounded by her only sister, a former OB nurse, and the wanna-be detectives known as Jessie and Maggie, it had been over the moment she ran away to vomit. What a time for *morning* sickness to find her.

She sent Mikayla a look that screamed "NO," but it was too late.

"You have something to tell us?" Mama asked. She was tight-lipped and quiet, which was the worst. Julie's jaw was practically on the floor.

Aunt Maggie, whose own daughter had experienced a . . . *spontaneous? unplanned? unwed? What was the right word these days?* . . . pregnancy, was eating her taco, eyebrows still raised.

Brittney exhaled as deeply as she could. Then she took a deep breath hoping new air would fill her with the strength and savviness she needed for this conversation.

"It seems you already know," she murmured. "Yes. I am pregnant."

Silence for several beats, and then:

Julie: "Welcome to the club."

Mikayla: Continued her somewhat frightened stare. She'd been Mama's daughter even longer than Brittney had been; she knew the deal.

Aunt Maggie: "Well, joy to the world, darlin'. Tell us everything, please."

Mama: "I don't believe this."

She doesn't believe this? She doesn't believe *it?* Of all the things she could say, after all the things that had happened the past few years, nothing in this family should be unbelievable.

"I am thirty-one years old, Mama. It's not like I was careless on prom night."

"I think the kind of night it was is so very much beside the point." She didn't even sound sarcastic. She just sounded angry, which made Brittney angry. She glared straight into Mama's eyes, trying to form the words.

"I am sure this is just another disappointment in a long string of them, but this is a child. A grandchild. You dote on them, don't you? Or is that only reserved for the ones born to marriages *or* descending from your precious first-born?" Travis had been conceived when Sam and Abby were dating in college.

"Don't make this about anyone else. You have the same opportunities in life as your brothers or Mikayla. Your choices are *yours*, Brittney, and now they are limited. It's plain and simple."

"You think I don't know that?"

"I think you know it in theory. I think you have no idea what it means to have a whole person depend on you. It isn't easy, and you won't find all the answers, or all the health insurance, or all the extra grocery money on TikTok."

Brittney shook her head, and though she didn't want to involve anyone else, there were three very enthralled spectators present. Surely one of them would be on her side.

"Do you see what I mean?" she asked, scanning the room, her eyes landing on Mikayla. "She thinks I am stupid and incapable. *Still*!"

Of course, Mikayla answered like the queen of Switzerland, "No one thinks you're stupid . . . "

"Oh my God!" Brittney yelled. "Can't you just take my side for once?"

"I will," came a solid voice from behind her. Julie's.

"You've more than proven you're capable of figuring it out. You went from a shitty job and a borrowed room to owning your own home and starting your own business in the span of a few months. And your business is mostly paying your bills, right? Of course you'll rise to this occasion, too. Congrats, Brit."

Brittney wasn't entirely shocked—disagreeing with Mama was probably still a little irresistible to Julie. But the mere thought of some solidarity bolstered Brittney. And then Aunt Maggie chimed in.

"*Congratulations* is really the first thing you need to be hearing right now."

Mama glared at her. Aunt Maggie stared right back before speechifying:

"No one in this room, not one of us, has done anything the simple way. And I daresay we all came out on the other side okay, even if we had to struggle and fight. And there ain't one of us who has had to struggle and fight *alone*."

Brittney held in a sigh. She wasn't sure how much her perfect big sister had had to struggle, unless she thought about Mikayla's utterly heartbreaking miscarriage the Christmas before Daddy died. Nah. Aunt Maggie was right. They all had *different* struggles, but struggles nonetheless.

"I am not going to apologize for wanting better for my kids," Mama said.

"But she's not a kid," Aunt Maggie retorted. She's a grown-ass woman with her business settled and is in love with a whole grown-ass man."

There was a pause as every eye in the room turned to Brittney. Her cheeks reddened. Here was the real beginning of the conversation.

"What did Harrison say?" Mama asked.

"Everything you would expect." She took a sip of water to fortify her resolve. "He's . . . as happy as we can be, considering the circumstances."

"Circumstances, indeed," Mama said.

"Mama! It's not like it's simple. He has two *children*. He can't just up and move back here to be with me, or he would!"

Mama stood. It made her stomach flutter a little bit, because Brittney knew this meant serious business, and she probably wasn't going to like it.

"Oh, FFS, Brit! That is exactly what I am talking about." Well, if she wasn't saying the actual F-bomb, maybe it wasn't so bad. "He has two kids *already*, in a different state. He has bonds and obligations and legalities . . . with others. Not with you. Do you have a plan? Or a promise of one?"

"What do you think?" she snapped. "It's new. We have a lot to figure out."

"I'm sure. And all I am saying is, if you were *married*, you wouldn't have to figure it out. Your family *circumstances*, however complicated, would be set."

"If we were married, I would have moved away with him," Brittney answered hotly, just as Aunt Maggie said, "Well, *look who's talkin'*, Jessie Rose."

"Wait, what?" Mikayla asked. Everyone now looked at Mama instead of Brittney, whose head was spinning.

"I thought a contract didn't really mean anything," Aunt Maggie continued. "Just commitment."

"What is she talking about, Mama?" Mikayla continued.

"I'd like to know, too," Julie added, an edge to her voice.

Mama's eyes were darts pointed at her best friend. Brittney couldn't imagine what the deal was, or how it had anything to do with her unwed pregnant girl status. Mama's own similar episode was about forty years in the past.

"I just mean, your mama sure as hell was against a contract, and that seems to be working out just fine for her."

10

I honestly could have throat-punched Maggie in that moment. Was there any conceivable way she thought she wasn't breaking a confidence?

"Maggie, that is a conversation for a different time. I don't think it's relevant to—"

"The hell it isn't!" Brittney responded. "*What* is she talking about?"

Maggie waved her hand dismissively. "Oh, I just mean that your mama and your daddy," she pointed at Julie for emphasis, "are Jesus married. No contract unless you count the unwritten one with the Almighty."

Three simultaneous female voices cried, "WHAT?" One of them added extra words at the end.

"You aren't married? You aren't *married*!" Julie was shaking her head and maybe shaking all over. Mikayla looked like she was about to cry. And Brittney was *seething*. I considered ducking behind the counter, so high was the hostility in the room at that moment. And if I was being honest, I couldn't blame them.

"How is this possible?" Brittney continued. "We were all there." Well, Julie hadn't been, and she was likely going to go right back to hating me after this. "We saw it for ourselves. Pastor Carter pronounced you *man and wife*."

"By the power vested in him by *whom*?" Julie asked. Ah, she was so clever.

"Who cares?" Brittney snapped.

"Because they tricked everyone," Julie continued. "And if Pastor Carter didn't say 'by the state of South Carolina' or some other legal authority, then *he* wasn't lying."

"He said by 'the Father, the Son, and the Holy Ghost,'" Mikayla chimed in. "I remember because it made Altan and me giggle. I always get a visual of something like . . . Casper . . . when people say 'Holy Ghost' instead of 'Holy Spirit.'" She looked down at her hands. "So, I guess we are all stupid for not noticing. Or questioning."

"Of course, you're not—" I started, just as Julie talked over me.

"Why would we question? We are supposed to be able to trust our parents."

The complicated oddities of their family were evident as the daughter who was enraged with me defended me. "Not present, no say!" Brittney snapped at Julie. Julie opened her mouth to retort, but Maggie talked right over her.

"You *can* trust your parents. You can also trust that not everything is your business."

"Are you saying my father's marital status is not my business?" Julie retorted, alongside Mikayla giving her aunt an exaggerated side-eye, and Brittney jumping back in the trench with Julie, saying, "This is absolutely, 100 percent our business, and you know it!"

"Okay, okay." I sat back down, resisting the temptation to swallow the entirety of my glass of sangria. "First of all, the question of whether it is their business is now null and void, Maggie, since you just made it their business. Second of all, marital status: Paul and I are married."

"Whatever *Jesus married* means," Julie muttered.

"Yeah, seriously. C'mon, Mama," Brittney added.

"Can y'all just shush for a minute?" I bellowed. "Please! How can anyone answer your questions when you keep trying to answer them yourselves?"

They went silent, which did nothing to help the tension in the room.

"We are, in fact, 'Jesus married,' thank you for that, Maggie." I paused dramatically to glare at her. "We decided that in order to preserve Daddy's pension, most of which is going to belong to you and your brothers" —I assumed they all knew whom I meant— "that we would keep our legal status separate. Our finances separate. But the house is in both of our names. We pay bills together. We just aren't each other's legal spouse."

Head shaking. Sighing. Wordless exchanges between my two daughters. I couldn't bear to look at Julie. I had wanted Paul to tell her, but he had his reasons. He always did.

Just as I had. Now they seemed . . . dumb.

"What about next of kin? Power of attorney? *Medical* power of attorney?" Julie asked, as I knew she would.

"Well, your dad has me in place for those things," I said, forcing myself not to sound small or apologetic.

"And for you?"

Now I couldn't bear to look at Mikayla or Brittney.

"Sam."

"Maggie!" If I could shoot lasers from my eyeballs at her, I would have in that moment. "Stop answering for me, for the *love of God*!"

"Sam!" Brittney cried, as Mikayla jumped from her seat. "Of course, Sam. Sam knows. It's always Sam. The rest of us are *idiots*."

"I can't believe this, Mama," Mikayla said, so soft and steely that I almost couldn't hear her. "I'm leaving."

"Sit down," Maggie commanded. Normally, Mikayla would have listened, but she was heading straight for the door.

"Could you maybe let me handle my own business?" I snapped, as I took off after her.

"If only," I heard Maggie say, while Julie threw in a "You're doing a bang-up job." Brittney scoffed.

My face turned red, but I caught Mikayla at the door.

"Kayla."

"Mama, I really don't want to hear it right now. I'm tired. I want to go home and give Josie her bath and tell Altan all about this. Don't worry. I'm sure he'll defend you."

I looked down. Altan and I did have a bit of a mutual admiration society. But I was sure even he would find my secrecy—my dishonesty—indefensible.

"Mikayla." Her expression softened ever so slightly. "I'm not going to try to make you understand. I just want you to know I'm sorry. I don't . . . I know it doesn't make sense, but . . . I just didn't want to make a big deal out of it. In my heart, I am married to Paul. We are living a married life."

"But why not tell us that?"

I wanted to say *You didn't ask*, but that's not the kind of thing one says to a daughter. And it was a cop-out anyway.

"I didn't want to explain myself." I said it like an exhale. I tried to sound more humble, less confident, but my mind just wasn't changed. "After everything that happened, moving too quickly, David and Julie moving away and breaking up, us breaking up and getting back together . . . I just didn't want to have to justify the decision over and over again."

She narrowed her eyes at me. She looked the same as she did when she was an eight-year-old quizzing me as to whether I hid veggies in the macaroni and cheese, which of course I had and of course I denied. *Damn.*

"Did you really think the legal versus spiritual status of your marriage was the hard part for us to swallow?"

I shook my head, disarmed. "Of course not."

"Did you think it would occur to any of us that *you*, a rule follower, would not be getting married *legally*? Come *on*, Mama!"

It had occurred to Sam. I let my silence speak.

"Did Sam ask you?"

At that moment, Brittney and Julie joined us at the door. They weren't holding anything, so they weren't leaving, just joining the conversation. *Bloody hell.*

"The truth is, Sam questioned whether getting married was a smart decision because of my age; if I remarried before the age of sixty, I would forfeit my widow benefits."

"So, are you going to get married when you turn sixty?" That looming event was coming up after the holidays, even though I'd been rounding up my age since Randall died.

My pause seemed to answer the question. All three of them were huffing in their own ways.

The traditional version of me wanted to answer. I wanted to appease them. I didn't even really have a reason to do anything *but* marry Paul at that point. But the version of me who had been through at least five levels of hell in the past two years was not interested in presenting a defense to people half my age, whether I'd given birth to them or not. There were many layers of complication, and I didn't even have words for all of them.

And there were factors I wasn't quite willing to admit. even to myself just yet.

I raised my chin somewhat defiantly and said, "We'll see."

Mikayla walked out the door. Brittney and Julie shared a look—God help me, I was not used to the solidarity forming between them, and I was both grateful for and pissy about it.

Brittney waved a hand. "She'll be fine." They walked toward the kitchen leaving me standing there and, not for the first time, unsure of where to go in my own house.

"Finish eating," Maggie called. But another thing that hell had changed about me: comfort food was no longer a stress reliever for me. It might have been my age, my radiation, or having a wardrobe that included size eight pants for the first time since I was a teenager, but my appetite vanished with stress, drama, tension, and/or hostility. And there was plenty of it going around.

I walked slowly back toward the table. Julie and even a recovered Brittney suddenly both behaved like young women eating for two. Maggie was pouring herself a second, or tenth, for all I knew, sangria. I watched Brittney carefully. Somehow the bombshell news of my youngest daughter's pregnancy had gotten pushed to the side by melodrama over my boring, third-maybe-fourth-quarter marital status.

If I were Brittney, I would be super pissed.

Even not being her, I was super pissed.

I sat in the chair next to her. She made a show of not looking at me, of concentrating *super* hard on the little crock of queso she'd set next to her plate of chips. I watched her carefully choose her dip-to-chip ratio as she had been doing since she was four-years-old. She got it from me. We took nachos seriously.

Each of us also had a special gift for making irrational decisions which we could justify with wit or poetry—except to each other.

"Brittney."

She didn't budge. Julie raised an eyebrow from across the table. Maggie brought the carafe to me. I shooed her away. This was all her damn fault.

"Brittney, I am sorry for my reaction. I am . . . congratulations on the baby!"

I meant it. I loved babies. I loved my babies. I loved the idea of *my* baby girl being a mother. But if she was the Cher to my Olympia Dukakis, well, I had to say that her life was going down the toilet.

"Thanks," she grunted.

I really wished the other two would go so we could fight it out. But no one else was giving in, so I gave up.

"We can talk when you're ready, about all of it. I'm . . . I think I'm done for the day. Julie—" I stood up, walked to her chair, and placed a demure kiss on the top of her head. "Take some leftovers for Robin." Julie was made of tough stuff. She would probably have a go at her father for the things he didn't tell her, and I learned that she would get over it in her own time if I didn't force anything.

I did not say goodbye to Maggie. And she had better clean up the kitchen.

Jessie

11

*T**witchy* was one word to describe my state after everyone left the house, and I was left to my own devices.

Anxious was another.

Abso-friggen-lutely panicked was another. I guess that was a phrase rather than a word. It was the closest match.

I had thought Paul would be home from dinner before all my girls left. I had expected an evening of más sangria for those of us not with child. I had expected the non-pregnant to pregnant ratio to be in my and Maggie's favor, not the other way around. And while I had certainly not expected news that my youngest daughter was the second of my offspring to be expecting a child outside of marriage, I expected even less that my own *outside of marriage-ness* would be exposed, much less be the hotbed topic of the evening.

Paul would be furious. If I was capable of singular emotion, I would be, too.

Instead, I went on a post-sunset cleaning binge, vacuuming every crevice of our 2,300 square foot house and organizing my sock drawer. Paul had turned me onto *technical running socks*. I barely wore socks, so it seemed time to get rid of every sub-par pair I had (most over ten or twelve years old) and only keep the good ones.

When I finished, I had a pile of random, including some unmatched, socks on the floor, and I was standing in front of Paul's open sock drawer contemplating if I should repeat the effort or if socks were too personal for such a task. And then he walked in.

"Whatcha up to, Jess?" he said with a knowing smile that melted my butter without fail.

I summarized my efforts for him, not the reason behind them. And since he was used to Jessie the Overthinker, he just nodded and sat on *his chair*.

Yeah. Suddenly, he was using it for sitting, quite often.

"How was dinner?" I asked, full of nonchalance.

"Good," he answered, offering no details, even though I always wanted to know what he ate, what everyone else ate, and any slightly relevant or interesting conversational details.

I watched him take off his shoes and then his socks. He stretched his legs out and did what we call a *squiggle*, burrowing into the chair and taking a deep breath, end-of-day relaxed and likely tired.

"How was yours?" he asked me.

I walked to the bed and sat on it, just across from him.

"Brittney is pregnant." That didn't need a windup. We were used to pregnant daughters.

"Well, I'll be John Damn Brown," he replied. Well, maybe it was a *bit* of a thing.

"Yeah. And before you ask, there is nothing else planned, *besides* a baby. I don't think she or Harrison are making any quick moves."

"Well, how could he?" Paul asked. "Movin' ain't cheap, and he's done it twice in short order, and a kid here doesn't change him having two kids there."

Usually, his ability to summarize blessed my overthinking heart. This was decidedly *not* one of those times.

"Have mercy, Jesus. Don't I know it?"

"Is Brit okay?" he asked. His attention was suddenly fully on me, his eyes intently studying me. In the light of his moodiness and distractedness in the previous weeks, it was alarming at first, and then immediately comforting.

"Well, she's, you know, she's *Brittney*. Full of piss and vinegar. Doesn't know anything, doesn't want to ask for help."

"That all sounds right," he said.

That's where I should have inserted something witty or wise. I should have done so with my daughter, too. Dang it, I was off my game. I wasn't sure I had any game at that point.

"She is physically okay," I said, though I realized at that moment that she'd run from the table to upchuck her dinner, and I didn't really have any clue *how* she was, other than justifiably quite angry with me.

Paul was still staring at me, but he'd begun the leg jiggle that signaled he was losing a bit of patience with the conversation. I wasn't being purposely coy, but I definitely didn't want to get to the next part.

"That's it?" he asked. "Really? I mean, how many weeks is she? How many days? What is the theme of the shower? Which restaurant's queso is the baby making her crave? Come on, Jess. Your baby girl is having a baby, and you're sorting the socks. What is up?"

I closed my eyes for a moment. I was not the same person I used to be. I was fully grown. Survived widowhood, cancer, major career change, buying and selling a business, untold adult-children dramas, our relationship drama, and a traumatic car accident in the past three years. I refused to be afraid to talk to my husband.

And he *was* my husband. Damn those kids for making me doubt what my heart had sealed.

"Hurricane Maggie . . . " I started. It wasn't a toss under the bus, but it did cut out the need for much introduction.

"Oh, sweet Lawd, what?" Like Randall had, Paul adored Maggie and was plenty comfortable with her. But he had far less history and patience with her.

"Well, me being me . . . Hurricane Mama . . . the subject of being unwed came up with Brittney, and I was angry, probably judgmental, to be honest . . . and Maggie took that opportunity to put me right in my place."

There. I was taking the blame.

"What does that mean, Jess?"

I couldn't tell if he already knew, but if I had to bet . . .

"Well, the phrase 'Jesus Married' was uttered."

Ugh. Being vague was so Past Jessie.

"Jessie Rose?"

I nodded.

"So they all know?"

"By now?" I said. "Probably."

"Who was here?"

I rattled off their names, saving Julie for last.

I swear, his sigh lasted a minute and seventeen seconds.

"Well. This is just fucking great."

I winced. Even if our family motto was *F-F-S*, and was uttered throughout most waking hours, Paul steered clear of profanity most of the time.

The word sounded unnatural coming from him, not to mention full of fury.

I wanted to say, "It's whatever. This is our life. Our business. We don't have to *G-A-F* about what any of them think." Wasn't he the one always telling me that? But that was not how I felt. I was embarrassed, and a little guilty, and also disappointed in myself. If we really thought being *just Jesus married* was just fine, why didn't we tell the people closest to us?

"I'm not . . . " My turn to sigh. I stood there, kind of ridiculously, amid the piles of socks, leaning against the dresser, not having any idea what to say or do next. "I'm not happy how they found out. But Paul, if it matters to them, whether we think it should or not, then I'm glad they know the truth. Or will, once those three get the news out."

"I doubt Julie will tell anyone," Paul muttered. "Maybe Robin, but I kinda doubt that, too."

"Why?" I asked.

"Because she'll feel stupid that she didn't know," he said, which was very apropos of Julie. "And," he added, after a heavy pause, "she will be ashamed of me for lying to them."

Well, hell. And ouch. The silence fell between us quite naturally then. If he had been a different sort of guy, one who didn't curate words, and Julie a different sort of woman, one who didn't occasionally use them like knives, I might have accused him of being melodramatic. But they were who they were, and I knew them both, so I knew better.

"I'm sorry it happened," I said quietly. He was looking at the floor rather than me, so I started dumbly picking up the socks and stuffing them in the waiting white Hefty bag that I would shove in my car until I made it to Goodwill. When I finished, I turned back toward him, and he had moved his gaze out the window. I thought of those women I had talked to in Georgetown and decided to be the person I said I was that night. I left him alone, moved to the kitchen, and put on water for tea. Dolly probably didn't need to go out, but I took her anyway. And I ticked off the times Maggie's big mouth and terrible timing had caused disarray in my personal life. Maybe that wasn't fair because certainly if I had been honest with my kids, there would be no news or *clarification* to spout. But it still happened. And I still had the fragments of a detonated bomb to deal with.

When Dolly and I came inside, Paul was standing in the kitchen making my tea. It was a mash-up few understood the appeal of and no one could make but him or me: cinnamon tea bag and equal dashed of cinnamon whiskey, honey, and cream. I was my mother's daughter in very few ways, but I never liked hot tea without milk. *Cheers, Mom. I am still a hot mess most days after all.*

"Thank you," I said, hating that I sounded kind of shy.

"You're welcome," he murmured, handing me the steaming mug and finally looking into my eyes.

"I'm not mad at you, Jess. I was close, but I'm not mad."

That was not a good start. What right did he have to be mad at me?

"What are you then?" I heard the edge in my voice, so surely he did, too.

"I'm just weary of all the emotional fallout all the time." Well, of course. It harkened right back to that talk I had with the ladies. He wanted buttoned-up, simple emotions, conversations, and relationships. How in the world, with three daughters, he ever thought that was attainable was beyond me.

"Well, Paul, I can't really control everyone else's emotions, and I did my best to control mine. I don't know what else to tell you."

I heard the note of finality in my voice, something I usually did not inject.

"I guess that's it, then. Conversation over?"

Yep. He heard it, too.

"What can I possibly say? I reacted to some upsetting news in some kinda way, and it ignited everyone else. This isn't unusual. Yes. I should have been more gentle with Brittney. But that isn't what you're concerned with. You're worried about Julie being upset with *you*. So maybe this time we just handle our own kids and let that be that."

Ugh. I heard it, the dividing lines, the *ick*, and I hated it.

"None of them are kids," he said. And that was all he said.

It was a constant sticking point between us. He was hands-off; I was hands-on. It was never going to change, no matter how many conversations we had about it. I was getting used to the idea of just letting it go.

"You're right," I acquiesced. "So let the cards fall. If they have questions, they'll ask. If we have answers, we can share them."

"What does *that* mean?" he asked. "Are you devoid of answers that I'm not aware of?"

I thought about it as I soaked in the tension that was between us. I didn't think I had questions, but hearing the judgment and outrage from his daughter and mine made me question why exactly we had made the choices we did.

I looked, really looked, into his eyes. Thankfully, he met my gaze because at that moment, I thought my skin might crawl if he didn't.

"Do you ever wonder why we decided what we did? Or whether we made the right decision?"

"Jessie," he said, not missing a beat. "Are you forgetting that I said we can change this status whenever you want to. Because I won't change my mind. And I haven't. I am married to you in all the ways that matter, and I will marry you in any other way that matters to you."

I didn't know why I couldn't verbalize a response. But every word I tried to utter stuck in my throat. It used to be so easy between us; why was I always second-guessing?

"And Jess?" he continued, letting me off the hook, "I mean what matters to *you*." He stopped there, but I could almost see the words stopping and starting in *his* throat. I could fill in every blank. *Not what the kids think. Not what looks right from the outside.*

I nodded, smiling at him in a way that felt deep but small. He rose from the chair, crossed to me, and brushed his lips against mine, barely pausing as he continued to the bathroom to start his nighttime routine.

It was all so familiar, his facial expressions, the cadence of his words, the way he looked at me, his bedtime routine. But the difficulty getting through was brand new, and I stood there wondering how to fix it.

Brittney

12

B rittney scrunched up her eyes as she did the math in her head for the sixth time, still picturing the screen display of her banking app. She had enough to pay her cell phone, the software bundle she used daily for her clients, and her car insurance, all her middle-of-the-month bills. But the private health insurance Mama insisted she needed? That cost more than those three combined, and if she paid it, she'd be eating all her meals at Mama's. And walking everywhere.

Can't have a baby without insurance.

Wait … can you?

Julie would know. Hell, Julie *could* probably deliver the baby herself, but Brittney wasn't sure she *would*. There had been some kind of traumatic event that caused Julie not only to drop the pursuit of her master's in nurse midwifery but also to leave OB nursing all together, and she rarely ever talked about it.

Well, Brit would bring it up the next time she saw her. In the meantime, Brittney pulled into the parking lot at the end of Garden City, where she'd been a whole bunch of times lately, sipping a club soda with lemon at the bar and generating her Canva images while listening to the banter around her and the ever-present mashup of Kendrick Lamar, Frank Sinatra, and Teddy Swims on the TouchTunes.

The Grumpy Mustache. She had become a mainstay there, so she might as well see if she could get paid for her time.

Lots of people had three jobs; this was the beach. Wages sucked. Being mostly-self-employed compounded that. Working at a bar after Labor Day compounded *that*. And a few more weeks with no clarity from Harrison compounded all of that.

"I'm so happy."

"I don't know what to do."

Those two mantras were on repeat from him. And besides a warm fuzzy, it did absolutely nothing for her. He'd had a row with Denise, with whom he was usually amicable, about Dakota's math grade and Playstation 5, and it seemed to take him a few days to get over that. Meanwhile, Ruthie was maybe going to have to get her tonsils out. She didn't want to press him in the middle of other stress, but she was also coming to terms with the fact that there would always be other stress. Always.

She tapped out to Katy, the only person who knew what she was planning.

Goodness. Everyone should have a Katy.

Brittney grabbed her bag, foofed her hair, and sauntered in. It was three in the afternoon, so the expected lull was taking place. She heard the sounds of Willie's Roadhouse on the satellite radio coming from the back. One lone ranger was at the bar, and when she looked closely, she knew it was that Nashville dude Morgan or Mason or Waylon or something, whom she always tried to avoid. An older couple was sitting in one of the booths with iced teas and cheese curds between them. LeeAnn came busting out of the kitchen with a jalapeño in her hand, beaming when she saw Brittney.

"What's uuuuuuup, girl?" She made a kissing sound and went to work on a spicy margarita. "You want one?"

"No, thank you, I'm just here to hang and get some work done."

"Cool. Sit down. You eatin'?"

"Oh, yeah. Baby really wants a cheesesteak."

What? What did she just say?

Brittney had already slid onto the red stool and felt LeeAnn's eyes snap directly onto her. For that matter, Waylon's did, too. *Shit.*

She sat up as straight as she could, as though that would turn back time or make her invisible, and simply said, "I am super hungry, LeeAnn. Extra white sauce, okay?"

"Got it, love." Like a consummate professional, she turned her back to Brittney, finished and served Waylon's drink, and entered Brittney's order. Brittney was watching intently, no longer caring whether these virtual strangers knew she was pregnant. LeeAnn might tell some people, but they'd all know eventually anyway. What she was really gauging was whether the POS software was similar to the one at Fishwalk. Ed's place was much more chaotic than this one. How hard could it be?

She picked up her phone and started texting everyone. Katy. Harrison. El. Mikayla, even though their interactions had stayed a little weird since the night of all-the-things at Mama's. She even shot a note to her brothers, albeit on the same text. She didn't have much to say to either of them these days beyond: *Hope you're well, thanks for abandoning the family when everything is constantly chaotic and you know, Daddy is still dead.*

She refrained from sending the last part. And it wasn't LeeAnn, but Betty, who appeared before her with her plate.

"You workin'?" she asked, grabbing a fry, which was one of the reasons Brittney loved being there. She felt like they were all friends, even if it was just in her head. The only friends she really had were El, and kind of the band, and her siblings, er, even the step ones these days. Katy had been her friend long before all the stuff that had changed all their lives.

It was still so weird.

"Yeah. Sort of, I guess. I should be anyway. Having some trouble focusing."

"Bwah. My life. You ADHD?"

Brittney smirked. Who wasn't? "Who isn't?"

"You have your brain scanned?"

"Girl, no. Self-diagnosed." She didn't know a single entrepreneur, or content marketer, or person who had a smartphone, who had an attention span longer than that of a flea.

"You should have it done. It's fascinating."

Brittney dipped a steaming hot fry in her Alabama BBQ sauce, a creamy concoction teeming with horseradish, and made a happy little sound as she chewed.

"I should. But in the meantime, I will trade you just about anything for food. Or another job."

Betty, who stood five feet even and carried herself like a defensive lineman—in a good way—put down her phone and stared at Brittney with her sometimes-intimidating intensity. Like, she never blinked.

"You really want hours? Don't you work enough?"

Brittney sighed. She felt like this was someone she could trust, and she was going to have to get used depending on people for things.

"I just need to make a little more than I am right now," she said.

"Well, Taylor's out. She made a big ass scene with one of the bar customers the other night *during* dinner rush and walked right out of here after I told her she was being an idiot. And she took Monty with her, so we were completely screwed."

"So, what do you need more, a cook or a bartender? Or a server?"

Betty's eyes dashed toward the kitchen, where her husband and co-owner spent most of his time.

"Yes." She shrugged. "Just depends on the day."

There was a contemplative pause. Brittney's heart raced a little bit. She hadn't realized how much she wanted it to work out. It felt logical and safe, and nothing else sure did.

"What days are you at Ed's?"

She looked down at her open planner, because simple answers were not coming as quickly those days. "Sunday brunch, usually every other week," she ticked off, "Close every Thursday, open every Friday."

"And you run your business?"

Come on. I can do this.

"Yeah."

"Hold on a sec."

She turned and walked into the kitchen. Hopefully that meant she was consulting with Greg, and they would take her on. Even one shift a week could make the difference she needed.

Thankfully, LeeAnn was talking to Waylon and was letting her be. Brittney listened to her own internal monologue *and* the angry growls from her stomach, which finally died down as she started to devour her still-steaming sandwich. She had two bites left and seven messages from Katy when Betty appeared back in front of her.

"So, if you could serve on Tuesdays, that would be a big help for me. And Greg would love for anyone in the world to learn his morning prep so he could take a whole day off some time. So, if you want to learn that, any day of the week, awesome. And bartend some Saturdays?"

Brittney felt her heart race. It all sounded good except for the Saturdays. Twice a month, for as long as she could sustain it, those belonged to her and Harrison. But most places would want her to work weekend hours. At least this was a safe place.

"I travel one weekend a month," she said carefully. "But I can make it work."

Betty's eyes flashed a little. Brittney knew the look. She was nice and young and probably understood, but she had a business to run, and things had to make sense.

"Two, maybe three Saturdays would be cool," Betty said, and Brittney felt her insides relax a little. "If you give Mr. Grumpy his day, it's worth it."

Brittney nodded. She'd been prepping her mama's kitchen her whole life. She could surely manage this.

"I feel like I haven't talked to you in forever."

Brittney heard the whining in her voice. She hated it. But it was true. She'd been hired at Grumpy on Monday. She served on Tuesday. She learned how to make Greg's potato salad, and all the homemade dressings, and even his famous meatballs on Wednesday *and* Thursday *and* Friday in between her shifts at Ed's while fitting in all her other work. She was exhausted at the end of every day but also couldn't sleep through the nights.

And now, on her night off, she was supposed to go hang out at Mikayla's for Thai food and *Outer Banks*. Instead, she was flopped on her couch at 6:00 p.m. trying not to fall asleep while she finally got to talk to Harrison.

"Catch me up, Buttercup," he murmured. He had just finished his end-of-day workout, the big weirdo, and she could picture him, his long brown hair pulled back and sweaty, his shoes and socks flung on the floor, a big, half-empty bottle of fruit punch flavored Body Armor in his hand. Their time together had been so brief, but his days and nights and habits were so achingly familiar; she just wanted him *home*. But that was a home that never really existed. They never really lived together. She was keenly aware that she missed something that she'd never had, and she wanted something that might be impossible.

"Well, let me tick it all off," she said, and launched into her week. She mentioned the new job casually, like it was no big deal because it wasn't.

"They said I could have one Saturday off a month, but I can maybe finagle another for when you're in town."

There was silence on the other end of the phone. She sat up, knowing it was about time to get ready to leave anyway, but also feeling something in the pit of her stomach that wasn't a baby flutter, or indigestion, or even the ever-present knot of grief that had sat there since Daddy died.

"Brit. You shouldn't be working so hard," he murmured. "Even if you feel great now, the more you're on your feet, you're just gonna . . . "

"Swell and be exhausted?" she finished with forced sunniness in her voice.

"Well, baby, yeah." He trailed off again.

She could feel the heaviness. It had always seemed to be there, before they even started, really, as wary housemates who didn't like each other, and then as a burgeoning couple with a shaky foundation, and now? He was a single dad trying to be there for his kids, so was there any possible way she wasn't going to wind up a single mom?

"You aren't going to want to make the trip here once a month much longer," he said. There it was. That pit in her stomach was a bullseye, and his words just hit it dead on. She felt her breath catch, and her heartbeat accelerated. *I'm losing him. I'm losing him.*

"Yes, I will," she protested. "Harrison, I'm fine. This isn't some high-risk pregnancy. I can drive a few hours to see—"

"You shouldn't have to, Brit!" he blurted. "I should be there with you, not seven hours away while you're working all these jobs and trying to drive here and carrying our baby. This is not how it's supposed to be."

She could hear everything he wasn't saying, mostly that he was going to fail someone no matter what he did. The thing was, she hadn't asked him, not once, to make a move or even a decision. Because the decision to have the baby was all hers.

"I don't really bother with how things are *supposed* to be," she said quietly. "I won't do anything that isn't safe, but I want to see you whenever I can. We'll figure the rest out." *How?* She could hear it in his voice, and that was probably Daddy's echoing it, too. But neither of them said it.

"I'm gonna check on flights for you for next weekend, okay?"

"Harrison, I can't aff—"

She didn't want to admit it, but he already knew. "I got it," he said, and they both breezed over it, because the fact wasn't lost on either of them, that even with his child support payments, his IT job kept him pretty solvent. Meanwhile, she owned her single-wide outright but still needed a third job to stay afloat.

"Thank you," she said, trying to keep the sense of defeat out of her voice. "Maybe you can stay until Monday?"

She smiled. "That would be amazing."

Their voices had gotten quiet. It was how they signaled the depth of their situation and, Brittney could admit to herself, of their feelings. It was her instinct to assume she loved Harrison more, that he was ambivalent about her and the whole thing. The huskiness of his voice as he told her about his day showed her how silly that was. He shared his heart by telling her something Ruthie had said in the car that morning that made him laugh, how he thought maybe he aggravated a shoulder muscle and was going to take the weekend off from boot camp, about how he wanted to make her the world's best avocado toast for breakfast next Saturday morning and maybe take her to the Smithsonian National Zoo.

Brittney giggled and relaxed. She hadn't seen the pandas since she was a kid, and she remembered Daddy buying Mikayla and her little stuffed ones to take home. Mikayla had named hers Cola, so Brittney named hers Coca, and she still had it somewhere in her small collection of blue storage totes, the few sentimental things she let herself store in her tiny home.

"Will you buy me a snowcone? And maybe a stuffy?" she asked.

"Anything, Brit," he murmured, his voice still husky and making her insides do flips. "Anything I can, I'll do for you."

She knew he meant it. She mostly even knew that he loved her. But there was still no commitment in that statement, no definition of what life was going to look like in their conversation. He was there with his kids; she was here with who was going to be her kid, *their* kid. And nothing he was saying or wasn't saying gave her a clue.

They lingered on the phone exchanging a lot of sweet nothings (the kind that meant everything) until she was sitting in Mikayla's driveway for fifteen minutes and Altan and Josie came out to get her. *Dang it.* She always cried at the end of her conversations with Harrison, every single time. But she was usually alone, and no one could see, and she'd make sure he couldn't hear. As soon as she was out of the car, Altan noticed the tears. He handed her sweet toddler niece to her and in his understated, stalwart, brotherly way, wiped the droplets from her cheeks and put his hand on the small of her back as they walked inside.

Mikayla was in the kitchen plating their food; she was channeling Mama more and more every day. Brittney watched her sister and Altan have a silent conversation— *about her*—and she didn't even care. Mikayla dropped the container of mango sticky rice to the counter and crossed the few feet to Brittney, embracing her fiercely. So Brittney let herself cry, feeling the weight of limbo, distance, financial woes, exhaustion, and the life growing inside her all at once. She didn't want to cry in her sister's arms, or at all, but it seemed the Fun Size Butterfinger—a nickname Harrison had bestowed on the baby not ten minutes before—had no tolerance for her silly emotional boundaries. She went ahead and let her tears leak during dinner, during Josie's sweet little good night, during the Pouges finding the gold, and during Mikayla's living room sermon assuring her everything was going to work out even though it felt like everything was absolute shit.

Altan brought them little bowls of gelato and sat next to Brittney on the couch. When Mikayla wrapped up with, "I cannot promise you anything about what Harrison will do, but I can promise you that you and this sweet babboo baby will not be alone. Not for one second." Brittney's quiet eye-leaking morphed back into an audible sob. This time, Altan wrapped her up, and she let it go until she was afraid of waking Josie or of actually needing IV fluids. There couldn't be much left in her.

"Why don't you spend the night?" Mikayla asked. "Can you even see out those puffy eyeballs?"

"Thanks, dumbass," Brittney muttered back. "I'm fine. Thank you. I am working early in the morning. It will just be easier if I go home."

The three of them sat there in silence for a moment, with the Netflix screen frozen on their dumb little message that might as well have read,

"I'm okay, you guys," Brittney finally said. "No better or worse off than yesterday, or before I talked to him. Nothing has happened. I just, well, anyway . . . " She sniffed into the last tattered tissue left on her lap. "It feels good to have gotten real with you. I appreciate it so much. But all I can do is wait. I am going to work hard to give Fun Size the life she deserves. Or he. I am going to be a good mom. And I am going to let Harrison do whatever he needs to. Because Ruthie and Dakota aren't any less important than this baby. I have to give him space and grace for that."

"You've gotten so old and wise, li'l sissy." His crisp, Turkish accent always made her smile when he said things that were decidedly southern. She rested her head on his waiting shoulder for a moment and then lugged herself up. Eight a.m. was probably not early for some people, but it felt like dawn to her.

Normally, the two-week span between her visits with Harrison felt like an eternity. That week flew, in a flurry of work, mostly. She had Taco Tuesday with Mama and Maggie and this time Katy, and that was just as awkward as she expected, because they were pretending like everything was okay. She went to The Salty Lips band practice Wednesday night, because El missed her and frankly, things with them had also been awkward because he was pissed at his brother.

Lots of people will be, if he leaves me here. Brittney tried not to think that way. *She* wasn't mad. *She* knew he was trying very hard to make the best decision in a complicated situation.

You sure, Brit?

Daddy's voice was ringing through a little more often lately. He wasn't happy with Harrison, either.

It's fine. It's fine. She told herself that all day, every day. And on a week that brought her a twelve-top for brunch at the Fishwalk that stiffed her, her first social media client in the potentially lucrative medical industry breaking their contract two months early, *and* her hot water heater deciding it would rather keep things cool, she needed the mantra for far more than Harrison's decision-making process. Nothing felt fine and lying to herself seemed to be the only resort. So she worked and she pep-talked herself, talked to Harrison until she fell asleep every night, took her vitamins every day and drank her water and wore compression socks for all her restaurant hours. She developed a fall drink menu for The Fishwalk and a fall social media contest for Robin and Julie's running store. She even learned how to make Grumpy Greg's "balls of meat," laughing like a twelve-year-old at all the silly inuendo of the popular menu item.

And then Friday finally came. She was all packed. El had given her a ride to The Fishwalk and Mama was going to pick her up at four and take her to the airport for her five-thirty flight. She'd be in DC and Harrison's arms by seven or so. *No problemo.*

Except it was. The lunch rush started late; the restaurant was practically dead until almost one-thirty, and then a storm brought everyone in from the beach and the golf courses and the Marshwalk and from whatever else people did on Friday afternoons. The bar was completely full for the next two hours. Brittney felt like she was making every cocktail she'd ever learned to concoct, and her arms actually got tired from all the shaking. She had to holler for Ed to bring her ice. *Where was everyone else?* Normally, Ainsley was early for her shifts, coming straight from her job at Wee Tots and changing for her night shift under the big oak. But at three-fifty-eight, though Mama had been sitting at the bar nursing a spicy marg for twenty minutes, Ainsley was nowhere to be found.

And neither was Ed.

Brittney couldn't text anyone. She was too busy juggling the drinks and the register and the food orders, and how long had she needed to pee, and *how long was Fun Size going to allow her to hold it?* Mama was looking at her with a mixture of restraint and alarm, and Brittney had to ignore her, or she was going to hop over the pine and make her drive the getaway car.

It was 4:05, and then 4:10, and by the time there was a break in the action, it was 4:30. Ed was walking toward her, and Mama was livid.

"Ainsley called off. Just now. I had no idea she wasn't here yet. I'll cover her. You go. I know you have a flight. Get outta here."

He said it all in one breath, his typical jovial smile eclipsed by a furrowed brow. Mama was already off her stool with keys in hand. Brittney grabbed the carefully packed rucksack she'd stowed under the bar and tried not to run.

It didn't matter.

They hit every red light. It wasn't summer, but it might as well have been. The Friday traffic was awful. No one in the left lane was even doing the speed limit. And then, of course, there was an accident at the 544 intersection. No one moved for four cycles of the stoplight.

Mama pulled up to the terminal at 5:19. It had taken them forty-four minutes to go ten miles.

"Be careful," Mama called out the open window. Brittney was already running.

She was afraid she was going to pee her pants, but there was no time. She entered the security line frantically. She double checked her gate number on the app one more time and then hightailed it there, hoping she'd put her driver's license somewhere in her pocket or bag, hoping she didn't wet herself, hoping . . .

"Oh noooooooo!"

She arrived at B6 at exactly 5:30. Not only was the door closed, but there was no one there. The gate must have changed. She turned around and through the blur of panic and tears, checked the nearest screen.

The gate had changed. A6. Myrtle wasn't a huge airport, but there was no way she would make it. Well, if she—

And just then, the screen changed. Next to her flight number, it said **DEPARTED**.

Her body went numb. She opened her Marco Polo app, asking Mama in a deadpan voice, "Please come back and get me." She made her way to the nearest bathroom, mentally composing her text to Harrison. She didn't think she could bear to hear his voice.

> Fishwalk was slammed. I got here too late and missed my flight.

She added three crying emojis and washed her hands.

His response was immediate.

> Buttercup!

And then a moment later:

Hold a sec.

She waited, trying not to stare at her phone as she made her way back out to the corridor. She knew Mama was on her way, though she didn't want to hear the Marco Polo pep talk that was inevitably being given. It felt like a lot longer, but in just a few minutes, Harrison popped back up.

There is a flight in the morning.

She already knew. It would be expensive, and . . .

Harrison. It's okay. We tried. I'll call you when I get home. I just need a minute.

With that, the ruining of the weekend felt final. She walked with much more energy and purpose than she felt to the terminal doors and waited outside. She felt like a teenager who got in trouble at a party. She prayed Mama would just let her go catatonic and not try to cheer her up. But when a car pulled up to the curb by her, it wasn't Mama; it was Mikayla.

"Get in, loser," her slightly older sister called from the driver seat. "Altan sent me on a date with myself tonight. I was just getting to Abuelo's, so Mama called me."

"I want gringo queso," Brittney said, throwing her bag with channeled gusto and disgust into the backseat.

"We can each get our own bowl."

Something about the offer, her tired sister's willingness to come get her, the idea of comfort food, even sans margaritas, undid Brittney. The little control she had left was blown away. She didn't cry or cuss or even say a word. She just let out a long, slow breath, and with it, any hope that things were actually going to work out for her and the baby . . . and Harrison.

> I'm sorry it happened. You wanna work today?

Brittney awoke to Betty's text with a headache that felt like a hangover, but that had not been brought on by anything nearly as fun.

Might as fucking well, she thought. And then, remembering that Betty was a different breed than any boss she'd ever had, that's exactly how she answered.

Since she was her Mama's daughter, she then immediately second-guessed herself. But the answer came back:

> Bwahahahaha. See you at two. The bar is yours tonight.

And so it was. From two until five, Brittney cut fruit, wiped the clean counter repeatedly, organized the coolers, played some songs on Touch-Tunes, helped Alice with a ten-top, and poured exactly four drinks. She was never going to recoup enough to pay Harrison back for the wasted plane ticket. Of course, he hadn't asked; and he'd tried half the night to get her to book a different flight. She just could not make herself do it.

Shortly into what was a calm dinner service, there was a squeal of tires and a loud crash outside. Brittney looked out the window to see a navy minivan and a gray-and-rust Kia tangled out on 17. Several other cars had stopped behind them, possibly all crashing into each other; she couldn't tell. It didn't look catastrophic, but it didn't look great either. She was looking for her phone to call 911 when Greg blew through the saloon doors.

"Gadzooks. We're gonna get hammered," he muttered. Then he grabbed the landline phone and stepped outside.

Brittney watched the action unfold. Two women emerged urgently from the minivan and began retrieving kids. Everyone was walking or standing, and she didn't see any blood or other visible signs of injury. No one had exited the Kia yet, but additional cars were stopping on the road and a few of them pulled into their parking lot.

Greg had correctly predicted the future. Within minutes, the restaurant was filled and every seat at the bar was taken. As the hubbub built outside, the door kept opening; the people kept coming, and entire parties exited in frustration after being told there was a wait.

Brittney steeled herself and took orders for cheese curds and burgers and Reuben eggrolls, while also trying to be inconspicuous as she followed recipes for some of the specialty drinks. She was certain that spicy blueberry-mint margarita was a disaster, but the platinum blonde lady who had also tried to order a pizza burger (off-menu items were an absolute *no*), didn't say anything about it. Brittney broke a martini glass, got espresso and Kaluha all over the floor, and seemed to set Greg right over the edge when the couple at the far end ordered steak nachos with *everything* on the side.

Finally, it seemed, things were in a calmer place. She sipped some ice water, wiped the counter because it actually needed it, and greeted two men who sat at the only available seats. One had closely cropped hair and wore a typical golfing ensemble, including a collared pink shirt and a smile that was bordering on flirtatious. But his counterpart had long brown hair, falling down his back in a loose ponytail. His shirt was black, his eyes were dark and moody, and their contrast reminded her so much of El and Harrison that she had to swallow hard and put on her game face before taking their order: a High Life for the rock star, a dirty gin and tonic for the golfer.

She handed them food menus and served their drinks. Her nerves were starting to calm themselves; it seemed the worst of the rush was over, and in an hour or so she'd be able to talk to Harrison. The guys ordered some crack fries and meatballs. The golfer didn't touch his drink, but when Brittney asked him if everything was okay, he beamed at her and said, "Absolutely." Someone, she guessed it was him, played Maroon 5 on the TouchTunes. Greg and Betty took turns coming out from the kitchen, the former telling her she did a good job even though she didn't agree, the latter welcoming her to her first official Grumpy ass-kicking.

But they were both in back when the guys, the last two patrons at the bar, asked for their bill. Brittney rang them up, taking note of the untouched gin and tonic in case there was a bad review later, and handed the golfer his change.

"Ma'am," his broody friend then said, "Are you the owner or manager here?"

Shit fire and save the matches. Here it comes. "No, sir. Is there a problem? They're right in the back."

"You'll want to get them," he said. The nerves in her stomach set on fire immediately. She peeked through the doors and summoned Betty.

He confirmed who Betty was and then announced quite loudly, "Are you aware your bartender is serving minors?"

Betty's string of expletives was immediate. Brittney wanted to throw up.

It happened quickly from there. Golfer was twenty years old. Long Hair was a cop. Brittney had been baited and fell for it. Betty was defensive of her and mad as a hornet, but nothing stopped the citation. There was a hefty fine, but thankfully, only to Brittney. It was a first offense, so the restaurant wasn't cited. Just her.

It felt right. It had been the worst thirty-hours she'd lived since Daddy died.

Once SLED and his buddy left, Brittney tried not to cry as Betty continued a rant about their little place being set up and Greg said logical, somewhat comforting sounding things. He handed Brittney a club soda with lime and told her to sit down. That was a mistake. As soon as she did, the flood of tears started.

You came to us as a friend because you needed more work. No one is mad at you. Shit happens. We will cover the fine. The two of them said such nice things, but Brittney felt the anxiety and tension anyway.

"Keep my tips," she said. "I'm done. You don't need me here adding to the stress. And there is no way you're covering the fine. I'll get it to you next week."

By the time they had closed up, cleaned up, and drunk up, Brittney was a soggy mess of sweat and tears, embarrassed and horrified, yet deeply grateful for the kindness of people who didn't owe her a thing.

She had texted Paul one key question, and based on his answer, she hoped she could make it up to Betty and Greg, who insisted she shouldn't quit. But—

You can't keep going like this.

Once again, the voices in her head merged with her own doubts about her capacity—as an expectant mother and as a human being. Was she being dramatic? Whom should she ask? El? Mama? Pick a sister? Who would tell her the truth?

No. She needed to own up to the one person who almost had as much of a stake in it as she did.

Harrison had already sent multiple texts checking on her. So with quavering insides, she called him.

"Hey, baby," he answered, halfway through the first ring. "Are you okay?"

She recounted the last two days in her head, imagining how she'd have felt that very moment being in DC, in his arms. At that, she let the last dam break.

"No."

13

Julie had visited the cemetery exactly twice: on her way out of town to live in Arizona, and the day after she got back, when she had to swallow her pride and ask Daddy if she could stay with him and Jessie.

She didn't give much credence to headstones, though Mama's was beautiful, with her name and dates and simply the word "Devoted." Danielle, in all her first-born daughter glory, kept flowers there in spite of her life being the most chaotic. Julie felt guilt and empathy wash over her; she and Katy needed to do more to help Danielle with that, whether it mattered to them or not.

She kneeled there now, wondering what she would do if she were armed with the same new information she had if Mama had still been *here*. Would she ask her point blank? Would she try to give her openings in hopes she would finally share? Would she not say anything at all, just carry the questions and confusion and surprise like she was already doing?

Leah's daughters had always known their mama was only a partially open book.

But the phone revelations?

It had turned out Mama's secrets were not very hidden at all.

"Tell me," she said aloud. "You're safe with me. I promise."

The night she searched the phone—the night Daddy had left the box—would be a core memory. Julie usually rolled her eyes at that term, but it made sense. Some profound moments would feel dramatic and then fade. But others etched themselves permanently, and she had now lived through enough to be able to tell the difference.

Mama's lock screen was her beloved Cane Creek Falls, just outside of her favorite place to visit in the north Georgia mountains. Her wallpaper was Christian, Danielle's first-born and the only grandson, sitting on Mama's counter with flour all over his face. Julie could recount only a handful of times she and her sisters had baked cookies or anything else with Mama; they just weren't a foodie family that way. But when Christian turned four, Mama had enrolled in a "My Grown Up and Me" cooking class at the park district, and they'd made all kinds of desserts and breads, and they seemed to have a blast doing it.

At first glance, all the normal apps were there. Mail. Maps. Photos. Facebook. Blah, blah, blah. Julie started to feel guilty. Everyone was entitled to privacy, whether they were alive or not.

Even with that thought in her mind, the green "Messages" icon beckoned. Sighing, she tapped it and started to scroll. There was not much there, threads with each daughter, a group with all three of them, Daddy, Mama's three sisters, a few work friends, even Jessie.

There was no one named Alex, no mysterious male names at all. *Of course there isn't*, Julie told herself. There were a zillion contacts, and Alex was there, but his company name was there, just like gobs of others in her list.

She felt the still-new flutter of Baby Bean moving, which seemed a better nickname than Tiny Queen Or King. In the lull of the breezy morning, she let herself sit cross-legged right there at the grave. No one was around, and she didn't have any place to be for hours. She tapped the music icon, looking for something Mama would have liked for a moment alone, outside, contemplative.

And there, Julie saw the playlists.

There were dozens of them, all with unique titles like *Mid-October Beach Run, Making Pancakes, Fold the Laundry and Try Not to Cry, Celebrate that Half Million Closing, Julie's Birthday*. Of course, Julie opened that one first, swiping at a single tear that had escaped down her cheek, her heart racing.

Mama was not a music fanatic. Was she? They'd never gone to a concert together. Julie couldn't even remember her fussing at the girls to be quiet because someone she loved came on the radio. How were there *so many* playlists? When did she make these? Why?

Her own birthday playlist started and made her smile immediately. "Baby Blue," George Strait. Family lore was that Julie had blue eyes for a full year before they turned darker, maybe hazel but mostly brown. Katy's had been brown since birth, and Mama sometimes called Julie "Blue Eyes."

It was a perfect playlist. Ten songs, each one packed with a memory, an inside joke, or simply meaning. She listened to each one, selections from the likes of Carly Simon, Stevie Wonder, and Pink, letting herself feel whatever came. She wasn't used to that; she usually kept her emotions in check and edited her own thoughts. But as soon as she stood and walked to her car, the reactions began like a ticker running through her.

These were so beautiful and personal and thoughtful.

And there were so many!

Why didn't they know Mama made these?

Why hadn't she shared them?

What else didn't they know about her?

Julie paired the phone to her Civic's stereo, fired up a list called *Driving to Work When You Don't Wanna*, and wondered if the most important woman in her life had actually been a stranger.

While her near-perfect husband was turning Julie's insides into an ooey-gooey center, she did not consult Robin when she knew he would advise her against whatever thing she was about to do. This was no exception.

She had gotten home and queued up another playlist: *Listen in the Gaps.* Mama had always used the term "gaps" when Julie was away at college and didn't check in for a few days, so Julie assumed she was about to hear some bright and shiny, family-friendly songs. Maybe a few country tunes about mothers and children. Maybe some Motown bootie-shakers that automatically lift spirits.

That's not what it was.

Instead, that list was filled with the kind of moody and morose selections Julie had listened to during her many numerous break-ups or disappointments in the world. Snow Patrol. Neko Case. Ray LaMontagne. Each song was intimate and full of longing, each sadder than the previous. How did Mama even *know* "Holocene?" Bon Iver's voice on the first line alone made Julie want to curl in the fetal position.

There's just no way, Julie thought. No way this complex music library was her mother's curation. She had to know what it was all about, so she put her shoes back on and headed to where her arrow always aimed: Daddy.

Once in the car, she thought to actually check in with him, and he wasn't home. He was at the Thursday morning arts and crafts fair by the library. Of course he was. Sometimes he was an unrecognizable creature now that he was *Jesus married* to Jessie. They hadn't even had that discussion yet! She was going to meet him anyway; he said they could walk to Benjamin's for something decaffeinated. He probably thought she was going to rant and rave about the secret lack-of-marriage, and maybe she would have, if she didn't feel so derailed by the phone.

She found him by Jupiter's Pies. Julie's pregnant stomach immediately did a little flip; she wasn't normally a big sweets person, but she was a southern girl and something about a strawberry rhubarb set well with her soul. Daddy knew this, and after taking one look at her, he turned back toward the table. A minute later, he stepped toward her with half a pie and a hug.

"Daddy. Not necessary. I've already gained—"

"You're gaining my grandbaby," he said. "And if it helps you, we can share it."

It would.

"Where's Jessie?" she asked.

"She's here, but she's meeting up with Maggie. So, I'm all yours."

Julie smiled. She and Daddy were once the best of friends. She knew life would move and change and so would the amount of time they had together. So even though she dreaded the conversation, she was grateful for the time.

After stopping at Julie's car, so she could grab a tote bag for the pie, they walked down the street toward Daddy's favorite little café. They stopped twice, once so he could greet Bern, Surfside's famous octogenarian rollerblader, and once so Julie could catch her dang breath. It was nearly lunchtime, and she—once a creature of moderate breakfasts, no lunch, salads for dinner—felt her stomach lurch in want of food.

They waited in the always long line before ordering their sandwiches and took up the last available table for two outside. The presence of strangers should guarantee good behavior. That's what Mama always said.

Who even was Mama?

Since they'd already covered the baby, the store, her sisters, and the weather, Julie decided to dive right in to the first of the hard topics.

"Daddy, did you happen to look into that storage tote before you brought it?"

She already knew the answer. And the look on his face confirmed it, so she continued. "Mom's hospital bag? Her stuff?"

A shadow immediately clouded his face.

"Daddy, her *phone* was in there. We thought it was gone. How did you not know?"

The pained look on his face gave her immediate guilt. He'd been in shock when Mama died; they all had been.

"Never mind," she said, reaching across the table to his hand, drumming anxiously on the painted beachscape of the table. "It doesn't matter. I just . . . I wanted to ask you about her music library."

"Her who?"

"Mama's!"

"Her *music* library? Jules, there were no CDs in the house. I swear. I would have noticed that."

"Daddy. For crying out loud."

And so it went. She had to meticulously explain what was on the phone. She hadn't brought it with her, didn't want to have to give it up if he'd asked her for it, even though maybe that was his right. Maybe.

After she told him, he looked away for an exaggerated period of time. She nibbled on a bagel chip, something she never would have eaten before Baby Bean started stealing all her minimal carbs, and she tried to be patient. Tried.

"I know what that's all about," Daddy said, in a tone that was almost deadpan but holding something else as well. "And before you ask, I am not ready to talk about it yet. I will. When I'm ready. And Jules? I'm just not."

"Daddy—" But before she even tried to continue, she stopped. His boundaries were always firm, and he rarely had to remind her. Katy was the one always riding roughshod over them. God knows she knew how it felt to have trauma to process before hashing it out like all the emos in their family. And now, especially, Jessie's family.

He put his hand over hers and completely surprised her.

"Jules. The mama you know, she started really loving all the running. And she made friends. Good friends. They went for runs and sometimes did breakfast or dinner or whatever."

"I mean, sure Daddy. That's what people do."

"She had a friend."

Julie stared at him. Mama was, well, she was not as introverted as Daddy was. She was *formal*. Her relationships reflected that, but she did, in fact, have relationships. So why was he saying this? There could only be one reason.

He didn't pause for questions. "Based on what I know and what I would surmise, he probably sent her the songs."

He? Someone sent songs to their mother? Love songs. Angsty songs. Dance songs. Running songs. Playlist after playlist, one seemingly more intentional than the last.

"Daddy?"

Daddy looked at her with somber but mostly expressionless eyes. "Honestly, baby, that's really all I know. How I know is a different story, and that's what I'm not going to get into right now. But there's your mystery. Mama didn't suddenly become some kind of pop culture superfan in her fifties. She had a running buddy. Clearly, he sent her songs. And she collected them. Good for her. Why not?"

Julie winced. There wasn't hurt or betrayal of any kind in his voice.

So why did *she* feel kind of misled, a little blown out of the water, and if she was honest with herself, completely humiliated?

Mama had been her hero and her best friend. Maybe, though, she hadn't known her at all.

14

My own mother used to use the phrase "stuck in your craw" quite a bit. She had a roster of similar phrases that she'd lob at my dad, brother, and me at regular intervals. Most of them made us laugh, and many of them were forgettable. But that one had been rolling around in my head.

Because Paul and I not being *really* married? That was stuck in my craw. So was his moodiness. That was on top of my own heartache over both my sons living far away, my lack of Taco Tuesdays and weekend sleepovers with Summer and Jacob, and how in the world Brittney was going to survive as a single mother.

And then there was Maggie, my sister-friend for the entirety of my adult life, becoming an unhinged, pain-in-the-ass, blabber of my secrets.

In spite of the latter, I needed her. We hadn't talked beyond cursory text exchanges since "Jesus Married Taco Night," which was how I had been thinking of it, so on another morning when Paul's long run seemed to be longer than ever, I showed up on her doorstep with two Benjamin's chocolate croissants and all the grace I could muster.

Maggie opened and stared at me with a side-eye, if that was possible.

"What's wrong?"

"What a greeting," I replied. "Let me in."

She opened the door with one hand and didn't say anything. I suddenly got the feeling that *she* was mad at *me*, which was beyond ridiculous.

"You got coffee?" I asked, marching toward her kitchen, my face already hot.

"Is this a coffee conversation?"

"You tell me."

"Feels like mimosa. Maybe bourbon."

"Maybe we should go for a walk," I said. "These are like 500 calories a piece."

"I don't give two figs about that," she fired. "How many miles did you already walk today, you psycho?"

"Doesn't matter," I said, crossing to her fridge. Orange juice, check. Prosecco, check. Screw the coffee. My insides were shaking. The two most important adults in my life—*yeah, yeah, I knew my kids were adults*—were on fragile ground with me.

I mixed two mimosas in Mason jars. Who had time to be proper? And then I slumped in a chair clutching a croissant, no napkin, no nothing. If there was anything my late-fifties, empty-nestdom, sudden widowhood, and dealing with the nonsense of new love had taught me, it was to be a little feral.

You're not that cool, Jess, I told myself. *Feral* would be telling all of them where to get off. *Feral* would be actually not caring what anyone else thought of my marital status. *Feral* would be taking Paul by his shoulders and shaking him and making him look into my eyes and finally get that I loved him and wanted him—could we just cut all the crap and noise already?

So, a little feral it was. Napkinless and getting chocolate flakes every-where, I stared at my best friend.

"Why does everything have to be so complicated?" I finally asked. "Why can't our daughters get married before they get knocked up? Why didn't Paul and I just get married? And why, for the love of God, did you have to tell them about us being Jesus married? Why, Mags?"

Maggie had done her share of hurricane-ing all over the past few years. I was not the only one living a new life; after being single since her late twenties, Maggie had married again. Moved upstate. Decided she hated at least some of that and moved back to the beach. Sheldon, the saint of a man who'd married her, was an almost-retired attorney who put up with her shenanigans and living apart; he cheerfully visited for long weekends. But something about all of it made her super spicy most of the time.

And I, who had always been drawn to her fire, maybe even a little jealous of it, was getting kind of sick of it. She needed to mind her own damn fires and stay away from mine.

Maggie did two things then, one unusual, the other unprecedented. The first was take a pause. She looked at her bare feet on the ceramic tile, then at me, then at her hands, not saying a word. But then, she crossed the room, wrapped me in her arms, and whispered, "I'm sorry."

"Maggie!" The woman had never apologized to me for anything, not for sticking Sam's hands in the cake at his first birthday and making him scream, not for taking Brit to get birth control when she was six-teen-dang-years-old, not for crashing family dinners with avoidable dramas or telling me my hair looked terrible on momentous occasions. *Sorry* was not her way.

"Are you dying?" I asked. "Am I? IS PAUL?" Those were the only reasons I could muster for those words coming from her mouth.

"You are such a dumbass," she said, letting go and taking a step backwards. "Let's walk."

She slipped her cement-inappropriate sandals on at the door, and we stepped out into the partly-sunny day. We had the street to ourselves and remained quiet for a whole block. It was so strange; maybe we were both dying and didn't know it.

"You're morose," she finally said, like she was reading my thoughts. She probably was.

"Am I?"

It was good that we were walking, and she couldn't see my face, because immediate tears popped into my eyes. I cursed them. I didn't want them. I didn't want this conversation. *I was sick of talking.*

"Jessie Rose, you know exactly what I mean. You and that man haven't been the same since you came home after that accident. And I know it was scary, and y'all are probably more traumatized than you already were, and more than you will let on, but is that all? I totally get you being pissed at me. But what else is up? For real?"

"I'm not sure," I said, surprised by the flatness in my own voice. "You're right about all of that. I don't know what else to say about it, though. I can't fix Paul. All I can do is work on me."

"Mmmmm-hmmmm." She was side-eyeing me, but I refused to look at her. Too many cracks in the sidewalk anyway. Eyes forward.

A moment later, she asked, "What are you doing to work on you?"

Eyes, stay forward. "You know, Bible study. Prayer. Long walks. A few books. Talking to you."

"You ain't been talking to me, so why should I believe any of the other stuff?"

Nope. Not answering.

"You should maybe see a counselor. Together. Separate. All the family. Hell, see one with me."

That almost did the trick and had me guffawing. Almost.

"I talk to Morgan," I said. She was my pastor's wife and friend. Stalwart. Honest. Tried and true.

"Yeah? What does she tell you?"

"To get a fucking therapist," I muttered.

"Oh no, she didn't!" Maggie said through a laugh. And then, out of the corner of my eye, I saw her stumble. She pitched forward, heading face first toward the concrete. Something in my current state superseded my normally clumsy instincts. I lurched forward just a tad more quickly than she did and caught her by the wrist and armpit. After she righted herself, in true Jessie form, I *then* buckled under the weight of her momentum and promptly fell on my knees, scraping them to smithereens.

"Ouch!" she cried. "Damn, girl. I think you broke my wrist!"

"But did you die?" I asked. "'Cause you were about to wipe all the way out!"

"Yeah, yeah," she said. "Thank you. My shoe caught on the crack. I didn't even see it."

"A likely story," I said, motioning to her flimsy sandals against my very secure Asics with the cute, glittery sugar skulls all over them.

"And you came outta nowhere, rescued me, and made yourself bleed," she deadpanned.

There was a little blood. I had attained what I used to tell the kids were "summer knees." The sooner in the season you scrape 'em up, the tougher you will be. There was a small sting in each as we turned around without consulting about it to head back toward her house.

I sat at Maggie's table while she fetched obnoxiously large Band-Aids, dark brown, so they looked "perfect" on my wrinkly, white girl knees. After I dabbed the blood away with a wet tissue, applied some antibiotic cream, and stuck them on, she handed me a fresh jar filled with ice water. And then she sat across from me and stared holes through my soul as only she could.

"You come out of nowhere, rescue, and make yourself bleed," she said.

"Maggie, not now."

"Then when, honey? Because I don't like what I am seeing here."

"Then don't look."

"Jessie. Rose."

I looked back at her, despite my preference not to.

"You haven't shrunk like this since you met Randall. Do you know that? You are acting like your pre-Randall nineteen-year-old, white-trash mama self. Why are you being small? Why are you being quiet? Why are you tiptoeing around that man who adores you? Why are you walking on eggshells with your kids? I thought we were past all that, baby girl?"

Oh, Mylanta. She hadn't called me that since Randall died.

"Everything feels super fragile," I said. Then I sighed for what felt like seventeen seconds. "My boys are gone. Who knows what Brit is gonna do? And Paul? Since our accident, it feels like he is systematically shutting down. Like, suddenly, I understand why he and Leah had such a seemingly sterile relationship. When he wants to be, he is a brick wall. And lately, he has a trowel in his hand most of the time."

"That's worse than I thought," she said. I didn't respond as she got up and fetched us each another mimosa.

"What are you gonna do?" She had sat back down, and her eyes simply bored right into mine.

"I don't, I mean, I didn't—" Ugh. "Maggie, until this moment, I didn't think I had to do anything. I didn't think . . . Mags, I didn't see what you're seeing."

"And you do now?"

I looked at my hands.

"You said I make myself small." And indeed, while I recounted this, my voice *was* small. "And that is one thing I won't be and won't do again. I promised that girl—Sam's mama, all those years ago. I won't make myself small to fit some mold that has nothing to do with me. I wouldn't do it for my parents or the uncomfortable church ladies. I wouldn't do it when I was wrangling kids by myself while Randall was away. And why in any world would I do it now?"

"Because you think you need to in order to hold on to him?" she asked.

I nodded. I thought of how my heart beat a little faster every time I was talking to one of the kids, and Paul walked into the room. He didn't say anything most of the time. But I felt the air shift. I felt myself shift. I didn't want stress, and I didn't want his judgement. I didn't know if I was being judged by him, but we'd had enough differences of opinion in the past that I had my defenses up.

"I don't want to lose him," I said, and just acknowledging the possibility out loud felt like a kick right to my stomach. "But I don't think that's all of it."

"Then figure out how to hold on," Maggie said, giving me her Maggie-stare. "Not just to him, but to yourself."

Buoyed by Maggie's admonishments, bandages, drinks, and pastries, I went home determined to have it out with Paul.

He was sitting on the front porch, his shoes and socks and ankle brace, all presumably sweaty from a run, on the floor next to him. There was a tumbler of water in one of his hands, his phone in the other. He looked tired. He looked at me.

"Hiiiiiii," I said, in my normal tone, like an exhale. My insides were melting at the sight of him, a little crumbled, but strong and healthy and a little more energized at the sight of *me*.

"What are we even doing?" I asked, before I thought about it. Well. I might as well sit down. I might as well have launched a torpedo, coming at him like that out of nowhere.

"For lunch? Did you not eat with Maggie?"

As a matter of fact, I was full of sugar, champagne, and indignation, which was not a promising combination on even a peaceful day.

"No." I tried to sound curt. I wasn't sure it worked or if it should.

"Okay." He set his glass down. "What do you feel like?"

I clenched my hands into fists and pressed them against my legs. So much of me was saying *Be peaceful. Don't say anything right now. Go have lunch at The Quay and enjoy the view and the tuna nachos and live your best life with this sweet man and shut up.*

But I couldn't just shut up. And it wasn't Randall's voice telling me that, or Maggie's, or any of the kids. It was mine.

"I feel like we aren't on the same page."

I let that ring out like a shot across the bow. Silence followed.

"So, we're not talking about lunch."

How I loved being retired with him. Being alone in our house. Not having plans. Heading out on spontaneous lunch dates to old favorites or new culinary adventures. But I needed to know whether I could count on that life or not before I continued in it.

"Not this time."

"I knew you weren't okay about the marriage conversation."

I slumped in the chair next to him. Then I self-corrected and sat ramrod straight, willing my voice not to waver.

"Then why didn't you ask me?"

"I was giving you time, Jess. And space. I thought—"

"You thought if you left it alone, I would get over it. Get distracted. Move on to the next emotional drama around here, because that's what I do."

That got his attention. He straightened his own posture, and his eyes were blazing. "Are you asking me or telling me?"

"I think you know."

"Don't play games, Jessie. You started the conversation, so have it."

He pissed me right off, mostly because he was right on.

"Fair enough," I said. I took a deep breath. I pushed aside the thoughts of how well Paul loved me most of the time, and I brought to the forefront of my mind the constant and mounting tension I felt between us and within myself. And then, I told him all about it in one nearly-breathless monologue.

I expected a counterargument of some kind, either heated and a little hostile or reasonable and deadpan. But instead, he stood, kissed the top of my head, and without a word, walked into the house.

At that point, I had a pretty good idea what was going to follow. And I didn't do a thing to stop it.

15

P aul was packed for his trip inside twenty minutes.

He hadn't even told Jessie he registered for that race. She would tell him a half-marathon seemed a little excessive. His age. His recurring ankle issues. His hateful, recent concussion. The deceptive level of humidity this time of year. The history of cardiac issues on his paternal great-grandfather's side that Danielle told her about over tea. If he wasn't acting how she thought he should, she would come up with a reason.

At least she pays attention to what you're doing. At least she cares.

He didn't want to go down that road, but he was being blown that way regardless. He waited until he heard Jess in the bathroom, and then he slung his duffle over his shoulder and left.

"We have a whole weekend. Where should we go?"

Four years or so before, Leah and Paul had tried to plan a trip, just a few days away. For no apparent reason, the effort had seemed monumental.

And when he asked her that simple question, Leah had looked at Paul from behind her issue of *Southern Living* and shrugged. "I told you to pick. It doesn't matter to me. The point is us getting away."

He wasn't sure what they needed to get away from. They had three grown daughters off doing their thing; if not settled, at least independent, even Katy, mostly. Meanwhile, Paul and Leah made their own hours, for the most part, so work wasn't stressful. Bills paid. Time for him to golf and her to run, time to enjoy the grandkids. Why did they need a break *now*?

"If we're going to plan something, it should be something we'll both enjoy," he said. *Let's not play games*, he wanted to say, but that would just start a fight.

"Well," he'd finally said, "you love Dahlonega. Let's look for something there, one of those boutique inns or a bed-and-breakfast, maybe."

Finally, Leah had put the magazine down. "You hate places like that."

He'd smiled at her. "And you hate Embassy Suites, so . . . "

She'd smiled back. That sort of exchange had been the closest they had usually gotten to achieving what he and Jessie had daily. But that was because Jessie was, as he liked to say, a quilt with arms: she naturally and willingly spread herself over him every day.

Sometimes, she nearly smothered him.

"You want to look for something, or shall I?"

The smile had vanished, replaced by Leah's get-it-done expression. "Why don't you look for places to stay, and I'll check calendars for what kind of events are coming up."

They'd been heading toward festival season, and Leah loved having things to do: berries to pick, wine to taste, 5K races to run, Fleetwood Mac cover bands to listen to. Without plans, Paul would read, golf, and nap, and she would be frustrated. The whole purpose of the trip would be defeated by the first night.

They never took the trip. There had been nothing going on in the north Georgia mountains that sounded appealing to Leah at that moment. Per his usual, Paul hadn't wanted to travel anyway. And per *their* usual, neither of them had made a grand effort.

And then, she'd died.

She hadn't been the first person he'd lost, but she was undoubtedly the closest, by far the most important. Mourning her was a mystery; he didn't even like to remember how cloudy those first days had been, the tension between how he felt—sad and confused—and how he was supposed to feel, devastated and gutted.

You're still sad and confused.

Julie and Katy had each told him recently that Leah was the voice in their heads. It made sense; they had lost their Mama during a formative time, still a little new into adulthood, before getting married and having babies was on their direct horizon. He hadn't asked Danielle if it was the same for her, nor had she ever offered the information. But he knew from Jessie that Brittney heard her dad's voice. And Jessie sometimes heard Randall, too.

Paul had only ever heard himself.

Until he let Jessie in. And now he heard her, all the time.

Usually saying something like, *You're still sad and confused.*

Forget that, he told himself, reaching over to turn up the radio. The *radio.* Not some sad-FM-curated playlist, like the kind Jessie made or apparently, the kind Leah had made *for her*. He wanted to hear Creedence Clearwater, maybe some Skynard. Instead, he heard the clear, twangy voice of John Denver, a song for Annie, a song for them.

He was transformed again. Twenty years old. Brand new to adulthood, for some. For him, he'd been couch-diving before it was a phrase, sleeping in alleys, stowing away overnight in Walmarts, and finally, living in his own car. But he was resourceful. He and his clothes and his maroon Buick Opel were always clean. He dated Leah for two months before she figured out he was homeless.

One night, after they'd gone to The Drive-In for burgers and shakes and a walk through Veterans Park, she mentioned that her parents were home, and she'd really rather be alone. Could they go to his place?

Paul had been good at many things, good at hiding things he didn't want people to see. But he was a terrible liar. So, it was only a matter of time, and Leah, for all the things about her he grew uncomfortable with over the years, was an excellent problem solver. She gently asked him some questions and swiftly made some calls. That very night, he slept on her parents' couch. The next day, he was in a studio apartment, where he stayed for the next nine months until they got engaged, and he upgraded to a one-bedroom in preparation for their life together.

Her parents had thrown a proper southern wedding, paying for everything down to their wedding bands. They'd had a grand dinner of chicken bog and pulled pork, macaroni, greens, baked beans, sweet potatoes, and banana pudding. There'd been a champagne toast and a live band, and Paul and his bride danced to "Annie's Song," with its vows of laughter and blue oceans and dying in each other's arms.

He loved her. And he felt completely inadequate and unworthy. And those two things, along with countless others, had not happened.

And he spent the next forty-some years trying to be what she deserved. Mostly failing. Kind of falling out of love.

And then she died.

The ride wasn't long, but it was fraught with the thoughts he didn't want to think and the feelings he'd tried to suppress. Paul considered things he usually didn't, like phoning a friend. But neither Carter, his pastor and friend, nor his bagel buddy Johnny picked up, and he didn't know what he would say anyway. He thought about Robin or Matt, as both his sons-in-law were pretty versed in the family history and pretty solid guys. But that would just involve the girls, and that was the last thing he wanted.

He needed Jessie.

But he didn't want to need her.

You're so stupid for that. It would be funny coming from her voice, if it wasn't so true.

He looked up and passed Wilson High School, which was not where he attended, but looked so much like it. For one moment that surely could not be measured in time, he swore he saw Walter there, his father, waiting angrily at the curb outside the main door, because Paul had not been waiting outside when his mom came to get him. He'd stayed after school to make up an geometry test, one that he'd missed two days before because

Walter had locked him out of the house for leaving a Coke bottle on the counter that morning, and Paul had slept on the porch, been defecated on by a *something* he really didn't care to know what, and didn't want to show up to school in filthy, smelly pants. Anyway. Walter had right and properly reminded him who was boss when he did come out of the building. The next day, Paul's A on the test did little to alleviate his sore jaw, his busted lip, and the fire growing inside him that said he had to get away. *Had to, had to, had to.*

Charlie had gotten away. His big brother had taken him with, and at first, for like a day, it seemed like it would work. But somehow, child services found him and stepped in, somehow deeming his abusive home a better setting for him. He had to go back, and now Walter was even angrier, and there was no other boy there to share the role of target for his wrath. No other son to share the guilt that their mother was too scared or her emotions too calloused to step in and help, much less protect them and leave Walter. Paul had it all to himself. Until he couldn't take it anymore.

Nearly fifty years later, passing that school, he felt his heart race, bile rising in his throat. He kept driving, not so far from the hotel now, but wondering why he thought he needed to do this race, revisit this route, pass this place, where he finally decided to run from his parents and a life filled with terror and pain and to be on his own.

For the rest of my life, his own inner voice said.

No, no. You are not *alone*, her voice said.

"Jessie!" He heard himself calling out loud for her, but of course, she couldn't hear him. She wasn't in the passenger seat, like he'd planned, like she should have been. And now, he'd likely made it impossible to reconcile with her. He'd likely ruined it for good.

The bed at the Hampton Inn was the only repository for his collapse. Fully clothed, wet from the sweat of panic, shaking from the stress of anxiety, his eyes swelling from the emotional release he was thankful no one else had seen or heard, Paul threw his bag on the floor and his body on the mattress. He looked at the screen and typed the only thing he could think of.

Then he sent it and let himself be done.

Jessie

16

Paul didn't come home that night. I woke up and knew it before I even opened my eyes. It sounds stupid, but I couldn't *feel* him in the house. I went ahead and performed a search, Dolly following, practically tripping over my heels. I checked every room, but he was nowhere. His Jeep was still gone. He hadn't come home, but of course, he hadn't fully been there in weeks.

I poured my coffee and creamer in a travel cup and put Dolly on her leash. She wasn't an early-morning walker like Cash had been, and we had a fence around our backyard anyway. But I needed one. Walking the beach was the only routine I'd carried over from my *old* life . . . before Randall died, before I moved, before I made a life with Paul. I refused to feel guilty for all the remorse, and nostalgia, and grief, and just plain anger I felt. One thing I had never ever felt with Randall was the uncertainty that he would come home.

Paul and I had broken up once. We had come together too soon after Randall and Leah's deaths, before either of us had healed enough to clear our heads. Julie and David had made some terrible decisions together, and when Paul and I argued over the fallout, I told him that we had different "relationship philosophies." And that had flipped his switch.

I suppose I thought our reconciliation and declaration of marriage meant we were more on the same page about the big things.

And it broke my heart to admit it, but that was proving to be an illusion.

Randall, I recalled as Dolly and I stepped onto the cold-packed sand, would never make me worry about where he was. Randall knew that feeling alone was a huge trigger for me. I always felt passed over by my parents in favor of my brother Tony. I'd had Sam by myself when his sperm-doner had dismissed me. I just barely trusted Randall enough to marry him. He had to do a lot of work to erase my doubts.

But he had.

Paul didn't know the younger version of me with those fears. But he did know about the others I lived with: that all my kids would eventually leave, that no one would need me, that no would want me around.

With that sobering thought, I paused right in front of the Conch Café, the scent of fried fish and beer still lingering from the previous night. With Dolly's leash buckled around my waist, I lifted my phone from my pocket and juggled my coffee as I tapped:

> This isn't who we are. Please let me know you are okay.

I shoved my phone back away and kept walking, because I knew better. Paul would not have this conversation via text. Paul would be very cognizant that I could see his location on Find My Phone anyway, that I knew he was a few hours away in Camden, where, per an uncomplicated Google search, I'd spotted a race was taking place that day. He would know that I would know he'd call me when he was ready.

I stopped walking again at the Garden City Pier. Dolly really didn't like to go this long, and now I was more than two miles from home. I'd end up carrying her for part of the way back. For now, I sat with her in the sun, avoiding eye contact with the fishermen. Soon, they and I would be the only souls on the beach this time of day for several months, and I would welcome their camaraderie. For now, I only wanted Dolly's company. She sat with me calmly, her head only turning when a newcomer to our plot caught her attention. The lady was super overdressed in gray sweats—not joggers, sweats, and anyone who doesn't know the difference can ask one of my daughters, because the description was beyond me, but I knew which was which when I saw them. She also wore Ugg-type boots, a navy cardigan, and an olive-green knit cap. Sure, it was around fifty-eight degrees, but the sun was moving rapidly up, and I just about could burst into flames from looking at her. She had stopped about twenty feet from us and was surrounded by seagulls whom she was carrying on a conversation with *and* feeding *bread*. Have mercy, Lawd. Someone would be snapping a picture and posting her as a cautionary tale on the Facebook pages. Feeding them is frowned upon by the Surfsidian crowd, but communing with them is perfectly acceptable.

Who would I be if Paul *didn't* come home? What would I do if he decided that this wasn't going to work after all? Could I even blame him? We had done nothing but navigate complications, conflict, doubt, and pure nonsense since the first night we'd spend together. All the easy things between us—coffee conversations, the daily grind, shared passions, strong affection—those were still easy. But in all the things that filled in the gaps, mostly the baggage and how we handled it, we constantly seemed to be at odds.

We didn't trust each other. After all this time. Was that normal?

I waited, that question looming in my head. Usually, one of my voices—Randall, Paul, or Maggie—would speak loudly and clearly with the very essence of the Savior. All I could hear in that moment were the waves and Dolly's breathing. She had fallen asleep in my lap, there on the shore, and I was in no hurry to get home. I had no one I wanted to talk to. And honestly, there was a mute numbness coming over me that hadn't been there since right after Randall had died. It felt alien and welcome to me at the same time.

I used to be afraid of silence and solitude. With all the kids and the moving pieces of a big family, and a husband who traveled, my life had never quiet, and I grew unsettled when it was. Then all the kids were gone, and the lack of noise in our home felt like an open invitation, a blank slate, a new notebook. I filled it with a vast variety of noises. Some did not stick: YouTube guitar lessons. Watching Telemundo in an attempt to revive my high school Spanish. A lame attempt at podcasting about trendy, abstract emotional topics I couldn't even pinpoint anymore. A few stayed, like my beach walks and all the cooking shows I watched and drew from to create the tea room and Sunday suppers.

In all of it, I learned to be comfortable with silence for the first time in my life. Quite unlike the tense silence that had existed around my parents' dinner table or the lonely silence of a house that used to be filled with kids and chaos and a long, lively marriage, my current bouts of silence mostly had been a simple lack of chaos.

But in the silence of late, Paul was always there, even if he himself was silent. He was a part of the air and of my unravelling fabric.

Ready to head back, I looked down at my phone. That's when I saw the lack of bars on the top right corner *and* the tiny little airplane. *What the heck?* How did that even happen? I switched my service back on and waited the requisite moments, cursing myself for not even noticing that anything I'd sent was stuck.

A few moments later, the dings started dinging. Maggie. Sam. Brittney. Mikayla. Abby. Morgan. Family Girls chat. And, yes. There he was. *Oh Paul*. He *had* communicated.

I'M SORRY.

I stared at the words, running my finger across the screen as though he could feel me touching him, trying to reach him, trying to soothe him. He had spent the whole night alone, thinking I didn't answer him. Did he think I didn't care? Was he running his race now? I looked at my watch. He must have been. And I wasn't there.

That wasn't how *we* did things, not my best friend Paul and me. Not my husband . . . *my husband*. If he was willing to try, willing to get help for whatever was haunting him, willing to come home and rebuild the trust between us, then that is what I needed him to be.

Brittney

17

One more week. That is what Brittney had agreed to, despite feeling completely inadequate, looking like an idiot, and being too exhausted to stand for even half a shift. That was also after Paul had put in a call to one of his fond former students at SLED and gotten their fine thrown out, and after Betty made a convincing case for her "working out her notice" and "leaving the door open." So, she took deep breaths and made very pristine drinks and carded every blessed person who walked in the door. Since most of them had gray hair, as was the demographic of Murrells Inlet, South Carolina, it became a bit of a joke by her last day there.

She did not care.

It was Tuesday, the supposed slowest day of the week. For whatever reason, the moon phase, the week before bike week, some sort of Reader's Choice sham of a contest somewhere, the bar was full. All afternoon, full. Most everyone was calm and easy, ordering beer or wine or something off the cocktail menu. Betty had made a cider-based sangria, the smell of which made Brittney nearly wretch at the beginning of her shift, but as the day went on, made her nearly swoon. One sip wouldn't hurt her, right? Fun Size was mostly formed by now. *Lawd, have mercy*. Thankfully, her normal wardrobe of boho-dresses and rompers was stretching so that her budget could, too.

Stop it, dummy, she told herself as she set another round down for the two women at the window end of the bar. They were hunched over their computers, supposedly "co-working," but also giggling and playing Pearl Jam songs, singing along. Honestly, Brittney thought they were a little unhinged, but Betty and Greg kept coming out to talk to them, so they must be regulars.

Nope. More than that. "Bestieeeeeee!" the shorter one called. Betty stuck her head out the kitchen door, laughing. She walked to their end of the bar, so Brittney stayed in front of the other customers. Two couples were there sticking to their hot dogs and salads and beer. Three ladies were on the other side of them; two were contemplating martini flavors, and one was on her third shot of Patrón. Everything seemed fairly normal, so she leaned back and kept an eye out, half-listening to her bosses' banter with the women on the end, who had moved on to 4 Non-Blondes. They should absolutely be friends with Brittney's mama.

Fairly normal. Brittney should have known better. The second she turned her back to grab a High Life for one of the men, she heard an ear-piercing shriek behind her.

Jumping out of her skin and rotating around at the same time, she saw the Patrón lady now standing next to her stool, a frazzled look on her face while she continued to scream, sounds, words, non-sensical phrases.

Betty jumped into action and walked next to Brittney, across from Patrón. "Ma'am, we need you to please stop screaming," she said calmly but in a firm and icy tone that meant business.

The screaming continued. Every new utterance sent a little shockwave through Brittney. She looked around to see if there was something she could do, but—

"Ma'am. MA'AM!" Betty stepped aside as a shot glass flew across the slick top of the bar toward her. It went right over the edge and crashed to the floor. Brittney jumped.

Greg appeared at her side and took her elbow. "Why don't you take a breather?" he said evenly. She nodded but also wondered where to go. Outside would mean walking right past Patrón. So, she wandered into the kitchen, where she could still hear everything. She went out the side door with the intent of leaving through the dining room to the patio. Greg was now standing next to Patrón, holding her hand and talking in Dad Voice, even though she looked at least his age or older. Brittney watched, with her panic now joined by a crushing desire to talk to her own dad. He would have been doing the same thing in the same situation, making everything okay.

She reverse-scurried into the kitchen again, standing right in front of the friers, which sort of provided some white noise and definitely made her feel warmer. Every few seconds, there was another shriek or yell, and every time it happened, she nearly came out of her skin.

The doors swung open, and Sofia, the other server that day, walked through. Even her tough-as-nails New York exterior seemed to be taking a hit.

"You believe this?" she asked, taking a sip from her lime-adorned glass and offering it to her. Brittney shook the head; Sofia didn't know she was pregnant, and it sure didn't seem like the best time to share the joyous news.

They listened for a minute, to Greg's murmurs and the intermittent shrieks. Then Betty bounced through the doors and said, "There's customers. Unbelievably." She said some other things in a string of expletives as Sofia followed her out. Then she took a deep breath and went, too.

Two police officers were coming in the door. Patrón didn't notice them until they greeted Greg, and he let go of her hand, an apologetic look on his face. They called her by name—Linda—and spoke to her just as calmly. She yelled, "Noooo! Noooooooo!" and then suddenly, it was as if the energy just left her all at once. Her shoulders dropped, her mouth closed, and then, to Brittney's horror, she started to cry. She didn't make a sound, but the big, gaping sobs shook her whole body. Betty had gone back to her friends, "Kel and Shanilla," and Greg went back to the grill. She didn't know what to do.

But she didn't want to stay.

Because she felt a little like Linda, depleted of everything.

And she couldn't scream, not here.

With a tight smile across her face, she walked behind the bar and checked on her customers. Betty's buds were packing up, apparently to get home to parenting duties. Maybe Brittney should befriend them; they seemed to be having a blast being working mothers. They probably had doting husbands or baby daddies in the same state, though.

She started in on two espresso martinis and quelled the butterflies in her stomach. She served them with the same pasted grin, refilled the couples' sodas, took an order for rice pudding, and started picking up the shards of glass on the floor. Of *course*, one of them stuck right into the palm of her hand. She watched the blood start beading up from the narrow cut. It didn't sting at first, but tears sprang into her eyes.

"You okay?" Betty spoke evenly and quietly right in her ear. She couldn't look at her.

"Not really," she answered, more quietly.

"There are Band-aids in the office. I'll meet you back there in a minute."

She rushed to the back, to the cramped and chaotic little closet that they called an office. She felt strange going in there, so she waited outside the door until a drop of blood fell on the floor. Stupid to let that happen in a kitchen. She rummaged through a few piles until she found the box of *Paw Patrol* bandages—leave it to Betty, an avid animal lover and rescuer. A stupid Band-Aid was not going to stay on the palm of her hand. She stuck one on anyway and grabbed a bar mop to hold over it. By the time she walked back out, the police and Miss Linda were gone, the two couples were ready to cash out, and the two ladies wanted to try apple-tinis. Betty took one look at her, and Brittney knew that she knew.

"Sofia will make the drinks," she said. "Go pick a booth. We'll talk in a few."

Brittney followed her instructions, humbled, exhausted, and grateful. She sat clutching a glass of water and waiting, her decision already made.

"I'm sorry it's so late."

Mikayla had hopped in her passenger seat this time, her hair in a crazy-messy topknot and her hands clutching a box of Hot Tamales and a giant tumbler, likely filled with club soda and a splash of apple cider. Her sister was weird even without being pregnant.

"It's fine. Josie has been asleep for two hours, and I don't know what to do with myself, besides worry that she must be sick if she's so peacefully sleeping. Anyway, who cares? What's up with you?"

Brittney took a breath and turned onto the bypass. She didn't know where she was going, only that she needed to drive.

"I quit my job," she mumbled.

"What job? You mean your business? Are you going to do something else? I knew that being a startup might be stressful with—"

"No, Kayla.

Mikayla didn't even know about the third job. So, she started there. By time she got in the drive-thru line at Cookout—*What did they put in those milkshakes to draw 8,000 people there at ten o-clock on a Tuesday night*—she had moved on from the SLED setup to that very night, how Betty had brought her out a fresh, piping hot Philly and told her, without Brittney having to say anything, that she knew it wasn't the right time, that Brit needed to chill a little while she was pregnant, that there were absolutely no hard feelings, blah, blah, blah.

"I feel like I made their lives worse just being there," Brittney said. "And they just kept being kind to me. And Harrison doesn't know about any of it, so I've been distant, which helps absolutely nothing in our situation. And why in the NAME of ALL are these stupid milkshakes so thick? I just want something peanut butter and chocolate and frozen, not to break a damn rib trying to DRINK it."

Mikayla was just starting at her, listening intently, in a rare stance of not asking clarifying questions or offering encouraging words. She contemplated what to say next, and then—

Was that...?

Was it the grilled onions? Was it nerves?

"Oh, my goodness! Mikayla! I feel it!"

The flutter in her tummy had to be, had to be, had to be Fun Size moving.

Brittney burst into tears.

"Buttercup. If you are sure, then it's amazing news.

Brittney nodded, as though Harrison could see her. He'd wanted to Facetime, but there was no way she wanted him to see her puffy eyes or red nose. She actually wondered if she could stop crying long enough to tell him.

"I'm as sure as I can be," she said, barely above a whisper. She was sitting on a rusty lawn chair on her front porch, Counting Crows playing on her Bluetooth speaker, with a perfect view of the moon and absolutely no idea if she was making the right decision or a desperate one.

"It's not so bad here," he said. "It will be pretty at Christmas, and plenty of marketing jobs, and—"

"And hopefully my mama survives it. Hopefully, I can find a winter coat to wrap around what I'm sure will be a gigundus belly. Hopefully your kids, whom I still haven't met, won't hate me too much."

And hopefully you won't resent me and your new kid and this entire situation. But she couldn't say that, even if she should.

"Everything is going to be okay. Every*one* is going to be okay," he said, almost convincingly. "I'm gonna come this weekend. Let me see what kind of airfare I can get. I'll spend Friday night with the kids and fly Saturday."

"Harrison, you already know that's going to cost a fortune. Save it."

"Baby, I need to see you. It's been too long, and we have to figure stuff out."

Let him. Daddy's voice? Mama's? Mel Robbins'?

"I'm not going to stop you," she finally said. "I miss you so much. And—"

It's so hard to do this alone.

"This is really hard," he said, like he was reading her mind. And though she didn't want him to feel anything but peace, she found comfort in hearing that she wasn't the only one, that he was struggling, too.

"Here," she said, tapping the speaker button. "Let's check flights together."

"Maybe for your next job, you can be a flight attendant."

She giggled, and didn't add that if they were living together, hopefully she wouldn't need so many jobs. By the time they ended the call, he was set to be in her arms by lunchtime on Saturday; they'd decided to have a sunset dinner at The Quay, and Sunday, at family supper, they would tell everyone that the third of Jessie Oakley's four children was moving away from home.

18

Aunt Sherron was looking in Julie's direction, but definitely not seeing her. She was somewhere else entirely. *Mama's secrets weren't dark. But they were real.*

"I know this must seem—"

"Sshhh. Please, dear." She held up her hand, and Julie closed her mouth in a rare act of compliance.

The beat went on longer than Julie's comfort level. She picked up her phone and answered a text from Robin, whose eyes were particularly watchful over her at the moment. She couldn't blame him; between Baby Bean and Mama's phone revelations, she was a little shaky.

Aunt Sherron finally broke from her trance. She took a long sip of wine, set down her glass, carefully wiped her perfectly-lined-and-glossed lips, and finally spoke.

"I think you mean Alex."

Julie's mouth dropped open. He had a name.

"So, you knew about this? The songs?"

"Honey, honey." She reached across the table for Julie's hand. "Let's not dramatize this. I promise, your mama was not wandering. She made friends in that running club she went to, and all that was just a little separate oasis from the rest of her life. And Alex was a friend. Nothing untoward at all. Nothing romantic. He was a musician-type, too, and he introduced her to bands and what have you. They ran a similar pace. Goodness, that almost makes me sounds like I know what I'm talking about, which I really don't."

Aunt Sherron smoothed an invisible wisp of hair along her French twist. She was Mama's eldest sister and somehow, even more formal. She would not have been caught dead exercising outside in the coastal South Carolina heat, sweating next to strangers, especially men. However uncomfortable Julie was with the conversation, Aunt Sherron had to be one hundred times less so.

"So," Julie asked carefully, "If he was just a casual friend, why do you know about him, and we didn't?" She was thankful for all her education and experience in healthcare. She could leave the emotion out, for now.

There was another weighted pause. Julie did not relent. She stared at her aunt until she broke the silence.

"Alright, Miss Ma'am. I understand. You are not a child anymore, if you ever really were."

Julie used to take comments about her maturity and solemnity as compliments; now, she smarted at them. She wished someone had told her to lighten up before she got to actual adulthood and went off the deep end.

"There was something like an attraction. Intrigue, maybe? Actually, I heard the term 'platonic soul mates' a time or two recently; it might could have even been something like that."

Platonic soul mates? "Platonic soul mates? What the hell is that?" She thought of Brittney and Katy's boyfriend, El. Brit would probably describe them as that. But her mother?

Aunt Sherron uncharacteristically fidgeted in her seat. If the stakes didn't feel so high, Julie might have found that funny.

"Julie Dawn, if we are going to speak like mature adults, then let us." She thought that was a reference to her spicy language, but her aunt surprised her again. "Everyone knew that your mama and daddy were not exactly . . ."

"Cuddly bunnies?" she offered. She had long made peace with the emotional sterility of her parents' marriage.

Aunt Sherron pressed her lips together. Okay. Julie would give her a break after that. "Yes. I suppose that's one way to put it. Anyhow, I believe Leah just found . . . fun . . . with the runner folks. And Alex was someone she knew casually through realty, so they had some things in common to start, and then..."

"He made her sparkle?" Julie asked, no trace of sarcasm or sass in her voice.

Once again, her aunt looked a little stricken. She sighed and picked up her wine. "Well, sugar, I suppose that is one way to put it. And without you explaining it to me, I have to agree that it's an appropriate term. He saw her in a way that most of us did not. He poked at her fun side."

Ouch. Julie knew what she meant, too. Someone also should have told Mama to lighten up. Maybe they could have helped each other. Maybe this Alex guy *had* helped her. Maybe she had some adventures or even just a sense of adventure before she died. Maybe she felt more beautiful or appreciated because of him.

"Do you know how my father knows about him?"

There was a cough that quickly turned to a sputter. Aunt Sherron pulled the cloth napkin from her lap and held it over her mouth. Julie pushed her water across the table, steeling herself for patience once again.

The coughing stopped. "He does?

"He does."

"Well, my dear, I have no idea. None. But I will tell you this: your mama was thick and thin with that man, your daddy. Of course, you know about the drinking and the recovery. But Julie? He was about as emotionally distant as a husband could be. And your mama, well, she was not the most nurturing all the time, either. She'd try, and not get through, so she would retreat. Multiply that by nearly forty years and add your defiant twin into the mix for some bonus stress. They probably should have had counseling or some such, but they didn't. She had Alex and your daddy had Jessie."

"What? What does that mean, he *had* Jessie?"

"Oh, my dear. Just more of the same. You call it sparkle. According to your mama, your daddy always sparkled around Jessie. And before you go rewriting history, she didn't mean a thing by it, nor was she any kind of way about it. She was simply cognizant that someone else made him feel more at ease than she did. And like I said, she had given up trying."

Julie sipped her water and set a hand over her stomach. The Bean wasn't fluttering; her nerves were.

"None of that is news, I suppose," she said. "But it's still hard to hear."

"Dear girl." Aunt Sherron reached across to her again, this time with more warmth and compassion on her face. "I know. Of course it is. But the main thing for you to know is, your parents were content. I know it sounds strange, but according to your mama, they settled into knowing who they were, and their roles to each other, and they were at peace with that."

"It sounds awful," Julie muttered.

Aunt Sherron, who had lost two husbands, one to a young dental assistant and one to cancer, squeezed her hand tighter. "You are happy and loved well, so of course it does. But I can attest there are worse things than calm companionship."

"I suppose," she said. She stared at the circle of condensation on the table and then at her aunt's hand, so much like her mother's. She had thought she knew Mama, thought she'd been her advocate, and now it seemed, there had been at least one person who knew her better. She had to find him.

Hours later, Julie was back in her leggings and her living room, baby Lexie cooing in her lap, and Mama's phone glowing in Danielle's hands.

Robin walked in carrying a whole charcuterie board. She flashed her most grateful smile at him, but he still admonished her.

"You're looking at it again?"

"Just feed her nitrate-free salami and tell her she's pretty," Danielle said. Julie shrugged her agreement.

"Of course we're looking again," Julie added, smiling at her husband as he popped a cube of Swiss cheese in her mouth. She chewed before adding, "Aunt Sherron knows more, but she wouldn't say anything else."

"I wish I could have seen her face when you used the word 'sparkle,'" Danielle chided.

"She used it too! You don't even want to know." Julie gave a little shudder thinking about everything her aunt had said.

"You two." Robin took a drink from his Modelo while passing one to Danielle.

"Don't drink that," Julie said, tracing circles on her niece's little baby belly. "Lexie won't like it."

"It's one, and I'm a serial pump-and-dumper," Danielle answered. "And I do want to know, but let's start here."

She had opened Mama's music app and was pouring through the playlists.

"Um, not for nothin'," Robin said. "If someone sent her those, can't you see *who*?"

"Wait a dang second. Here. Take this." Danielle giggled as Julie handed the *this*—her third child—to Robin. "Gimme the phone!" She snatched it from Danielle and immediately started tapping through the Apple music app.

"There it is!"

"What? His name?" Danielle squealed.

"Well, no. I mean, it's his user name. Chance62."

"Chance?" Robin scratched the back of his head. "That's gonna be a tough nut to crack."

"Is it?" Julie snapped.

She dropped her mother's phone and picked up her own. Danielle started tapping away at hers. Robin stared back and forth at them, patting Lexie's back and picking at the charcuterie until approximately two and a half minutes passed, and—

"ALEX CHANCE! MYRTLE BEACH! HIS NAME IS ALEX CHANCE!"

"I'll be John Damn Brown." Danielle stared at her own phone. The sisters had found pay dirt at the same time.

"His Facebook," Julie said, now just above a whisper.

"He has a YouTube under Chance62," Danielle added. "He's a musician!"

The initial adrenaline had evaporated into a hushed awe.

Julie stared at his profile picture, a professional headshot like most re-altors around had. He was wearing a crisp white shirt and standing on a balcony with the beach as his background. He also sported a neatly trimmed mustache, beard, and long gray hair that was tied in a ponytail, flowing in enviable beach waves down his back. He wasn't overly distinct looking other than he was the complete opposite of Paul Jameson.

She passed the phone to Danielle, and looked over at Robin, who was swaying with the baby and looking back at her, wide-eyed and waiting. Danielle, already staring at his picture, handed her phone to Julie.

"He's from Louisiana," Danielle said.

"He plays piano," Julie said.

"He has two sisters."

"He used to do shows at—" Julie gasped. "The Surf Mist Pavillion. Back in the day! Danielle, look at this!"

The sisters smooshed together on the couch, mesmerized by the mu-sic. A few predictable covers played from the tinny speaker of Danielle's iPhone. Foreigner. Tom Petty. Counting Crows. And then—

Robin heard it with them and could tell something grave was happen-ing. He sat beside Julie and handed her the baby like a gift or a peace offering or a healing balm.

"I don't know if love and destiny are the same.

I only know I'm home

Every time you say my name.

I don't know if we're dancing

Or just dreaming

Or just here

All I know, Amelia, is I always want you near."

Julie stared a little stricken at the phone. Danielle rose and crossed the couch, scooping Lexie into her arms.

Robin peered over Julie's shoulder. "Amelia's Song," he said out loud.

"Our mom," Danielle said quietly. "Amelia Jean. Leah was all anyone ever called her."

"She *hated* 'Amelia,'" Julie said.

"Well, he wrote Amelia a song, that's for sure."

Julie gaped at her husband. "Thanks, Captain Obvious."

"You . . . do you think she *knew*?" Danielle's voice had gone up in volume and octaves.

"It's a really beautiful song," Robin said.

Julie shrugged his hand off her shoulder and stood. "Why are you being such a dumb ass right now?"

"Julie!" Danielle admonished.

"It's okay," Robin said, a slight, stony smirk on his face. "I probably deserve it, and she doesn't really mean it."

"You don't think?" Julie seethed. "How can you make light of this? Who cares if the song is pure poetry or pure crap? Some other guy wrote it for *our mother*. He knew her real name and who knows what else about her. And this is like . . . he didn't even try to hide it!"

"Jules," Robin said, in a softer, more even tone that even quieted Lexie's blubbers. "Look at this video. It was probably made fifteen years ago. Maybe more."

"And?"

"I doubt this was . . . I mean, I can't say what their relationship was, but he used a code name, basically. A pretty melodic one, at that. It fits the song. He shared songs with her. I know it's a reveal, and it's weird and probably stings a little, but don't let it raise your blood pressure too much. "

Danielle spoke into the tension. "You're only allowed to be logical if *she* is being logical."

"Shut up, Danielle!"

Julie's vitriol silenced her sister and her husband, but Lexie took the moment to begin crying, loudly, as though something had hurt her. As if she knew.

"I knew Daddy kept a lot of his stuff behind walls," Julie said quietly. "I thought I knew Mama. I thought she was fully ours, not a mystery. And she had this whole thing, this whole life, that didn't have anything to do with us, and we can't even talk to her about it."

"I know, sweetie," Danielle said. She patted the couch cushion and looked at Julie until she disarmed her. Julie sat back down.

"It's not fair," she said, barely above a whisper. "At least you had her here for two of your babies. I feel so . . . " Julie looked from her sister to her husband to her own hands in her lap, her arms still wrapped around Lexie. "I know I am surrounded. But I feel so alone."

Paul

19

Miraculously, the half marathon was not a disaster. He didn't break any land speed records, but he also didn't fall and break any bones, so he counted that as a positive.

Just as miraculously, Jessie was waiting at the finish line. She was supposed to ride with him, but of course, he'd shown his backside to her, had a meltdown, and ended up texting her anyway. So he wasn't sure why she came, but he was a little thankful for his back-of-the-middle-of-the-pack pace, because she made the two-hour-and-fifteen-minute drive, and when he crossed the timing mat nearly three hours after he started the race, she was holding a sign, smiling, and fully there for him.

He had barely slept. It was so unlike her not to answer him, and he really believed he'd gone too far that time.

But just like her, she hugged his sweaty, wrung-out form, walked him over to the water and bananas, fussed over his medal, and pretended like everything was fine. He let her for a little while. He smiled and agreed to go get lunch. He told her about how it felt to pass that thirty-year-old wearing Nike super shoes in the sixth mile and how it felt when he got a cramp in his quad in the eleventh mile. She scrolled through the official photos until she found his and *oohed* and *ahhed* and saved them so he could send to his girls. He hated them, but she seemed to love them. And he believed her.

It wasn't until their plates were cleared and Jessie was having probably her sixth cup of coffee that she reached across the table, took his hands, and said, "I don't know if I can bounce back from this, Paul."

His own hands went limp in hers.

He had done the one thing she asked him never to do: retreat.

And so, she was doing the one thing he'd hoped she would never do: telling him she'd had enough.

They sat there wordlessly for who knew how long. There was a radio playing over the pancake house speakers, '90s country, Pam Tillis, maybe? No. Suzy Boguss. Why did it matter? Jessie was going to leave him.

"You don't have to say anything," Jessie finally added. "I'm not . . ."

She trailed off, but she didn't let go of his hands. He strengthened his grip, hoping it communicated something: *I can be stronger. I can do better. I can hold on.*

Please, don't go.

"I'm not going anywhere. I'm just not convinced, Paul, that this is what you want. That this domestic, blended family, almost-married thing—the way I want to do it and am trying to do it—is what you really want."

He couldn't meet her eyes. He looked at their hands.

"I know we have talked about it ad nauseam. And listen, Paul—look at me, please?"

He raised his eyes to hers, willing himself not to allow anything unshed to spill over. Not then.

"I know you love *me*. I even know you want me. It's the whole package that gives me pause and doubt. I come with a lot, and it adds to your lot, and maybe it's just too much."

She looked so earnest and compassionate, so wide-eyed and worn out, that he couldn't look at her any more. As soon as he shut his eyes, they overflowed. And just like Jessie, she squeezed his hands to reassure him.

"Don't," he managed.

"Don't what?" She squeezed again, harder.

"You don't have to try to make me feel better or make it easier for me. It's not your job."

"*Paul*!"

His name rang loudly in the thankfully crowded restaurant. He wanted to cower, but he looked at her because he knew she would insist again.

"Don't you know? Or is that exactly what you don't understand? It *is* my job."

"Jessie . . ."

"Paul."

He waited her out.

"I don't know a lot of things. I don't know all of your past or how it affects you now. I don't have to know more than what you want to share. But I do know that the only way I can move forward in our relationship is if we do it together. If we talk things out. If no one retreats. And what I'm saying, Paul, my darling, is that if you run away from me again, I will likely have the desire, even the desperation, but I may not have the strength to follow."

This was the part when softer music should have played, when the light should have shifted, when everything should have been made clear. But his brain was foggy, his sweaty clothes had dried and were sticking to his tired, cramping limbs, and he smelled really bad.

"I don't know how to do this," was all he could say.

She smiled wanly, and she let go of his hands. "I know."

Then she stood up, kissed the top of his head, and said, "You get this one. I'll be waiting at home."

He had taken a lot of drives that were much longer. One of them was even halfway across the country with Randall. But the two hours and twenty-two minutes back home felt quite eternal as he replayed Jessie's words, the ones from the pancake house and basically every word she'd said to him since a fateful night on the beach right after their spouses died.

She's not trying to fix you. She is trying to love you.

He'd be hot-damned if the voice in his head still wasn't Leah sometimes. But hearing her talk to him about Jessie was a new one.

You didn't let me love you.

He was making the same mistake. He didn't need Leah's ghostly voice, or his girls' real-life ones, or anyone else's to tell him what he already knew.

What you need is a good kick—

He knew that, too. So, for the second time on his ill-advised trip, he pulled over. Then he scrolled through his phone. Dialed Carter again, ready to ask him a question he'd been avoiding for months.

The phone rang twice before Carter answered, voice already warm, already steady. Paul almost laughed at how predictable that was, how some people seemed built for answering calls when others were falling apart. He opened his mouth, closed it again, stared out at the stretch of road ahead of him; the overcast sky that had been perfect for thirteen-point-one miles was now just a gray, fatigued void.

Paul had rehearsed this, or at least thought he had, but the words he'd prepared felt flimsy now, too careful, too polite. This wasn't a question that needed to be asked gently.

"I think I already know the answer," Paul said finally, before Carter could say much of anything. "I just need to say it out loud to someone who won't let me pretend it's simpler than it is."

Carter didn't rush him. That, too, felt like grace. Paul stayed quiet for a beat longer, not explaining or defending, but simply listing it all, the wanting, the anxiety, the exhaustion, the way doing nothing had started to feel less like faith and more like avoidance. When he finished, there was no lightning bolt nor any absolution spoken into the space between them. There was just Carter's calm voice, telling him that love didn't require permission from the past, only honesty in the present.

That choosing to stay numb was still a choice.

That God didn't ask people to survive their lives.

"He simply calls us," Carter concluded, "to life, abundantly."

When Paul ended the call, he sat there for another minute, hands resting uselessly on the steering wheel. Nothing outside the car had changed. The road was still the road. The future was still uncertain. But something inside him had shifted, maybe even settled. He wasn't ready to push or explain. But he was done pretending this was something that would simply pass if he waited long enough. He started the engine again, pulled back onto the road, and drove on, steadier.

The trembling inside him was gone, not because he was avoiding the next step, but because he finally knew he was willing to take it.

20

The drive home was uneventful, but I was tired, and my mind was so loud that I only craved quiet. But that was not the home I created, and as soon as I got there, the house was full in its familiar, chaotic way. My phone kept lighting up with questions I hadn't agreed to answer yet. Mikayla stopped by unannounced, responding to David's text led me speak to T-Mobile about a problem on his line that only I could fix, and Dolly had had an upset stomach all inside her crate.

It took over an hour to reset. The coffee pot had been refilled, and I moved from room to room on muscle memory alone, tidying things that didn't need tidying, nodding at the replayed conversations in my head, reminding myself that this was normal, that this was what it looked like to be needed. And still, beneath the hum, there was a low, persistent awareness I couldn't shake.

Did I break up with Paul?

No. But something had shifted, not loudly or visibly, but definitely inside me, just enough that standing still felt more impossible than usual.

He would be home any minute, I supposed. I sort of thought he would be right behind me, but I was also glad he wasn't.

If I saw him break again, all resolve would leave me.

But I needed to stand firm on what I wanted for my life, which held less time in front of me than behind me, no matter how much protein, collagen, creatine, or magic elixir from TikTok I ingested or how many weighted-vest squats I did.

I had made most of my life decisions based on what was happening to me or around me, even the great ones. I couldn't afford that anymore. Time is an unrenewable resource, and I would not spend it with someone causing me to second guess my place in his life.

Even if I loved him breathlessly.

He found me in the backyard, nursing a fresh bee sting on my hand. September always surprised me with its intensity. The heat was hotter. The humidity was wetter. And the bees were swarmier. September was the perimenopause of months.

I looked up at him and said, "There's tea in the fridge."

"I don't care about that," he answered.

I raised my eyebrows. "Alright," in my exaggerated southern accent.

"Jessie."

And before I could answer again, he was on his knees in front of my chair. *On his knees.* People who have not reached their sixties do not appreciate that gesture. Once you're down, you have to get back up, and he had just run thirteen miles and then driven a hundred and change. But there he was, *on his knees.*

He took my hands.

I shut my eyes. I just couldn't.

"Please don't give up on me."

I was certain he had more to say, likely had words teeming like those bees in a busy hive, but restraint had always been part of his hero energy. Whatever he could have said would not have undone me like those six simple words did.

I let go of his hands and covered my face, and without any care for what I looked or sounded like, I let sobs absolutely wreck me. I could tick off three years of utter craziness and grief, starting, quite honestly, with Mikayla's miscarriage right before Randall's fatal accident. Cancer tried to screw with me. My kids were spread out all over the place. I bought and sold a business and was trying to have a writing career. And God help me, this new marriage had all the intensity of a high school infatuation, all the trauma of a *Chicago-Something* show, all the weight of Shekinah glory.

"Baby."

Paul wrapped his arms around me. I wasn't angry with him at all. I wasn't even *two-thumbs-down* disappointed in him. But it didn't change his effect on me. I was sad and hurt and so freaking tired, and I knew he was, too, but I couldn't help him. I had exhausted myself trying.

My sobs gave way to a few deep breaths. I could feel my tears soaking his T-shirt, and he smelled very much like a man who ran a half marathon and then drove for three hours. But I didn't want to lift my head. I wanted to just stay and exhale and at least pretend we were fine, that love was enough.

I waited a beat, and then sense won over. He needed to stand up, and we needed to have a real conversation. I slowly leaned back, untangled myself from his embrace, took his hands in mine, and stood, making myself the brace for him to stand with. He made it seem effortless. He was good at that. Too good. He had hidden behind that for too long.

"I will never give up on you. Ever. Okay?" It was hard to choke the words out, but I badly needed him to understand that before I continued. "But Paul, we need—"

"Jessie." He put a finger over my lips before cupping my face with his hand. "I'm going to tell you everything, okay? But not alone. You're not going to just carry it. I'm ready to ask for help. Real help. Because you can't do this anymore, and I don't *want* to. Okay? *Okay?* Please give me one more chance. Please."

I could not stop crumbling. I could not get myself together. I knew exactly what he was saying, and it had been an unspoken prayer in me for months, maybe forever. There was a part of my brain telling me he had to do it on his own, that I could not be a crutch or companion in whatever recovery he needed. But the rest of me insisted that was the single dumbest thing I had ever heard, and I would march to hell and back for the man standing in front of me, wanting to try.

21

Therapy is hard.

I don't know what I expected. I had never really done it before. A little grief counseling after the stillbirth of our son Jamie. Pastoral care sessions regarding Randall's passing. Nothing formal or appointed. No notes taken or insurance claims filed. But here we were, Paul, who was a little worse for the wear than I had seen or may admitted to myself, and me, my own heart a more battered and bitter than I had wanted him to see.

Carter had referred Paul to Mallory Mullins. He felt that a female counselor would feel safer for Paul. Her office was smaller than I expected. Not cozy, exactly, but not clinical either, with two chairs angled toward a low couch, a lamp instead of overhead lights (always a plus in my book), and a box of tissues that made sense but also made me nervous. Paul chose the chair closest to the door. I noticed, filed it away, and didn't comment.

Paul had spent his first few sessions alone. He'd been immediately referred to a neurologist who diagnosed him with persistent post-concussive syndrome. He didn't want anyone to know. He didn't want me to know either, but since he was also going to see a cognitive therapist, he didn't try to hide it. In turn, I didn't tell him exactly how horribly guilty I felt that I didn't know just how much the accident and concussion had affected him.

He also told me matter-of-factly that he and Mallory went through the good, bad, and serious ugly of his childhood, his homelessness, his alcoholism, and his marriage to Leah. He didn't share all the details, and I managed to be okay with it.

That was the shaky foundation we had started from. I summed up our working-friends history, our tentative start, our early and devastating break-up, and our chaotic first two years of being, ahem, Jesus-married.

I fidgeted in my chair a lot; I was cognizant of it and wondered what meanings it conveyed, but my lower back and chronically uneven hips always caused me to cross, uncross, sit on my foot, use an ottoman, blah blah blah. I wasn't going to edit myself, too much, at least.

As for Mallory, she listened more than she spoke. She appeared to be somewhere between thirty-five and forty, old enough to relate, young enough to seem like one of our kids. Her long, brown hair was shiny, and her smiles were intentional but reserved. When she did speak, it was slowly, like she was placing something fragile on the table between us.

"Paul," Mallory said, "when nervous system decides something is un-safe, it doesn't consult the present. It consults history."

Paul nodded once, eyes fixed on the floor. I felt the urge to reach for him and resisted it, the way I was learning to resist a lot of things lately.

"And Jessie," Mallory continued, turning to me, "your instinct is to move toward connection when things feel uncertain. That's not wrong. It's just very different from Paul's." She paused. "The trouble starts when one of you needs quiet to regulate and the other hears that quiet as aban-donment."

I swallowed. "It does feel like that," I said. My voice almost broke. I was not accusing, just not editing.

Mallory nodded. "Of course, it does. And Paul, when Jessie presses, what does your body tell you?"

"That I'm about to fail," he said, before I could brace myself. His voice was steady, but his hands weren't. "That I'm going to say the wrong thing. That I'll make it worse."

A heavy silence settled between us. Mallory let it sit.

"Here's the work," she said finally. "Paul, your job is not to disappear when you feel overwhelmed. It's to stay visible. Even if all you can say is, *I'm flooded and I need ten minutes,* that will be a springboard to satisfy both of your instincts. And Jessie, your job is not to chase clarity or closure in that moment. It's to trust that pause isn't a withdrawal. It's a bridge."

I let out a breath I hadn't realized I was holding. Paul glanced at me briefly.

"You don't need to fix the past," Mallory continued gently. "You need to learn how to notice each other faster in the present. Healing doesn't mean *this* stops happening. It means it doesn't last as long."

I felt mostly okay about that. My problem was that I could understand everything Mallory and Paul were saying intellectually. But –

"I just really want to fix it," I blurted. "I know that I can't. I get that it's not my job nor do I have the ability. But when he is visibly shaken or hurting or shutting down, everything inside me goes KABLAM, and I need to *do* something."

"And you make it worse sometimes," he blurted.

Ouch. Also, *touché.*

Mallory looked at me and asked the quintessential therapy question: "Jessie, how does that make you feel?"

In the moment, all of it made me feel like running away, just like Paul had done. I wondered how *he* would feel if I did that, but I didn't feel like I could say that. In fact, I felt a little like they were ganging up on me.

"It makes me feel alone," I said with a shrug.

"So back to *quiet* feeling like abandonment," Mallory surmised.

"I suppose." I looked at my hands.

"But you're not. You're just giving him the space he needs."

"Well." My defenses flew on up. "The person I love and have given my heart to telling me I make him feel worse in his crisis moments sure *feels* like I am alone. What am I supposed to do with that?" I finally dared to look at him, and he was already staring at me, his expression both soft and a little confused.

"It's not you," he said quietly. "It's me, Jess. You know that."

"Just because you tell me it's not me doesn't mean I process it that way," I said. "I'm trying, Paul. I really am. I know you're still not used to me and how I do. I don't expect Snickerdoodles and hugs to make it all better. But it will never feel great to know I make it worse." Damn it. There went the tears, hot and coursing down my cheeks before I could even attempt to nonchalantly swipe at my eyes.

"I'm trying, too, Jess." He said it with such defeated resolve in his voice that my heart cracked a little more.

"Am I even what you need?"

I asked it out loud before I could stop myself, and the words seemed to suck the air out of the room a bit.

Mallory was looking at her notebook. Ah, this was for us to work out, not for her to counsel. Thanks for nothing, Mal.

After an uncomfortable pause, Paul answered with a bit more passion. "Of course you're what I need. That's what I'm trying to tell you. You didn't cause any of this."

"But I make it wor—"

"I shouldn't have said it that way," he interrupted. "Can we please leave that go? I'm sorry. You don't make it worse. You definitely don't make *me* worse. It's just that when I am trying to process, I talk to myself. I have a checklist to go through. Mallory has made it a more productive checklist, because it used to be things like, 'Is this worth a drink? Am I worth the fight? Should I just stay away from everyone forever?'

"So when you add to that, and start telling me how amazing I am and how much you love me, I feel worse, Jess. I feel unworthy of you. And it all gets muddled in my head. I am just trying to un-muddle. Because most of the stuff that makes me spin out doesn't matter one bit anymore. I know I'm better than my father. I know he can't hurt me or take away anything I have. I know I didn't give Leah a completely shit life. I know my daughters are great in spite of our mistakes. But just like you say, I can't always separate that in the moment. That's why I need a minute."

After a momentary pause he added, "That's why I need you. I just also need you to wait for me, if you can."

Mallory gestured to the tissue box, as though I would have missed it on the little round table next to me. Haha. I had missed it. I was sitting there sniffling and making myself a soggy mess. Every sentence Paul finished brought a fresh wave of tears. His way with words was one of the things I loved most about him. I wonder how our relationship would have developed if we'd both been engineers instead of writers.

I blew my nose, completely devoid of dignity, before I answered.

"You have me," I said. "I'm sorry if I made you doubt that. I will always wait for you. And I'll try to be quieter about that."

He smiled at that, almost like he was going to giggle. I smiled back at him, and we continued.

When the session ended, I felt, well, tentative. A little shaky. Informed, beaten up, and hopeful all at once. I was a little afraid to look at Paul or say anything in case it was too much. But that was the whole point. *I* was not too much. Life just was sometimes.

As we walked to the car, Paul reached for my hand. There was nothing apologetic or urgent in the gesture, nor did he seem to be asking me for anything. His hand simply felt natural in mine, comforting, like a perfect fit. So I let that be enough.

Julie

22

"Jules, at least let me come with you?"

Robin had to know it was a futile plea, but he also had to try. Julie had braided and unbraided her hair three times while he listed all the ways her meet-up could be a bad idea.

She didn't answer him.

"Did you tell your sisters?"

At that, she turned from the mirror and glared at him.

"No, I didn't tell my sisters. Danielle would do exactly what you're doing, and I only need one. Katy would insist on coming, probably with a case full of dynamite or something. Robin, don't act like I haven't thought this through."

It had not been difficult to reach Alex Chance. One never could know if someone would read their message requests, but they had a few mutual friends, and Julie had picked up a few light-internet-stalking tips from Brittney.

What was difficult was his immediate response. *Immediate.* Like he had been holding his breath and waiting for a sign.

What was difficult was Julie's equally immediate instinct to meet with him. She knew it was her own heart reaching for her mother, any part of her she could still grasp, and Alex certainly seemed to hold some part of Leah that Julie had never seen before.

What was difficult was keeping it from her dad. She would of course tell him—eventually. She told herself she was protecting him; he had a whole lot going on in his head since that accident over the summer.

But she was also being selfish and keeping Alex and his secrets about Mama to herself . . . just for a moment, Mama all to herself.

Robin had stood behind her and waited until her hair was braided. Now, he put his arms as far around her burgeoning waist as they would go. She let herself lean back into him.

"I can drive you and wait in the car," he said. "We don't know anything about this guy."

She sighed. "I'm meeting him in a public place. The worst he can do is make me cry. And the hormones will see to that anyway."

"Jules." One of the things she loved most about her husband was that he didn't insert an ellipsis when the situation called for a period. He knew when her mind was made up. If he disagreed, he let her know and then moved on.

As soon as she walked into the diner, Julie saw him. He was sitting in the booth furthest from the door and facing it. Just like in the pictures, he could not look more different from her dad. He wore a fitted, black leather bomber, his head covered by a black fedora with a plaid hatband, his long gray ponytail hung down his back. He had a goatee and mustache, like everyone did these days. She started walking toward him, and like a southern gentleman, he stood.

She blushed a little. She didn't want a scene, and God bless it, she definitely didn't want any emotions.

"Hi, I'm Alex," he said quietly. His voice was deep and a little gravelly. She wondered if he smoked. It seemed to go with the biker motif.

She shook his outstretched hand before sitting. It seemed silly to say her name; he already knew.

"I've never been here before," he said.

Julie looked around. "Me either, honestly. My stepsister suggested it. She used to work here." She shrugged. "Are you . . . do you want . . . ?"

He chuckled. "I always want to eat."

With that, they spent a few minutes silently perusing the menu. Julie tried to ignore the ticker tape of questions running through her head. She had most of them documented in her Notes app, but even she knew that pulling that out and firing away at this stranger was awkward at best and ridiculous to its core. He owed her nothing.

When his chili dogs and her salad had been ordered, he took a long drink of his tea and looked straight into her eyes. "Thanks for meeting me," he said.

Now she chuckled. Not heartily, just . . . *what the hell was the mood for this meeting?*

"I'm the one who asked."

"Then thank you for asking."

His eyes were dark and serious. Intensity dripped off him in a way that caused Julie to rest her chin on her hand and stare back. Looking at him emphasized the bottom line to all she had discovered in the past weeks: she didn't know her mother half as well as she had thought.

"It became obvious to me as I . . . well, as I read a few of my mother's messages—and it's important to me that you know I did *not* read them all—that not only were you special to her, but that you . . . held her in high regard. Cared for her well. Saw her for the amazing person she was. And even though I don't understand all of this, I appreciate that. I don't have delusions about the kind of marriage my parents had."

Umph. That felt like too much, too heavy, and too private of a thing to say, so she paused and took a calming breath, searching for the intersection of her loyalty to her family and her own need for insight, for resolution.

"Julie." His voice was a mixture of gentle and steady; she couldn't help being comforted by it. "I will answer any question you ask me the best I can. But you have to steer this conversation. Do you understand?"

She did, and she was impressed by his directness. People did not usually appreciate that quality in her.

"Yes. Thank you. So . . . how did you meet? The realty office?"

Julie already knew that, of course, but he indulged her in a few details of the work they did together.

"And you just became . . . like, work friends?"

Alex exhaled for what felt like a minute and a half. Julie sat up straighter, anticipating a much more than simple response.

"We became very distant best friends. Or to use the phrase your mother preferred, platonic soul mates."

Really? That phrase again? Her mother did *not* say things like that. That sounded much more like a Jessie-ism. But Aunt Sherron had been right after all.

"What does that mean?"

He sighed again. Julie supposed she should feel a little guilty, putting this guy through a total investigation. But he'd *said*, "ask anything," and this was her mother they were talking about. Her dead mother. Her dead mother's *secret life*.

"It means that we were close. We worked together some, and we ran together some. We chatted a lot about a lot of things, most of them fleeting, like training and favorite musicians. Some of them more serious, like family events or family history or . . . bad days."

The bad days will bond you, Julie thought. She'd had a few right after she met Robin, with him almost literally picking her up off the ground. And here she was, with his ring on her finger and apparently, the world's most ravenous unborn child raging in her abdomen, demanding snacks.

She opened her mouth to respond to Alex but then closed it again and nodded.

"There was not a physical affair between us," he said carefully and bluntly all at once. "Beyond a few" —he looked away with a tinge of embarrassment on his face— "hugging incidents, we never laid a finger on each other. We never went out together, just the two of us. We rarely even said 'I love you.' And Julie, as hard as this probably is for you to hear, I want you to know that it feels *ridiculous* to say out loud."

Her instinct was to feel sorry for him, but she remembered the context and swallowed, trying to steel her resolve. The things that had possessed her mama to keep this man a secret were betrayals to her father and to her and Mama's relationship.

"You don't have to tell me anymore," she said abruptly. "I know you're offering it freely, but I can't sit across from a grown man and hear how he loved my mother. Because Alex? If you talked like this about her, with this look in your eyes, when she was alive, you have to know that *everyone* around you was on to you. I have zero doubts about that."

A rueful little smile spread across his face. He immediately said, "Sorry."

"I don't think that matters at this point, do you?"

He sighed and shook his head.

The silence turned awkward. The food, thankfully, came. Julie messed with her salad, rearranging the tomatoes, cutting the lettuce, spreading the dressing just so.

"You do look like her," Alex said, his own plate untouched.

Julie didn't look at him. Of course, she heard that all the time. She was the daughter who looked *and* acted mostly like Mama: driven, serious, devoted, *together*. But Julie had struggled through her twenties to settle her heart down. The harder she worked, the more she had been distracted by some dumb guy or the idea thereof, it'd seemed.

Apparently, that was another way she and Mama were alike. She still wasn't over the shock, especially being here in his presence.

"Thank you," was all she could say.

They ate in oddly companionable silence, the whole meal. Julie kept ticking off the questions in her brain, but none of them felt appropriate. She observed him as subtly as she could, making all the perfunctory comparisons. He was about the same age as Daddy, she guessed. He was much more chiseled and styled. Daddy was more formal back when he was a principal, but since he retired and became a writer, and adjunct professor, and sometimes-running-store-associate, he was more laid back by the day. Alex wore a Blank Brand shirt, fitted, sleeves carefully rolled up. He sported platinum rings on each hand, black ink tattoos up both his forearms (she didn't want to stare long enough to figure out what they all were), and an earring in his left ear. He emanated a sophisticated, reserved air that was similar to Daddy's, but also a particular openness that would unnerve her if she wasn't careful.

The server was a thin, ageless woman with a curly ponytail who introduced herself as Gina and crouched at the table when she spoke to them. She collected their plates and checked on whether they needed anything else. Alex, without consulting with Julie, asked for refills, rice pudding, and time—smoothly, like he was used to setting the room at ease.

After Gina brought the drinks and dessert, Alex asked quietly, "Is there anything else, Julie?"

There was both steel and sadness in his voice, like he knew these were the last moments he would be connected to Leah. Something inside Julie understood.

Even though she didn't need to, she wiped her mouth carefully with her napkin, looking into his eyes for just a moment. They were a dark gray, tinged with green, almost slate colored, and somber. She shook her head. She didn't want to offer any empathy to him.

But there it was.

"Can you . . . maybe just tell me one thing. Anything. A story? Something about my mother that . . . lets me know her a little better?"

Alex stirred a little in his seat. Julie figured it made him a little more uncomfortable, but why should she be the only one? Anyway, she really wanted to know. She waited patiently, sipping her tea and noting "Eighteen Wheels" playing on the radio. The Mama she knew had listened to a great variety of music a lot of the time but hadn't been a music fanatic. Alex knew someone different.

"We had office hours together once or twice a week," he finally started. "That is when we really got to know each other. It was almost always quiet in the morning, so one of us would bring or make coffee, and we'd just catch up a little."

Julie nodded. Work friends. Nothing intriguing there.

"One day, she came in clearly stressed. Tight-lipped. Quiet. It had been her turn to bring coffee, and she had made a deal about the coconut latte from some new coffee truck, but she'd forgotten them. It was very unlike her."

"Probably something Katy did," Julie murmured. Alex laughed a little, knowingly. It pierced her heart a little.

"She didn't want to talk about it," he continued. "And that was an unspoken rule between us. No pushing. No expectations. We were definitely a sounding board for each other, but advice was given only when asked. So, I let her be and went to fetch coffees myself. But before I left, I choose the music."

Julie's heart fluttered a bit, though she couldn't pinpoint exactly why.

He shrugged, like he was trying to stay casual in his reminiscing. "Music was, I suppose, the language between us. It was usually me sending her songs, live clips, little noodles I had written occasionally. And then, as you know, I would make playlists for her. After a while, she started reciprocating. She was a little embarrassed about her taste and her experience, because of growing up a little sheltered from secular music. It was so fun to show her new things, even stuff she hated."

"What she hated surprised me sometimes," Julie said, thinking of a playful and ongoing debate in which Daddy always defended "classic country" and Mama called Johnny Cash and Waylon Jennings drunken warblers.

Alex's eyes twinkled. "Well, that day, I teetered on the edge. There was a song my dad used to play to cheer me up, and I wanted her to hear it, but it's Allman Brothers, and that classic bro sound just wasn't her thing."

Julie felt suspense building. Mama was polite but so vocal. Did she turn it off? Hurl a speaker? Break down?

"The song is 'Soulshine,'" he said. "Do you know it?

She shook her head.

"I put it on repeat," he said with a grin. "Not only is it southern rock, but it is relentlessly down-home and positive."

"So not her jam." Julie smiled.

"Yeah. So. I was gone for maybe fifteen minutes, and when I came back—"

He broke off, seeing it. Julie wished she could, too, whatever it was.

"She had her shoes off. She was sitting at the window seat where no one ever sat. She was looking out the window where the pond was, even though it was a foggy morning. And she was singing, *'When you can't find the light that got you through a cloudy day, when the stars ain't shinin' bright, you feel like you've lost your way . . . '*

Julie didn't respond. And Alex was no longer really talking to her.

"Soulshine," he continued. "'It's better than sunshine. It's better than moonshine. Damn sure better than rain.'"

Silence fell for a moment. He looked torn between continuing or letting the image hang there.

"You can leave it," Julie said. "Or tell me. It's up to you."

His eyes widened as though she'd read his mind. He stammered, making her wonder if it was indeed better to let it conclude.

"She was a little teary," he said softly. "You know. Unusual for her. And she caught me watching her, which should have been a little embarrassing for us both, but it just wasn't."

He paused again. "I am sorry. I don't want this to be hard or awkward."

There was no other way for it to be. And she told him that. "But it doesn't mean I don't want to hear it. Because she's gone, and you *knew* her, and . . ."

She didn't have to finish that part. She let him finish instead.

"We just didn't say anything. The song kept playing. She stopped singing. And when she stood up, we danced a little. Not anything super intimate. Not the whole song. Just for a minute. And then we drank our coffee and went about our day."

Julie swallowed. In spite of all the pep talks she had given herself, she blinked until her tears fell freely down her cheeks.

He knew Mama. Really knew her. And she was reminded that joy and intimacy was not something that came easily for Leah, but something she fought for and chose. Just like Julie.

"Thank you for that," she said, her voice small.

The warmth in Alex's eyes was glazing over as well. He reached his hand forward, almost like he wanted to take hers, but then he stopped, cocked his head, and asked, "Can I tell you one more thing?"

"Sure." She nodded to convince herself that it was okay.

"I was at the funeral."

That seemed like an odd declaration. Julie assumed he had been, after all that. And also, he was Mama's colleague and friend, so it was perfectly appropriate.

"I sat with some mutual friends," he explained, reading her mind. "But around the time that song played, I had to leave. My level of grief was not, oh, *proportional*. And that song undid me."

"Mama *loved* her some Amy Grant," Julie said absently. She and her sisters had chosen the song "Where Do You Hide Your Heart?" and played the recording—no other voice would do—with the obligatory slide show, a sliver of a lifetime hopefully reflected in 100 pictures and four minutes.

"I was hiding *my* heart," he said. "It felt like a sign I should leave, grieve privately as long and as deeply as I needed to, and then move forward. And I did. Hardest thing I will ever have to do is kill the pain of not being able to reach my best friend when I couldn't even miss her out loud. This was still . . . " he paused for a deep breath, "It was just absolutely amazing to hear from you. And to see her one more time, in you."

She sighed and dropped her defenses just a little. "It was equally amazing . . . this, for me. Sorry. My words aren't coherent. I didn't expect to feel this way. I should probably be mad at you or resentful, and I'm not sure I will ever tell my father about this, but somehow, I feel like I got to see her today, in a brand-new way."

"I feel the same," he said. "It's been a gift."

Julie's heart beat a little faster. She had a choice to make, quickly. She didn't want to stay in touch with Alex; that was too much. But based on this once-in-a-lifetime encounter, she decided almost easily.

"I actually have a gift for you," she said, pulling the baggie out of her purse, her heart racing from adrenaline and her mind racing from all the recognition. "There was a file, kinda buried. I don't know if she meant for you to see it. I didn't read it. But it was called 'Soulshine,' and when I opened it, it started 'Dear Alex.' So, here it is."

Alex looked as if he had seen a ghost. He reached across the table, accepting the baggie from Julie, and then clenching it so tightly his knuckles whitened. In that moment, he looked so desperate, so devastated, that she sincerely hoped there was something meaningful on that tiny USB drive.

"I should go," Julie said, reaching in her purse, hoping the distraction of paying the bill would keep her eyes from overflowing.

"I have this, Julie. Please."

Normally, she would have debated on several principles, but the heaviness of everything else seemed to vastly outweigh her compulsion to cover a forty-dollar tab.

"Thank you," she said, more softly than she wanted to.

"Thank *you*," he echoed.

"I . . . I don't expect we'll see each other again."

She slid out of the booth, feeling off-balance in every way. She avoided his gaze while she smoothed her pants and picked up her bag, slung it over her shoulder, and swiped at her eyes. They weren't teary. They were just threatening, and she had to be sure before she looked at him.

His eyes were glassy. She nodded and walked toward the door, knowing he would follow. Once they reached the covered porch, thankfully devoid of other customers, she stopped and looked again.

"There is nothing I can say that is peaceful or simple. It's all complicated."

"I know this," Alex answered.

"I'm about as warm as my mother," she said, with a tiny giggle.

He shook his head. "Soulshine."

She nodded. "Soulshine." And with that, she stepped forward and let Alex hug her. She didn't hug back, and she didn't quite relax, but she accepted it, knowing what it meant to him and probably to Mama, somewhere.

Julie didn't go straight to Daddy. She called Robin on the way home and told him *almost* everything. He hadn't known Mama, and a few of the details, like the "Soulshine" story, just felt too private to say out loud. She had no idea how much to tell Daddy, so she got dressed for a run.

She had copied all of Mama's playlists to her own account; they'd been all she listened to for days. Now she scrolled more methodically, searching, and it wasn't hard to find: One entitled "Window Seat" was there, and the very first song was, of course, "Soulshine."

She hadn't heard it before, that she remembered. It was mid-tempo and bluesy, perfect for the pace she was capable of in the October afternoon. The humidity had relented, but the sun and her hormones had not. She made it just over a mile before she shrugged and turned around.

You have nothing to prove, Mama's voice told her.

She'd had it on repeat: *"We all feel this way sometime. You got to let your soul shine, shine 'til the break of day."*

Neither do you, Mama.

"I'm not sure I wanted to know this, Julie."

Daddy's words stung. She knew things were tenuous with him; she had accepted how much he loved Jessie and had moved forward, but she had really believed he'd want to know at least a little about Leah's other side.

It hadn't occurred to her for a single second that he didn't want to or more startlingly, that he already did.

Deflated, she answered, "I'm sorry. I should have realized how different it would feel for you."

Paul sighed. She'd asked him to come outside and walk. They made it to the bocce ball park on Lakeside—she never remembered any of the real park names—before she needed to sit again. It was calm and pretty there; there were benches by the pond, and the flowers were still hanging on. She practiced being grateful that her legs were still carrying her around and not mad that she couldn't seem to do all the things she was used to.

"I know she had a friend named Alex. I saw Alex. I *met* Alex. She adored Alex."

Julie let the silence speak as that sunk in. Maybe the discovery of Alex in Mama's life wasn't that big of a reveal. Maybe everyone knew but them, her daughters.

"Oh."

"Julie, I can't even begin to tell you how much I don't want to talk about this."

She stiffened. "It's fine. You don't have to. I'm sorry." And when he didn't answer in the very next beat, she added, "Let's walk back."

"Julie Emma."

"Daddy—"

"You have to give me a minute," he said, sounded exasperated but also, nearly laughing.

"Daddy?"

"Jules, I have some things to tell you, too. The first is that I'm sorry I haven't been strong enough to talk about these things before." He reached across the green grooves of the bench and took her hand. "Because mostly, I might have been a pretty good dad, but I was not a great husband, and your mom deserved a great husband, someone to know her better and rise to her standards and grow with her.

"I loved her. You know that. And she loved me. We just never quite let each other in all the way. And that leaves gaps. And we both let other people and things fill those gaps."

Julie allowed her unasked question to linger in the air.

"There were no affairs or scandals," he answered it. "You know about me and booze. That was the biggest gap-filler I ever allowed in. And after that, honestly, Mama didn't try so hard, and I didn't blame her. We focused on you girls and our jobs; we found hobbies, and we absolutely, both of us, allowed other friendships to take up some of that lost and lonely space."

Julie nodded, mostly not surprised by an of it.

"The shameful part of it," he continued, more quietly, "is that we both knew, and we both allowed it. Because letting things be, letting Alex be your mama's friend, her letting Jessie be mine, was easier than finding our way to each other and taking risks and healing. Believe me."

"How did you know if you hadn't tried?"

Paul nodded and gave a sad little laugh. "Great question, Jules."

She wasn't sure he was actually going to answer, so again, in spite of wanting more, she gifted him a long pause. He squeezed her hand and then let go as he spoke again.

"Sometimes, one of us *would* try. And when the other didn't respond at that time, it cut like very deep rejection."

Ouch. She knew that feeling.

"The other part is that I'm trying now."

Julie looked at his profile. His weight always fluctuated just a little bit. He was blessed with squirrel-like metabolism and also a powerful sweet tooth. Being outdoorsy had always helped him stay lean. Running almost made him skinny, and the last few months, since his car accident in the summer, he was thinner than she'd ever seen him. It accentuated his age, the lines in his face, the weariness that always seemed to shadow his eyes.

"What are you trying, Daddy?"

He closed his eyes briefly before he turned to her. "To heal."

That stole her breath for a moment. She heard birds flapping their wings. She felt Baby Bean flutter. And she felt Mama, too, a tiny, familiar nudge inside.

"I'm proud of you, Daddy," she said, and rested her head on his shoulder. He leaned his head against hers and let out a deep sigh. There in the sunshine, with the first man she ever loved, she felt the peace she had been fighting to find.

23

"Remember when I came here to visit for Christmas, and Paul brought us the most amazing breakfast tray out here?"

Maggie's favorite memories were always random. There was a laundry list of things about that first Christmas – the one *after* Randall and Leah had died, *after* Paul and I had gotten together, broken up, and then moved in together, *after* David had moved to Arizona with Julie, *after* Maggie had married Don and moved away – that I remembered quite well. It had been the *utterest* of chaos, from my brother showing up unexpectedly *decades* after leaving Maggie and their girls to Maggie's daughter Nora announcing she was pregnant from a one-night stand named Abe, who happened to show up at our Christmas Eve dinner via a connection to Brittney.

Nah. I had kinda forgotten Paul's lovely charcuterie board, and I told her so.

"Well, I would love to have that right now," Maggie murmured lazily, stretching out her legs toward Sparrow Drive, also lazy and quiet in the afternoon haze.

"I would love to have a lot of things right now," I said, still caught in the space of two hours before, the hand holding mine, the silent car ride, the going of separate ways when we got home. Paul was running. I was both craving and resisting a giant mimosa. Hearing more about his relationship with alcohol was making mine a bit tenuous. "Peace. Certainty. A three-month cruise."

"The cruise seems attainable," Maggie murmured, sipping *her* mimosa without a care in the world. Well, that wasn't true, but it felt like it in the moment.

"Mikayla and Josie will be here any minute," I said. "If she needs me to babysit, will you stay for a bit? I'm actually not sure I'm up for it, sister."

Maggie gaped at me as though I said I was giving up Mexican food forever. "Who are you? Surely not my Jessie Rose who lives to bounce grandbabies around. Not my Jessie Rose who never asks for help with anything."

I gave her the birds'-eye, respectful of Paul's privacy, version of going to therapy.

"Babyyyyyy!" was her answer. And for the first time in a long time, I was willing to accept her big sister energy. She sighed, still staring at me. "Why didn't you tell me it had gotten so tense?"

"Because I could barely admit it to myself until he took off for Camden, and the aftermath was just . . . I needed to process and not just drink about it, you know? This is honestly a question of how I am spending the rest of my life. Because Mags? If it is not with Paul, it's gonna be just me. That is one thing I am absolutely sure of."

"Here, here," she said, taking a swig. Her first year with Don had held its own doubts, all hers, because she *had* been on her own for so long. "I got baby Josie. And Mikayla if need be. Why don't you take yourself for a nice long walk on the beach or something?"

I shrugged.

"Sheesh. Ambivalence is downright scary on you."

Before I could answer, Mikayla pulled into the driveway. And before she had Josie unbuckled form her car seat, Brittney's car followed.

"Lord, you didn't call an intervention, did you?" I asked.

"No, ma'am. I didn't know we needed one."

"We don't," I snapped. "Hey, Kayla! You need help?"

She was already walking toward us with her toddler in one arm, her bag in the other, and her key fob in her mouth. She managed a smile through that, and I took Josie from her as soon as she reached the stairs.

"I didn't know Brittney was coming, too," I said. "Do you all want lunch?"

"Jessie!" Maggie scolded at the same time Mikayla said, "Mama! We don't just come here to eat. And it's three in the afternoon. We are pregnant. We ate all the things already today."

"Damn straight," Brittney said, coming up from behind her. "But if you want to throw together something . . . "

"No, ma'am," Maggie repeated. "I am sending your Mama to the beach. I'll take y'all out if you need to flap your jaws."

"Maggie!" I said. "You're not the boss of me."

"Someone needs to be. At least sometimes."

"Mama, what's going on?"

"Oh, for the love. Nothing. Nothing I want to talk about right now."

There was a collective sigh around me.

"Fine. Everything is fine," I said, trying not to sound as frustrated as I felt. "Paul and I are ... we are seeing a therapist. Today was our first session together. And if you must know, it's hard. It sucks, actually. And I am exhausted, but we all know how I feel admitting that, so let's just get the chips and salsa out and live our lives, okay?"

I knew they were all exchanging glances and having silent conversations, so I focused on Josie's malleable little body in my lap. Mikayla dressed her in quintessential first-baby-girl fashion, and today was no exception. She was in patchwork overall shorts that were bright pink, aqua, orange, and yellow. No shirt underneath. No shoes. Matching kerchief on her head that she magically left in place. I could have gobbled her up.

"Maybe I'll take Josie for a walk?" I suggested, expecting resistance and for them to tell me to take a nap or some nonsense.

But amongst the din of their alternative suggestions, Brittney worked to meet my gaze. There was purpose in her eyes that stopped everything for me. Everything.

"Brit," I said, feeling my heart flutter a bit more rapidly. "What's up?"

Brittney

24

"I wanted to tell you sooner," Brittney started, settling into one of the Adirondack chairs that made her burgeoning belly stick out a little more. "But Harrison and I . . . our plans keep getting thwarted, and I don't want to wait any longer."

His impromptu flight from DC had gotten cancelled. He was going to drive, and his battery was dead that morning. Brittney believed in signs. It hurt to be away from him, but seriously. They'd each ordered pizza and spent the whole afternoon and evening on their FaceTime, like teenagers. Watching movies, laughing, crying a little, and making their plans. And now more time had passed, and she was facing her music, alone.

"Oh my gosh, let me see!" Mikayla squealed.

Aunt Maggie swatted her arm, but it was too late.

"See what?" Mama asked, and Brittney instinctively tucked her hands under her thighs, a hint of shame burning her cheeks.

"It's not that, Kayla," she said with a hint of vitriol. "Jeez."

As "Mama" as Mama could be, she said, "Why don't I get you some tea first, and then you can tell us? Or you can just tell me, and we can send these two away?" She stood and handed Josie to Maggie.

"These two?" Mikayla said, in mock outrage. But they all watched Mama flit through the front door, forcing a reset, calming Brittney. It was Mama's specific brand of magic.

The three grown-ups sat wordlessly and let Josie take the lead. She was babbling to Maggie about the "punshine" so they couldn't help but smile at her with her little bandana and the sweetest little bare feet and painted piggies in the world. Brittney wasn't sure if she wanted a boy or a girl and was certain it didn't matter, but Josie made a strong case for daughter vibes, even at the same time Mama's own two daughters were about to drive her completely insane. The boys did, too, after all.

Mama returned with one Mason jar filled with tea, mint sprigs, and a wedge of peach on the lip for good measure. One jar. Aunt Maggie and Mikayla must have really pissed her off. No one said anything as she handed the drink to Brittney and grabbed Josie back up, presenting her with a frosted animal cracker.

"Alright Brit," Mama said, looking her dead in the eyes but with softness in her expression. "What did you want to tell me?"

Even while clasping the cold jar, Brittney felt her palms sweat. Would it have been easier with Harrison by her side, with the whole family around instead of the three most likely to ask her hard questions? Maybe. But like everything else lately, this was the circumstance she was given, and she'd delayed the moment long enough.

"Things aren't really working the way I thought they would," she said, and the stupid tears immediately sprung in her eyes. She wanted this to be a moment of empowerment. Not weakness. Not pity. Not surrender. But, hot damn, the hormones always had the final say these days. "And regardless of that, Harrison and I delayed some of our decisions as long as possible, because, well, they are really fucking hard decisions. Sorry, Mama, but they are."

Mama nodded, silently, patiently, and with a look of resolve on her face that unnerved Brittney completely. She stood back up and handed Josie to Mikayla, took the jar from Brittney's hands, and pulled her upward.

Brittney could barely meet her mother's eyes. She was only just beginning to understand what it meant to really hold another human, their well-being and their heart and soul. Mama had done that, times four, and adding in all the in-laws and grandkids and everyone else her heart adopted along the way, Brittney could not fathom how she had the capacity for it all.

She didn't want to do this. She didn't want to hurt the heart that had held all that space and all that burden, who was now the one making this easier for her.

Mama put her hands on Brittney's face. She felt like she was eight years old again, asking if Mama was sure it was still okay if she went to Samantha's birthday party, because her baby brother Jamie had been born already dead and everyone was so sad and careful and quiet, and Brittney had made it her mission to ensure Mama was good.

She was not going to be good about this, but Brittney couldn't help it.

"I know," Mama said, tears welling in her eyes. "I know you have to go, baby. And I know that's how it should be."

"Mama—"

"I don't want you to do this alone," she continued. "I know you have us. I know you've been trying so hard, but Harrison is the daddy, and he has his other kids, and he loves you, Brittney. I know that."

"I never wanted to disappoint you this way." Brittney's eyes overflowed then.

"Brit, even if you got married and then got pregnant, Ruthie and Dakota would still be there. *He* would still need to be there. I get it. Don't mistake me." Her voice got shaky, and she took a moment to compose herself. "I hate it." She let go of one of Brittney's hands and started smoothing her hair instead. "But I get it. And I will help you however I can. Okay, baby? Okay?"

Brittney let her hug her then, and Mikayla and Aunt Maggie stood. In a different family, they might have walked inside and given the mother and daughter a moment. But that's not who they were. They piled right into the embrace, until Brittney couldn't tell whose arms were where, whose tears she felt, what voices she was hearing.

But for the first time since that positive pregnancy test, she started to feel like maybe things were going to be alright.

El's voice absolutely killed Shinedown. Brittney was a little mad The Salty Lips hadn't covered them sooner. Now they'd added at least three songs just as she was going to start missing some of their gigs.

All of their gigs.

She'd told Katy that morning. Took her to breakfast at Neal and Pam's, splurged on extra potato cakes, tried not to be jealous of Katy's double mimosa, and told one of her best friends that she was leaving. She fully expected Katy to be cool. She'd run away to the other coast when she was barely eighteen. As soon as she recovered from that utter disaster, she'd move to Wilmington. Katy was the freest spirit in their makeshift family by far.

But no sooner did Brittney say, "I'm moving to be with Harrison," did Katy lay her blonde head right on the surfboard table and *boohoo*.

"Katy!" Brittney somewhat awkwardly put her hand on Katy's head. Katy was not an Oakley. The Jamesons did not cry in public. They did not cuddle. Brittney had no script for how to comfort a sister that didn't come from her Mama.

Katy said nothing. Neither did their favorite server Kim when she set down their plates, grimaced at Brittney, and walked away. Everyone knew them there. The band played there every month. Katy was no stranger to making a little scene; it just didn't usually look like *this*.

"Kakes, come on. Please don't."

"Don't caaaaallllll me thaaaaaat," she sobbed. Brittney stifled her giggle. El had assigned Katy the nickname, and whether Katy liked it depended entirely on the day, the weather, her mood, who was saying it, why they were saying it, and if there was any cake around.

Brittney took a sip of decaf from her styrofoam cup and stared across the road at the ocean. It was a typical autumn late morning. The air had started out a little crisp, but the sun blazed bright and unapologetically until everything was warm. Brittney had never lived anywhere but right there, in Surfside Beach. And she wasn't one of those natives or long-timers who dismissed it, took it for granted, or pretended it wasn't amazing. She loved the beach, the salt air, and the sand. She loved the kitschiness of a tourist town. She loved the little mobile homes like hers and the grand, new beach McMansions popping up in the middle of them. She loved the staggering number of ice cream shops and thought sand dollars and starfish made just fine décor. She loved beach bars and drinks named after sea creatures and all the motorcycles zooming into town twice a year. She loved wearing flip flops in December and taking golf cart rides on New Year's Day.

And she loved her chaotic, makeshift family.

How the hell was she ever going to manage this?

She squirted ketchup on a paper towel and dipped a potato cake in it. The crunch snapped Katy out of her sorrow. She lifted her head, looking like a wounded pre-schooler, swiped at her eyes with another paper towel, and reached for the other potato.

"I can't believe you're leaving me. After I moved here for you!"

Relishing the salty goodness, Brittney answered without emotion. "You moved here for El. And maybe the band. And *maybe* your nieces and nephew. So—"

"Alright," Katy broke in, exaggerating her southern accent. "True. But still."

Brittney threw a grape jelly packet at her, and Katy laughed, her cheeks still wet and her eyes still puffy. "You think you're gonna have to live there forever, because seriously, Brit. DC? It's cold up there. No ocean. And one too many ex-wives."

That was for damn sure.

She'd made Katy promise to let her tell El herself, and she was nervous but confident Katy would keep her word. Though the stepsister was known in some parts of the family as "The Mouth of the South," Katy respected Brittney's bestie-ship with El.

Brittney kinda wished she could pin it on Katy, though. Because telling him would be almost as hard as telling her Mama had been.

El was singing the opening lines of "I'll Follow You." It was a perfect song to end the set as they'd opened with "Symptom of Being Human."

Brittney was frankly *so sick* of her own tears, but she was going to miss the band and these nights almost as much as she would miss El.

Per her norm, she hung out while they finished shmoozing with the crowd and breaking down their set. She even helped Ringo and carried a few of his lighter bags. And then, El found her sitting at a picnic table near the fence, trying to keep her distance from some of the dogs that always populated the Tidal Creek beer garden. She wanted to be as alone as possible. If she could have piped in her news to El from somewhere else entirely, she'd have done so.

"Brit," he breathed, when she finally got the words out. "Damn it. I knew. I knew it was probably going to happen, but I hoped . . . "

He stopped himself, looking away to the streetlights. She pretended not to notice the glassy sheen over his eyes. They weren't that way. Their closeness was solid and unwavering, but emotions were understood rather than expressed most of the time.

"Why didn't he tell me?"

"Because I insisted," she said without a pause. "He might be your brother, but I'm your—your—*yours!*" she said, and then a tiny sob broke her voice. She took a sip of her stupid soda water and let the moment pass.

"How pissed are you that you can't drink right now?" he asked with a smirk.

"If I were in a state to drink, this wouldn't be happening." She said it before she thought it through, and as soon as she heard it, she winced. El pulled the lime from his gin and tonic and tossed it into her soda and let her bask in her own words.

"You are mine," he finally said, gently but with sternness in his voice. "And I told you, I'm here for you no matter what. You won't be alone, no matter what. So be sure, Brit. Because you don't *have* to do this."

Brittney felt her cheeks redden. El and Harrison hadn't been reconciled very long, and though she appreciated El's loyalty to her, she didn't want any bitterness or wariness between the brothers.

"I know," she finally said. "I . . . know. I'd be fine here. I have you, and the sisters, and God knows, I have my mama. But El? I do have Harrison. I love him. And I want my baby to have a real family. It's not ideal. It's not, I mean, you already know . . . of course I don't *want* to move. This is my home. But Harrison . . . he's my home, too, now. It's been a rough couple of months, but it's taught me that. I don't want to do this without him."

They both pretended not to notice the tears pouring freely from her eyes and landing on her laced hands. He reached across the table and covered them with his own hand, giving a gentle, reassuring squeeze.

He cleared his throat before quietly asking, "Do you know when?"

She shook her head. "Just that it will be soon. I'm going to try to secretly rent out my place. I'm not ready to sell it; I just got it . . . "

El looked into the flames of a nearby fire pit for what felt like minutes. Brittney had wanted him to understand, though she didn't really expect it. She felt relief wash over her. And a fresh wave of sadness.

"I'm having a tough time imagining all of this without you, punk," he said.

She refused to notice the glisten still in his eyes.

"You made this feel like home, you know?"

She nodded. "Now you can make it feel like home for Katy."

He snickered. "She grew up here, dummy."

Brittney shook her head. "Yeah, but ask her. She felt so alien here she ran away the first chance she got. *You* have made all the difference for her. Just like you did for me. Well, not just like, but . . . I can't imagine all of 'this' without you, either."

"What, your preggo belly? That's kind of weird."

"Shut up!" She reached into her glass and launched an ice cube at him.

"You're sewn into the fabric of my life, El. I might have heard that in some country song my mom played over and over in the Grand Caravan, but that doesn't make it less true. So I am not going to consider this a goodbye. Just another housing crisis. Temporary. Because you and me, sir? We are ride or die. Period. Exclamation point!"

He nodded solemnly and kept his hand over hers while he glanced away. El was the one person in her life who shared silence with her. Life was loud; it always had been for her. And she knew this next step, moving and having a baby and becoming some sort of stepmother, was going to make it even louder. So she relished this form of silence, the two of them under the stars, their drinks melting into the picnic table, the laughter and banter surrounding them but not touching them. The tension she'd have to live with was palpable: She couldn't wait to go to Harrison, but she was in no hurry to leave this.

25

Paul stood in the doorway of one of their sunny guest rooms, the one where Jessie had a desk that was painted a faded, dusky blue, its surface a curated display of antique desk lamp, a framed picture of the Mikayla and Brittney around age four, and a ceramic mug crammed with pens and pencils she never used.

She never used the desk either. He watched her sitting in the easy chair in the corner, a linen blanket over her legs, not her feet, lest she melt from the heat, holding her laptop. Dolly was crammed between her hip and the side of the chair. Some acoustic playlist was setting a somber mood. He just wanted to look at her.

Whether she didn't notice him right away or wanted to preserve the pause, he didn't know. But Damien Rice finished his whole sad, repetitive song before she looked at Paul, her face as crestfallen as the lyrics.

"Hi love," she said softly.

"Hi baby," he answered, realizing he'd been holding his breath.

"Wanna sit?" She scootched her feet over to one side of the ottoman, patting a spot for him to sit. He almost raced there from the other side of the room, but he paced himself. Sat. Put his hand on her foot. Looked into her eyes, drowning in everything he had missed because they were being so damn careful with each other.

"Jessie Rose."

She was staring at him, her hair in a low ponytail thrown over her right shoulder, a smidge of black liner smeared under her eyes, and a look of cautious hope in them.

He reached over and cupped her cheek. "I miss seeing you sparkle when you look at me."

Her eyes turned downward. "You do?"

"Yes."

"You see my sparkle? And my lack thereof?"

"Of course I do."

She looked out the window, still away from him. He felt a little sting at that, even though he knew he deserved it.

He was afraid to ask, but he did anyway. "How can we bring it back?"

"Paul, it isn't your responsibility." He knew she would say that. "I'm a grown woman. I've seen it all. I've done it all. My sparkle is always gonna ebb and flow. But maintaining it is on me, not anyone else."

He moved his hand from her face and squeezed her hand. And he resolved he would sit there like that, one hand holding her hand and one holding her foot, and he would wait for her until she was ready to let him back in. And he prayed she would.

"I'm not anyone," he said. "I'm your husband. Sssh. Don't say it."

She closed her mouth.

"I *am* your husband. I am *yours*. And I know I hurt you. I know the way I deal with my demons has been to build a wall around them and me to keep everything from spilling over. But now you know. You've seen it all. I don't have anything left to hide or any reason to hide anything. And you haven't run away. So that tells me, Jess, that you still want this. That maybe loving each other is actually enough, if we're still willing to try."

He heard the sob that caught in her throat. She pretended like it hadn't happened, kept looking out the window as water poured from her eyes. He would let her pretend. He wasn't looking away.

"I gave up, Jessie. Years before Leah died, I gave up. I watched you and Randall, I watched Danielle and Matt even, and I knew I was never going to have that kind of fulfillment in my own life. I was resolved. Whatever I had was good enough; it was already more than I ever thought I'd have."

"And then they died. And you know the rest of the story. I realized I wanted you long before I was ready to have you, Jess. I didn't know it could be this way. I didn't know love could be so . . . much. I didn't ask for a damn thing, and life gave me you."

He swiped at his own eyes in frustration. It was hard for them to cover much ground with both of them blubbering.

"I don't say I need you lightly," he concluded. "I don't think I have ever said that to anyone before."

She nodded emphatically. "I know. I *know*! I want it to be enough," she finally said, taking breaths between each word.

"Baby, *you* are enough. It's me. I'm the one who's broken. You just . . . you made me want to quit ignoring the things that are wrong and actually fix them."

She smiled, her eyes still running over, and squeezed his hand back. "That part makes me very happy."

"Then why all the tears, my Jessie?"

He heard himself, turning into absolute goo. The feeling wasn't new; the ability to allow himself to melt around her was. His heart was thudding in his chest, a little sweat running down his back. He hoped he wasn't too late.

She had gathered herself, chin no longer trembling, eyes no longer filled. With a calmer resolve she said, "When you find yourself whole, and Paul, I hope more than anything that you do, you may also find you don't need me anymore. Or want me."

"Jessie!" He felt the frustration rise in him but tamped it down. Why wouldn't she feel that way, like he was going to leave her? He almost had. "I don't need you to fix me. I don't want you to heal me. I need you because I love you. I want you because ... life is beautiful with us together, in a way I have never known. Please don't be afraid to walk through this with me. Please forgive me enough to try."

Her eyes widened. She stacked her things on the little side table and shifted her whole self, scooting forward in the chair, toward him. Then she took his face in her hands and looked into his eyes, into *him*, before she responded.

"Paul, I am afraid of many things. Most of them have already happened, and I lived through them. But let me tell you: I would rather face down every single one of your demons with you, whatever they may be, than spend one more day with you out of my reach. Because you are my best friend, I *want* you. I need you, and I love you. I will fight with you. I will fight for you. But please don't make me wonder and don't make me chase, because losing you is what scares me most of all."

"Jesus, Jess." His eyes were profusely leaking as he took her in his arms. This had happened before between them, some intimate take on life with them sitting in the most awkward position. But his bars had been lowered, and all he wanted was no space between them. His arms grasped her tightly, and he pulled her into his lap, not letting go. "You're not going to lose me. I'm not going. I won't go. Jessie! My Jessie . . . "

She had done this for him since the beginning. Held him together. Reassured him. Just said his name aloud, reminding him who he was. Now he was relieved to have the strength to do the same. She was radiant. She was strong. She was *his*.

Jessie exhaled. Paul reveled in her satisfied sigh. They were all about her happy place, sharing the Irish Delight charcuterie board at Whistling Duck, a scoop of Peanut Butter Oreo from Drippy's, and a walk on the pier now that the tourists were fairly scarce. Afterwards, they sat—plopped right in the sand, under the stars—where they could hear an Eagles tribute band playing from Scotty's Beach Bar but were otherwise, thankfully, all alone.

He had his arm around her, and she had her leg draped over his. It was the closest he'd *felt*—not been, but felt to her in months.

Since the accident and concussion and all that.

Since the revelation to the kids about their brand of marriage.

Since Julie made him face truths he'd buried.

Since therapy made him deal with all of it.

Jessie nuzzled right into the crook of his arm. He felt her inhale sharply and then exhale deeply, a telltale sign that she was editing herself, beginning to speak thoughts aloud and then deciding against it. Sometimes, he edited her editing. Tonight, he would trust her and let it go. It seemed a secret to their survival, that sometimes they would do it her way and talk everything out as immediately as possible, and sometimes they needed to do it his way, with some brooding, some silence, and then as few words as were necessary.

"I think I know what you want to ask," Paul murmured. His lips were near her ear, partly because he loved to linger there, and partly because who their age could hear above the sound of the ocean waves?

"You probably do," she answered lightly. He could barely hear her. "But you don't have to answer. Not tonight. It's okay. We're okay."

He leaned away just a little, because he was going to tell her, and it wasn't a *whisper in your ear* kinda answer.

"I don't think Leah cheated on me." He had been turning it over and over in his head, since his talk with Julie, and since years before, when it became obvious that he and Leah were never going to be what the other needed. "Neither of us would blink. Neither of us would give up or leave. And I'm not sure either of us wanted to, but her having other relationships that filled her up, even if one was a guy who wrote songs for her, I'm not sure I can begrudge her that. I wasn't enough, Jess. I just wasn't."

She stiffened, drawing her legs up toward her tummy, but she didn't speak.

"You can say whatever you want," he told her. "I'm not twisted up about this. I mostly made peace with it all long ago."

"There's not a lot for me to say." She unraveled herself completely from his arms, only so she could turn and look at him. "Because obviously, I think you are the most amazing human and more than enough for anyone. I didn't know you *before*. I didn't raise kids with you. I didn't have to deal with your addiction, but it's hard for me to imagine loving someone so much and not fighting for them. I mean, Paul . . . I would fight *you* for you, you know?"

He couldn't help the laugh that escaped him. "Baby, I know. You *have* fought me for me, over and over again." He paused before adding, "With a helluva a right hook."

She narrowed her eyes at him, and then wordlessly smooshed back into his side. His arm automatically went back around her shoulders, and he almost thought he heard her purr.

"You know me so well," she said. "Now please, stop making me fight."

He pulled her tighter and looked out at the water. She had made him fall in love with the ocean, with the smell and the view but mostly the sound of the waves, especially at night like this, and all the serenity it brought. He craved it almost as much as he craved her, and it didn't bother him to admit it. Not anymore. His lips found her ear again.

"Jess?" he whispered

She didn't answer. She waited for him, and because he knew her so well, the gesture was perfect for the moment. She had been waiting for him for two-and-a-half years, and maybe he was finally caught up. There was only one gesture left for him to make.

"Will you marry me?"

Brittney

26

"**I**'m sure he'll take good care of it, Brit. Just leave them."

Brittney was staring at her favorite thing about the cozy single-wide that she'd rented, made her home, almost lost, then finally purchased with her inheritance money. She'd completely covered one living room wall in band posters, like some '90s college kid. She stared at it whenever she felt lost, or worried, or—increasingly common— unable to sleep.

Now, it would belong to Travis. Her nephew said he would leave the wall untouched. And even if he didn't, what could she do? Her makeshift wallpaper was never meant to be moveable. At least it would stay for a while. She wasn't sure what Travis's taste in music was, but she knew he had zero taste in interior design.

And at least she didn't have to sell the whole house just yet, even though she thought it would never be her home again.

Well. As long as everything works out with Harrison . . .

She was getting more used to the voice in her head being her own, but she got on her nerves quite often.

"It's going to be fine," Mikayla said, flopping next to her on the couch while apparently reading her mind.

"You say that, and yet—" Brittney threw a nod toward her sister's tear-stained face.

"I just . . . I wish they could grow up together." Mikayla spoke so quickly that her sentence sounded like one long word. She shielded her eyes. "Oh, I know we are supposed to pretend like this is all fine, but Brit! I don't even know how to function without you close to me. Remember when you had the chicken pox and I didn't, and Mama still made me go to Sunday School, and I had to lead the pledge to the Christian flag and peed in my pants?"

A different collection of words crammed themselves together in Brittney's head. She wouldn't repeat them. They were not Sunday School words.

She scooted closer to her sister and put her arms around her. She didn't cry, likely because she was hella dehydrated, and she tried to save her tears for the shower rather than keep parading them around for the world, the town, and her family to see. Speaking of which—

"Is this a bio-sister only moment, or may I also be sad?"

Katy came and sat on the arm of the chair, on the other side of Brittney. Without ado, Brittney yanked her by the arm until she was smooshed into their sister-pile.

"Pretty safe to say we're in this together," Brit said.

"Sure. You say that thirty seconds after I just packed a drawer full of hair clips and half-used eye shadow palettes," Katy whined. "I have never in my life seen you wear eye shadow."

"Oh, but she did," Mikayla said, with a sudden spark of joy. "She rocked smoky eyes at our great-uncle's funeral and our dad came *undone*. She rocked that look everywhere for about three years."

Brittney rolled her eyes. "About how long you were dying your hair black 'like your soul,' you ridiculous Hufflepuff."

"Oh, I remember that," Katy said. "My mama thought maybe you were worshiping Satan."

"What?" Mikayla cried. "No, she didn't!"

Katy pretended to ponder. "No . . . she actually didn't. But she did think maybe you needed to get to the altar. Or try some Prozac. In our family, it's always a healthy balance of the two."

"In our family, there definitely should have been more Prozac. Daddy didn't really believe in therapy."

"He was the only one of us who didn't need it," Mikayla added.

And then the three of them grew silent, the momentary, simultaneous realization sinking in: that two of the main people who shaped them were gone forever, and that one more thing was about to change forever.

Katy was staring at Mikayla.

"What?"

"Are you gonna hang out with me when she's gone?"

Mikayla winced. "Do you *want* to hang out with me? My toddler is about to be my oldest kid. The only gigs I go to are called Music with Mommy, where I sing alternate lyrics to Beyoncé songs."

"Would my band be considered sitter-worthy for you?" Katy asked.

"Sitter worthy?"

"I have a Danielle," she said, as though Mikayla was a stranger who didn't know her older sister and had also never left her home for the public, at that. "She has come to *one* gig, and she left at intermission, citing her three children and average of two hours sleep. I get it. Mostly."

"I'll come to a gig if you want me to," Mikayla said, and there was a sulk in her voice. "Nobody ever asks me to do stuff like that."

Brittney gaped at her. "The hell I *don't!*"

"You asked me *once!*"

"And you said no."

"Josie had hand-foot-mouth disease."

"WHAT IS THAT?" Katy looked horrified.

"She's always going to have something," Brittney continued, ignoring Katy entirely. "And now you're gonna have two. So rashes and stomach bugs and pox and lice and scurvy."

Mikayla finally doubled over laughing. Katy continued staring at them with her mouth open.

"Scurvy!" Mikayla yelped. "I can't breathe!"

"What is scurvy? What are these things? Why do the children have them?"

Brittney dissolved into a cackle.

"I mean, I think it would be fun to hang out, but don't come if there's scurvy," Katy continued.

Mikayla was still shrieking. "Deal!" she managed.

Katy looked satisfied. She jumped off the couch, phone in hand.

"I'm ordering food, sisters. If we are really going to finish everything-but-the-essentials today, I need more than Chex Mix and club soda, Brittney."

"Whatever. Hurry! And no pickles, not anywhere near me." It made her stomach lurch just to think about it.

"Or coconut," Mikayla added. "Or soy sauce."

"Oh, my gawd!" Katy answered. "Should we just have peanut butter and jelly?"

Mikayla wrinkled her nose. "Ew. Only if it's strawberry," at the same time Brittney said, "Just pick something; I'm starving!"

"When is he getting here?" Mikayla asked. Katy had gone to the other room, and now Brittney had popped her feet up on the ottoman, and Mikayla had rested her head on her shoulder.

"Tomorrow," Brittney said, every bit of conflicted emotion betrayed by her voice. "He's leaving at some ridiculous time, like four in the morning." They were not leaving their plans to the airlines anymore. Time was far too short. "We should have a full weekend with the kids to work on, you know, a brand new life and family unit. Then I'll fly back. Then it will be one more week until . . . "

"Until you break Mama's heart," Mikayla finished.

"Shut up."

"And mine," her sister continued.

And mine, Brittney wanted to echo, but she just leaned her head over on her big sister's and didn't say another word.

Traditionally, Brittney loved everything about a road trip. Mama had instilled it in her. Dress in comfortable layers. Wear slip-on shoes. Bring a few car snacks with the knowledge that you absolutely will stop at a gas station for something ridiculous, like BBQ Corn Nuts or Gardetto's, just the rye chips, and that super-sugary French Vanilla Cappuccino that isn't even real coffee. Have a playlist ready, so you don't get stuck listening to some stupid game. Bring a paperback, *and* a well-stocked e-reader, *and* a few magazines, because we are a reading family, and you need to be prepared.

Also, car naps are a religion.

Also, hold hands with the driver and occasionally give a little neck rub to show your appreciation for being the passenger princess.

This one felt less adventurous and more daunting. She hadn't seen Harrison in so many weeks, and though they texted endlessly and talked every night, the idea of meeting his children—with her own child now visibly showing on her very person—left her a bundle of nerves.

He knew it, though. He squeezed her hand again as they turned into the Buc-ee's, most of Florence now behind them and finally, the interstate close by. She needed the cleanest public restrooms on the planet as well as some edible cookie dough and maybe, just maybe, a brisket taco. She probably needed him telling her one hundred more times that it was going to be okay, and then, perhaps, she would feel a little less shaky about the whole entire world.

She came out of the bathroom—without giving into the impulse to grab a giant framed photograph of a sunflower field off the wall—and found him at the soda fountain, trying to choose between cream soda and ginger ale. She walked up and hugged him from behind, as close as she could get with their growing little melon in the middle.

"What kind do you want?" he asked, turning around with a smile and brushing a flyaway hair from her eyes.

Brittney felt her stomach flutter, not from Fun Size, but the kind she felt back when she and Harrison first fell in love. He smoldered when he looked at her. She melted.

"Just get a big one, and I'll share with you," she said, actually batting her eyes. "Whatever you want."

He leaned down and kissed her, softly, but with a promise of more, before he chose cream soda.

"Let's get out of here," he said, pressing the lid on their drink, taking her hand, and leading her through the maze of fellow rabid brisket-eaters to the register.

They walked out into the sunshine, and Harrison paused on the passenger side of his truck to open the door for Brittney. She clamored up, and before she could swing her legs in, he folded her up into his arms. He buried his face in her neck, took a deep breath, lingered. And it wasn't that Harrison wasn't affectionate, but after all the missed connecting and talk of logistics and kids and the baby, she had almost forgotten what it felt like to be wrapped up together. She sighed and squeezed him back.

"I love you," he whispered. "I know how hard this is. Thank you for trusting me to take care of things, to take care of you."

She swallowed against any renegade tear that might have been forming. She was sick of crying. "I love you. It's gonna be good. Let's enjoy the ride!"

It sounded like something her mama would say.

"Not that it hasn't been worth it every single time, but I'm a little sick of this particular ride," he half-grumbled.

Brittney let that fly over her shoulder. She already felt guilty all the time, about all of it. Being another unwed parent in the Oakley line. Being another one of her mama's kids to move away. Making Harrison shuffle back and forth and now to cause more upheaval for his Dakota and Ruthie. The list could go on forever, and she would never be able to carry it all. She was taking this burden from him. He was flying in to move her the following week, and then he wouldn't have to make the drive anymore.

"I read this thing," she said. "Okay. It was a meme. But it said something about people with the most peace being people who always, no matter what happens in their lives, hold on to gratitude with one hand. So whatever is going on . . . your job woes, got a health thing, a break-up, your kid sprayed fart spray in the middle of Spanish class and they had to evacuate the school, your dog ran away, your dad died, your brother died, you're getting kicked out of the trailer park . . . whatever horrors have befallen you, you keep those in one hand, 'cause you have to. You hold on to gratefulness with the other. Always."

Harrison squeezed her hand in reply. "You remind me to do that," he said. "It's hard for me not to look at all of this as a huge failure on my part, Buttercup. But you don't have to remind me to be grateful for you. I know what this means to you. I know you don't want to move away from our home and your family—"

"But you are my family," she said, her right hand on her burgeoning stomach. "You and this one. And I hope Ruthie and Dakota will be, too, but I know it's gonna take time."

He smiled, the first really hopeful one she'd seen from him in a bit.

"And it will be worth it," she added.

With that, they sipped and snacked, mostly wordlessly. His sunroof was open. Her shoes were off. The 2000s playlist was immaculate, everything Salty Lips-esque. By the time they reached I-95, the road trip vibes had infiltrated. They were singing along to Black Stone Cherry. Brittney leaned over to kiss his neck, and he laughed when he heard her stomach growl. It was 10:30 in the morning, and Fun Size was ready for second breakfast.

The screen changed as Harrison's phone rang. He had it set to play "Santeria," and Brittney immediately started chair-dancing a little. She was scrolling for a restaurant. There was a plaza nearby with Chipotle and Mod Pizza and all the things.

"What? Dakota, I can't understand you, buddy."

The call was, of course, on speaker. There was a lot of background noise, and Brittney had never really heard Dakota's voice before, but she was certain it didn't normally sound so high and squeaky and . . . waily?

Her heartbeat immediately accelerated. Harrison's face was turning white. "Pull over," she said.

He did.

"Dakota?"

The words kept coming and were unintelligible. Harrison listened without speaking for more seconds than Brittney could fathom, and then he finally said, sternly, "Dakota. Who is the closest adult to you?"

"Mom." His voice had gotten tiny.

"Put her on the phone!"

"She caaaaaaan't!" Dakota was on the verge of a wail again. And then they heard the sirens.

Harrison looked at Brittney and mouthed "What the fuck?" She squeezed his hand.

"Dakota, where are you, buddy? Please try to be calm and tell me."

"We were driving to the zoo. Ruthie wanted—"

"Ruthie is there?"

Brittney put her hand on his arm, hoping he would shush and let his son try to finish. *Dear God, please, please.*

Dakota didn't speak again. There was all the noise they expected, because now they knew: this was happening. It had to be a car wreck. Denise must be incapacitated. And they had no idea what was happening.

The call disconnected. They sat on the side of the road for untold minutes. Harrison hit the steering wheel, and then he looked at Brittney with sheer terror in his eyes. "I'm sorry," he said, and she shook her head. They were not her children. But she was also terrified.

He tried to call Denise's parents. No answer. He tried to call back Dakota's phone, and then Denise's, to no avail. Brittney's stomach continued to make obnoxious noises, and he finally looked at her and said, "I guess we just keep going. We have to get there." While every nerve ending inside of her felt like it was rapidly firing, she reached for her inner Randall Oakley, whose voice in her head was mysteriously absent, and made their plan.

"I'll drive," she said, unfastening her seatbelt. "I am going to have to grab some food, but I will be quick. Keep trying to call her parents and also the highway patrol. If you have her license plate somewhere, that will help. Okay? Okay, Harrison?"

He nodded, looking at her like he'd seen a ghost. She reached over and held his arm, trying desperately to steady both of them. They waited in silence until traffic seemed clearer and then switched seats. All thoughts of food forsaken, except for what the baby needed, she ran through a Cook Out, ordered grilled chicken sandwiches and peach milkshakes, and kept driving while she listened to Harrison make all the calls, not getting very far, and sounding more shaken by the minute. Finally, just after they passed Raleigh, Harrison's phone rang again.

"Harrison Cory?"

"Speaking." Brittney reached for him, with her hand, with her soul.

"This is Harlee Lancaster. I'm a social worker at Inova Alexandria Hospital. Your children, Dakota and Ruth, are here in my office. They're safe."

Brittney had already pulled over. A relieved sob escaped Harrison's throat. She realized she'd been holding her breath and exhaled deeply.

"Thank God," he said. "Oh, thank God. Thank you, ma'am. Are they okay? May I speak to them?"

"Of course. I just need a moment to update you on their circumstances. I just need to verify a few pieces of information with you."

His frustration was palpable. Brittney held onto his forearm again as he listed dates of birth, his own social security number and address, even their health insurance provider. Finally, Harlee continued.

"I appreciate your patience, Mr. Cory. First of all, your children are mostly uninured. They were in a vehicular collision about three hours ago. Some cuts and bruises have been treated. Their maternal grandparents are on the way here, and I understand you are already en route back to the area as well?"

"I am," he said, his eyes closed, his head leaning back. "We are about—" he glanced at Brittney, who mouthed *Four-ish*, "—four hours away."

"The children said you and their mother, Denise Cory, are divorced?"

"Yes, ma'am. How is she?"

There was a pause, and Brittney's breath caught in her throat.

"Mr. Cory, I regret to inform you that Ms. Cory did not survive the accident."

"What? I—what? How?"

"The impact was primarily on the driver's side," she explained gently. "Dakota was in the passenger seat, and Ruth was behind him. Ms. Cory, unfortunately, suffered a catastrophic brain injury. She likely lost consciousness immediately. I am so sorry to say that she died at the scene."

"Oh my God. My God." Harrison handed the phone to Brittney and put his head in his hands.

"This is Brittney Oakley," she said softly. "I'm Harrison's partner, and we are traveling there now from South Carolina. He's . . . He's gonna need a minute to collect himself. Thank you for the call. Is there anything else we need to know, or need to do?"

"I need the kids," he said.

"He would really like to talk to his children."

"Of course," Harlee answered. "There isn't anything else to be done. When their grandparents, um, Mort and Jane Scofield, get here, we will need to verify that it's okay for them to leave the hospital. But right now, I think a video call might be the best thing, as soon as he is ready."

She placed her hand on Harrison's back. He was sweating and shaking, but she knew him. "He's ready."

Julie

27

Five Months Later

"Thank you for coming with me."

Julie had never thought she'd be a talk-to-a-headstone kind of person, but losing her mama and everything after had changed fundamental parts of her, so she was learning to embrace the notion of surprising herself.

Having Ayden had changed her, too. Twenty-seven hours of labor, one for each year she'd had Mama near, and she felt her through each contraction, almost audibly heard her saying, "Come on, my girl. Stay strong. You have this!"

She did.

Ayden Nicholas was perfect. When he was ready to greet her, with Robin and Danielle at her side, he emerged after three pushes. Even after witnessing and assisting in dozens of births, Julie could not have predicted the euphoria of it. In the midst of feeling clobbered, torn, and completely drained, she held her son and laughed and cried.

He had Robin's nose and her daddy's hairline. But his round, curious eyes one hundred percent belonged to her and her mama.

I'm still here.

That was what radiated in her brain every time she drank in those little hazel eyes. *Mama is, somehow, still here.*

Robin, their son in his arms, was sitting on the still-cold, early-spring ground next to her, one hand squeezing her shoulder.

"Darling, where else would I be?"

She smiled, her hand covering his.

"Mama." She set the box on the ground. It was sealed. Didn't matter. The contents inside were shredded, symbolic. Julie wanted her mother to have her secrets back. She had printed out the pages and pages of song titles, sent to her by a man who wasn't Leah's husband but certainly someone who knew her at a soul-level, who saw her and loved her.

"I tried to measure you by what I thought I knew," she started. "And now, I've spent some time calculating the distance between how I saw you and who you actually were. Turns out, it's not very far. And your emotions and your relationships and these private . . . thoughts . . . between you and Alex, between you and anyone else, for that matter, those belong to *you.*"

The tears had started to fall, as they did more easily these days. She'd thought losing her mother made her softer, and it had. But nothing could have prepared her for how becoming a mother would lay her heart wide open, exposed for whatever the world wanted her to feel. She had already grown to understand Jessie a little better, because she seemed to feel *every-thing* these days.

"So, I'm giving them back to you, Mama. I ask your forgiveness for prying, for doubting, for thinking it mattered that I didn't understand. The truth is? You've been my hero, and I always wanted to be just like you, and

. . . I failed. I failed because I thought *you* were perfect, and since you died, I've been reminded over and over again that I am *so* not perfect. That—"

Her voice completely broke then. Robin put his arm around her, steadying her. The words came out in heaves and pauses, but getting them out was the important part.

"That broke me just as much, Mama. I was so mad at Daddy for marrying Jessie that I wanted you to be perfect all the more. It was so ridiculous, I know. But nobody is perfect. And none of us has to be. And that's what I wanted to tell you. You were the perfect mother for me. You taught me to be strong and gracious, to appreciate beauty and excellence, and to love how I need to love. That it's enough. Because Mama, it may not make sense to anyone else, but the way you loved us was perfect."

Her face and her shirt were soaked from her tears. She wished she could bury the little box in the ground right there, but it didn't matter, and it wasn't right anyway. Too many things had been buried and needed to come to light. Too many things had been bottled and needed to be freed. She used her braid to wipe at her eyes before she stood and then gratefully accepted the little sleeping bundle Robin handed to her.

"You sure you're ready, darling?" he asked, a tentative hand still on her shoulder.

She managed a smile at him. "I think this was everything I needed to do."

"You still up to meeting Dad and Jessie?"

"Well, I am starving, and there will be food, so . . . "

They started walking toward the car. Robin looked sidelong at her and chanced it.

"I think it's more than dinner," he said. "I mean. I think you are starting to trust Jessie. Maybe even enough to rely on her a little bit?"

Julie stopped midstride. She shifted Ayden from a recumbent position to resting his little head on her shoulder. "So?"

He widened his grin at her. "You're not going to argue?"

Placing a kiss on Ayden's head, she shrugged. "There is nothing left to argue about. My parents loved us. They respected each other. They stayed. But they were never really happy together, not like Daddy is now. That's not Jessie's fault, or anyone's fault. But I think it's a lesson." She started walking again.

"Aren't you going to tell me what the lesson is?"

"You already know," she said. "You learned it with me, I think. We love who we love. We love big. No apologies. And don't run away when it gets hard or scary."

They reached the car, and he unlocked the door, facing her, his hand reaching for her braid, tenderness on his face.

"If you ever do run," he said, "Just remember two things: I'm faster, and I'm going with you."

He pulled her and Ayden into his embrace, and so much unlike who she used to be, she melted into him. That was how she would move forward.

28

"Last one, Mikayla. Take a breath and then push as hard as you can!"

I held my daughter's hand, just across from Altan, who was holding the other.

What an honor, for the first time, to be present at the birth of a grandchild. They filled my heart: Travis, Summer, and Jacob. Sweet little Josie, almost a big sister. The ones Paul brought with him to the marriage: Christian, Vivi, and Lexie, now joined by baby Ayden. In some small ways, and hopefully more in the future, Dakota and Ruthie, and the baby still coming.

But right now, it was Mikayla's time. She and Altan had chosen to be surprised, and with all Brittney's turmoil six hours away from us, with Julie's blessed event a few weeks behind us, we could focus on the little world unfolding in that little room. A tired mommy, a nervous daddy, and me, a thankful crone and doting Mimi, watching my first-born girl in absolute awe.

The guttural sound she made was barely audible. She was reaching inward for the last of her strength, and it was absolutely amazing to watch. I squeezed her hand, but then she let it go, gripped the bed, and that was it.

A tiny wail filled the room. Maureen, the midwife, smiled broadly, the newly-emerged little body in her arms. "You have a daughter!" she said. Altan beamed, his hand on Mikayla's cheek. She put her trembling hand over his. My tears erupted immediately. A little girl, a baby sister, a miracle.

I kissed the top of Mikayla's head, then Altan's, lingering in the room for only a few minutes before I took my leave. They could, and should, do the next part without me. I was there for my baby; now, they'd be there for theirs.

I walked down the four flights of stairs and out into the sunshine. It had been an unreasonably cold season, harkening me back to my Chicagoland winters, with their endless gray skies and biting cold. No, it hadn't been quite as bad, but I was older and more used to sunshine and mild temperatures, and my tolerance for anything below fifty degrees was at an all-time low. Finally, with March almost drawing to a close, spring seemed to be keeping its promises, not just of more light and warmth, but more hope as well.

Without even having to look, I unlocked my phone and called Paul.

"How is she?" he said, instead of "Hello." I warmed up from the inside out.

"She's perfect," I said. "The baby *and* Mikayla."

"Haha. Yaaaaaay!" My husband's hearty laugh came through the phone, reached my ears, and travelled to my weary heart.

"Her name is Ainsley Joy." I loved it so much. She wasn't named after anyone She was just gonna be a little giver of happiness, forging her own way. "Can you pick me up?" I asked, knowing he probably already had his keys in his hand, jangling them at his side.

"Of course. You need anything?"

I sighed, my face turned upward toward a cloudless blue sky. "Just you."

"Maggie asked if we wanted to have brunch with her and Sheldon tomorrow. Maybe at the Creekhouse?"

Paul shook his head, wiping his mouth with the cloth napkin. We were sitting at The Quay, enjoying the best sunset view around, the ocean on one side, the marsh on the other, gold and pink and purple and red *everywhere*. He reached over with his fork for a bite of my shrimp and grits, his she-crab soup bowl empty, his crabcakes gone. Waiting on another grandbaby must have made him ravenous. I beamed at him, pretending to swat his hand away.

"The hallmark of this family is planning our next big meal event in the middle of a big meal event."

I was slumped in my chair, exhausted. I smelled like I needed a shower, because I did. I was also hungry, but my adrenaline had crashed and eating felt like it required a bit too much energy. At the same time, I also felt sparkly, thinking of the baby and noticing how excited Paul was.

"Is this an event?" I teased, pushing my plate toward him for ease of access.

"You need to eat, baby," he said, taking another forkful and smiling.

I dipped my own fork in the luscious gravy. Maybe I could just sip that, because *yum*.

He reached for my other hand. "Any time I get to spend surrounded by beauty with my gorgeous, amazing wife constitutes an event."

Wife was a loaded word. And a true one. On New Year's Eve, with little ado, we had made it real. The two of us, Maggie the notary, the moon. She snapped a terribly-lit photo of us afterwards, and we texted it to the kids before we strolled over to the Conch for tourist-priced drinks and fried seafood by the lull of ocean waves, right where we'd started and woven into the fabric of *us*.

"I guess I'm so used to fun meals and the beach and gathering that I forget sometimes: These are events. They're memories in the making."

"They're how we do family," he concluded.

I raised my eyebrows at him, though in my head, it was always the cool gesture of one eyebrow that I never could pull off. "We?"

He caressed my thumb with his.

"Yes. *We*. I like your way, Jess. It took me time, more time than it should have. But it's all worth celebrating. Being together is worth celebrating."

I felt a twinge at that. He was right, of course. I had staked my whole life philosophy on it, with recurring themes and made-up reasons for parties and countless little and sometimes formal traditions. But it hadn't kept my kids safe from loss, and it hadn't kept them from scattering. In fact, sometimes, I wondered if I had done too much to try to keep my family close. They were all I ever wanted, but maybe I'd smothered them. Maybe you can love too much?

"Please stop," Paul said. "I see your wheels turning. You did so much *right*, Jess. So much. I'm sorry it took me so long to catch on and open up to your way of seeing things."

Damn him. A tear escaped my tired eyes, and once that seal was broken, there was no telling what would surge from me next.

"I never needed to try to change you," I said carefully. "And I want you to know, Paul, for real, that this? You and me? This is enough, to fill my days and my heart. I promise."

He squeezed my hand, tilted his head, smiled at me, and said, "Aw, Jess. I love you. That is such a lie."

I was going to at least pretend to be appalled, but he was already shaking with laughter. And he was kinda right.

I let him have his moment, took a sip of my Long Island, and looked at the blazing colors over the marsh. The view simply never got old, nor did the smell in the air, salt and water and seafood and sunscreen. So many things about home had changed, but even so, it was still home. And I loved where I lived.

"It's not a lie," I said resolutely. "It's a hope, Paul. It doesn't mean I'm not a little heartsick. Doesn't mean I won't long for some things, like all my kids back in the same place. But my soul is at peace. Here. With you. For the rest of our lives."

He raised an eyebrow. Just one. *No fair.*

"For the rest of our lives?"

I nodded. There was nothing else I needed to say.

29

Brittney stood in the doorway of a kitchen that still felt a little foreign to her, even after nearly five months of Life with Harrison and the Kids. Life with a stressed-out dad and his two broken children. Life as a very pregnant person who traded one set of overwhelming circumstances for some that were even more so.

She wouldn't and could not drown, though.

Harrison was sitting at the kitchen table, his shoulders slumped, his head in his hands. He was keeping up with work, and his firm was so generous with his hours. He worked from home anyway, but now there was the added therapy appointments to his schedule. The emergency school pick-ups or visits that seemed to happen at least once a week. The well-meaning check-ins from teachers and church folks and Denise's friends and the parents of the kids' friends . The days that Denise's parents couldn't handle dance lessons or soccer practice, and Harrison still refused to have Brittney do any of it.

He had returned to Crossfit, finally, and it was so good for him, but there was no room in his life for music or travel. Barely room for romance or any time alone with Brittney. Only a tiny bit of space for prepping for Fun Size. Brittney tried so very hard not to feel like a burden, but when weariness eclipsed every moment, every look on his face, it was hard not to take it personally.

"Are you asleep?" she finally called, trying to keep her voice light.

He didn't answer, which seemed to be the answer. For weeks now, she'd been boxing herself in, trying to give him space with his grieving children, trying to stay out of the way, to wait and listen and learn. She worked on settling in, found a favorite coffee shop, made a few casual friends at pre-natal yoga, focused on her marketing clients, on eating well for the baby, on asking Mama everything she wanted to know. But she was weary too, of being so careful with the kids. Not overstepping. Not making them sadder. Trying, trying, trying. And now?

All she wanted was Harrison. For him to be okay, and for him to be close to her.

She uttered a silent, one-word prayer as she took a few steps forward: *Please*. Then she placed her hands on his shoulders and bent herself very methodically to bury her face in his neck.

Her prayer was answered by one hand, reaching up and resting on the back of her head.

"Buttercup," he murmured.

"Yeah," she whispered. "I'm here."

"You wanna go to bed?"

That was all the leaning down her burgeoning belly and achy back would take. She stood, hating to break the moment. But he stood immediately after and faced her.

"Baby." A sad smile crossed his face.

"What? Do I look that haggard?" she chided.

He cupped her face with his hands. "You look like the person who's supposed to be taking care of you has been neglecting you."

"Harrison—"

"Brit, no. Don't." He took a deep breath, and she felt her calloused heart, which she had been reinforcing for the worst, melting like a marshmallow in a Fourth of July bonfire. "I know there haven't been a lot of choices, but you've made the hardest ones. I see you. I promise. I see you, and I got you. I *promise*."

Even in the midst of all the grief and tragedy, he was not prone to shows of emotion, so the sheen over his eyes caught her off-guard. Through all the turmoil, she'd had been determined to stay strong, to ask for very little. And now he was reminding her of how very strong he was, how little *he* had asked for, and somehow, this was helping her believe that maybe everything was going to be okay after all.

"I haven't been mad at you, or felt abandoned, or anything like that," she said. "You know, mostly I'm just trying not to be homesick and to make sure I am personally ready for all this." She grandly gestured to her stomach. "'Cause I hear babies change everything."

His hands moved to her bare shoulders. It was still in the forties out-side—a reality she could barely fathom in March after living in the coastal South her whole life—but she was running hot all the time, she presumed because she was a human incubator. He caressed her skin with his thumbs and smiled at her, his eyes still glassy.

"They do, Buttercup." He exhaled slowly. "I know it's been a lot. Par-enting is a lot. I don't have a playbook for this, but I think it's going to get easier. The baby will be a great distraction for everyone."

She smiled a bit more stiffly. "I hope so. We have to make sure the kids don't feel . . . more displaced. Or replaced. That's key."

"It's all key," he said. "I was just sitting her thinking about how to tell them, when to tell them."

"Tell them what?"

"That when school is out, we're gonna spend a month in Surfside Beach."

Brittney's head nearly snapped off her shoulders. "We're what?"

"I talked to your mom," he said. "And Travis. He's spending the summer in Georgia with his parents, so we're gonna move back into your place for a bit. See how everyone likes it. Show the kids what beach life is. And then as long as everyone is cool, I thought . . . well, babe, I thought you might want to get back there. Raise our baby there. Raise our *family* there."

"Harrison!" Her knees actually felt weak, and she must have swayed a little, because he grabbed her harder and held on tighter. She tried to put her arms around his neck, but they felt like lead. The next thing she knew, he had her sitting in a chair, kneeling in front of her, bracing her.

"Geez, babe. I know it's exciting, but don't be so dramatic. You scared the hell out of me."

"I'm fine. I just can't believe it. Are you serious? You think they'll really be okay with this?"

"One thing I know," he said, "is that they will be okay if I am okay. If *we* are okay—you and me, Jane and Mort—then they will know they can be, that they're allowed to miss their mom and still have a happy life. We have to show them."

Now her eyes filled.

"Did you talk to someone about this? Like a professional something?" They had had some family counseling through social services, but Harrison had been pretty resistant to it, all bootstraps and *we got this*. He was a child of trauma himself, so she supposed maybe he was right. Maybe.

He nodded. She felt reassured. And then he said, "I talked to your mom and Paul."

"What? Harrison! They aren't professionals, by any stretch. Come on!"

"Brit, they've been through some shit. They know a thing or two about how to move forward."

"Oh, I know, I know, just . . . " She sighed. Maybe he was right. Maybe they were more relatable with their evidential wisdom than a therapist could be. Maybe she was too close to give them enough credit. "No, you're right. Sometimes they even make it seem easy, even though I know it's not."

"It's pretty tough for them, I think," he said. "Anyone could assume because they're so happy together that it's easy. But joy doesn't mean a lack of hardship. They have all their baggage and all of ours to carry."

"You know, they went to therapy back in the fall. Might still be," Brittney said.

"He is," Harrison said, and she felt bad, that he knew something about her mama's husband that she did not. But her threshold wasn't the same as Mama's.

Two nights before, Brittney had eaten Chipotle with the hot red chili salsa and was awake half the night with relentless heartburn. That same night, Ruthie had woken up screaming with a nightmare. She and Dakota had tried to get their mother's lifeless body out of her seatbelt, out of the car. It would haunt them forever, and Brittney didn't know anyone who had the capacity to deal with that, to bring peace to that. But she could concede that if anyone did, it was her Mama.

And probably Paul.

That night had been the first time Ruthie let Brittney hold her. Not just hug her. Not just say comforting things. Brittney had held her, and rocked her, and dried her tears, and attempted to soothe her into the wee hours so Harrison could get some sleep. She thought maybe it had been a step in a good direction. She couldn't think of a *right* direction, because who knew what was correct or not for those kids and what they'd continue to go through? And she couldn't think about the fact that she was the only mother figure they had now. They weren't bratty kids who told her "You're not my real mom" when she reminded them to take a shower or do their homework. They were polite. They all knew she wasn't Denise. It was painfully, obviously true every single day.

"That's good, then," she said. "Paul is a wonderful human. He deserves peace. And so does Mama."

"We all do, Brit," he said. "I think that's one of my takeaways from all of this. I could spend the rest of my life feeling guilty about what I've done wrong, about the kind of husband I was to Denise. But the truth is, what happened would have happened, no matter if I was a better guy, no matter if we'd still been married. And I'm a much better father now than I was, than I would have been. So . . . I don't think everything happens for a reason, Buttercup. I don't think my kids living a nightmare was *supposed* to be. But I do think maybe God prepared me, you know?"

Brittney was feeling steadier, and she moved her hands to his knees. "For such a time as this?"

"Yeah." He rose up on his knees and pulled her into him. "That is exactly what I mean." His hands smoothed over her hair and for the first time since that horrible day, she didn't feel any barrier between them.

Except for the baby in her belly. Fun Size sure took up a full-size space anymore.

That was totally okay with her.

That was the night. They talked for a while. They loaded the dishwasher. They went to bed. And around two in the morning, she woke up in a puddle. The cramping started. The race was on.

They briefly contemplated calling Jane and Mort; that had been the plan, but something about their earlier conversation had buoyed them both. They had a chance for a different kind of life-changing moment, and they took it.

"You really want us to be there?" Ruthie said, her hair a mess, her eyes wide open.

"I do," Brittney said, trying not to show her discomfort. "This is your brother or sister. You should be there! Like . . . the best welcoming committee *ever*!"

"Ever!" Ruthie exclaimed, and she threw her arms around Brittney, who kinda felt like throwing up, but she reveled in the moment. Harrison was right on; this was going to be good.

They loaded into the car. Of course, he was driving, but he also left a voice memo for Mort, basically saying *Meet us at the hospital when you get this.*

Was this life now? Brit, her partner, his kids, their baby, and his . . . ex-in-laws? If so, so be it. Mama had taught her well; it was all about the family you gather.

And seven and a half hours later, their family was gathered. Their. *Family.*

Brittney held Randy in her arms: Randall Paul "Stone" was their perfect, amazing baby boy. She was so sore that she was also numb. She was so happy that she couldn't stop crying. She was so in love that she couldn't remember what life had been like the thirty seconds before their son was born.

Their son.

Harrison's arm was around her. He was still collecting himself, having been heaving sobs just a few minutes prior. The medical team, apprised of their family's situation, had let Dakota and Ruthie stay until the very last minute. And Jane and Mort had been the real MVPs, getting there at five in the morning to make sure the kids had a place to land besides alone in the waiting room.

"Mama!" Brittney used what was left of her energy to FaceTime the person she most wished could be there. She answered on the first ring, laughing and crying with a mug of coffee in her hand and Paul at her side.

"I can't believe my baby had a baby," Mama said.

"I can't believe it either," she said. The weight of Randy in her arms felt so natural, so perfect, and so soothing. She knew this was the thing that Hallmark cards and memes talked about. Motherhood. It immediately transformed her soul.

After they hung up, after the cleaning up and measuring and assessing was done, it was just her and Harrison and Randy for a few more minutes. Brittney felt like she was in a bubble, self-contained and warm and weird and perfect.

Perfect.

For the rest of Brittney's life, she would remember this night. How Dakota played all of her favorite songs. How Ruthie made up little rhymes and cheered for her during her worst contractions. How Harrison had laughed nervously during every minute of all the above. How Brittney felt, for the first time in her life, sure of herself and her path. This was her journey. This was her family. This was her whole heart.

"Mama," she said, tears running down her cheeks. "Why didn't you tell me?"

"Tell you what, baby?" Jessie asked.

"That I could love somebody this much?" She looked down at the baby yawning in her arms, his perfect little form swaddled in a hospital-issued blanket, his daddy's tattooed and sinewy arms encircling both of them.

"You never would have believed me, "Mama said. "So, I want you to know, that this thing you feel right this second? I still feel that way about you. Every time you roll up in the driveway. Every time your name lights up my phone. Every time Facebook pops up a damn memory of your beautiful, cherubic face? I feel exactly how you feel right now holding that amazing little miracle."

"Really, Mama?"

"Baby." Mama was beside herself. "I promise you. That is true. That is real. That is lasting. You and your brothers and your sister are the most lasting, the most beautiful, the most miraculous, the very best things that have ever, ever, *ever* happened to me."

Brittney laughed, because Mama was cheesy as hell, but she knew this was nothing but true. Right in this very second, regardless of all the things that had gone wrong and would stay wrong, regardless of all the things that had gone wrong and were yet to be fixed:

This was the best it would get. This was beyond her wildest dreams.

She reached backwards with what was left of her strength and put her left hand on Harrison's grizzled cheek. Her right hand held their boy. Her whole heart held their family. She had no idea what was about to be, how everyone would do, but what she did know—beyond any doubt—was that they would figure it out together.

EPILOGUE

Leave it to Katy to be late.

Julie wanted it small. She had a specific vision. She had surprised them all by asking for "just the family" but meaning the blended family.

She had opened her heart. Well, Ayden had opened her heart. On some days since his arrival, Paul almost didn't recognize his middle daughter. So many of her sharp edges had been rounded by the tiny hands and big, brown eyes of her firstborn child.

Paul held Jessie's hand as they walked the parking lot, facing the storefront. With the exception of Jessie's sons, all of their brood was there. He held the door open for his wife and followed her inside to behold a whole store full of people before it was even open for customers.

They were immediately greeted with a loud form of happiness and the smell of coffee alongside hints of cardboard and fresh paint.

Danielle smiled tiredly at him as he kissed her cheek. She had Vivi and Lexi settled into their double stroller, the former animatedly attacking a spill-proof bowl of Cheerios and Goldfish crackers, the younger blissfully asleep. Christian was hopping from one foot to the other while his dad timed his ability to balance. In that instant, Paul could vividly remember having three little kids, the exhaustion and exhilaration of every waking hour. Every time he wanted to say, "Don't blink," he felt like an old man. But these days, he also thought vaguely of his own lack of a father during that new-parent stage of his life, and he gave thanks that he was there for his daughters.

Robin was behind the counter trying to fix the register printer while Julie laughed at him from across the room. She was wearing Ayden like she usually was, strapped to her in a perfectly fitted, perfectly ergonomic carrier, a soft shade of ocean blue covered in navy anchors. Ayden was blissful.

And so was Julie.

Brittney stood near the front windows bouncing Stone against her shoulder. In one breathless ramble, she told Ruthie not to hang from the Brooks shoe display and inexplicably asked Jessie where the wipes had gone.

Jessie ignored her and distracted Ruthie with the box of donut holes they'd brought. Then she picked up a canister of Clorox wipes that were sitting next to the foot scanner.

"Not those wipes," Harrison said, already digging through a bag. "The baby wipes."

"There are too many wipes in this family," Brittney muttered.

Paul had helped himself to the coffee and smiled into his paper cup. Nobody noticed. And that was okay. Their family's brand of happiness was a little weird and a lot loud.

Sunlight poured through the big front windows, catching dust in the air and turning the concrete floor into a shade of gold. One of the associates — Paul thought her name was Meagan — had propped the door open. The sounds from downtown Conway were different from the beach he'd became achingly familiar living near, a melody of traffic and footsteps on the sidewalks and the occasional bark or chirp or part of a conversation. Lenny Kravitz was playing over the speakers. Paul was glad they played real music and not some canned workplace mess.

Julie, with Ayden now fully asleep, moved through the store like she belonged there. And rather than the new location, the customers beginning to wander in, the shiny sign hanging outside, Paul was struck hardest by Julie herself — how alive she was, how at ease.

Robin looked up from the register finally and caught her watching him struggle.

"You gonna help me or just let me suffer publicly?"

"I think publicly," she said.

They both laughed as she walked toward him.

Laughter was not effortless. Paul knew better than that. Grief had changed all of them too thoroughly for effortless anything. But it no longer looked like Julie was dragging herself behind life hoping not to lose her grip. She had both hands on it now.

Jessie appeared back at his side and stole the cup from his hands.

"This is *terrible*," she said.

"Then give it back."

"No!" She giggled. "Remember that horrible Fourth of July when Julie and I finally came to blows over the coffee?"

"Mama, no one will ever forget that Fourth of July," Mikayla said. "Here."

With that, Jessie released Paul's cup back to him and opened her arms to accept Ainsley Joy. The lines around her eyes had grown a little more prominent in the past year. He would never tell her that, and he didn't care. She'd earned them, and they made her all the more beautiful to him.

At that moment, Katy came in, typical wrecking ball fashion. El was strolling behind her, looking unsure of whether he should be there, but sister energy took up all the space. He needn't have worried.

"About time!" Julie said. "We're open now. I wanted to have everyone here *before*. Robin, do you have the box?"

"Lemme get it," he said, disappearing to the back room.

"What box?" Paul asked Julie at the precise moment Stone started wailing.

"Hold!" she said, and Paul knew his question would not be answered until she was ready. Meanwhile, Harrison took the baby from Brittney automatically before she even asked. Their baby son settled against his chest immediately, a tiny fist curled near his collar.

The sight hit Paul sideways: Brittney standing in a sunlit room with a baby and a man who looked at her like staying had never been a question, with those two kids of his starting to heal and maybe thrive. They'd been through so much to get to that point, and Paul was relieved that sometimes, good things piled on top of bad.

Robin came back to the front, and Julie motioned to her sisters. Before Paul knew it, everyone had gathered around the counter where a worn file box sat, familiar handwriting scrawled across the lid.

Leah Jameson.

Paul felt his stomach twist before anyone moved to open it or said a word. He immediately took a deep breath.

"I found it when we cleaned out the storage unit," Julie said quietly. "I thought it was old tax stuff."

Danielle stepped closer. "But it wasn't."

The phone hadn't held Mama's only secrets.

Julie nodded, and Robin opened the lid carefully and started pulling out folders.

Paul frowned. "What am I looking at?"

Julie looked not at Paul, but at Jessie. She stepped forward and took his hand.

"You sure this is the time?" Katy asked.

"I hope it's about to get busy," Julie snapped. "Maybe you shouldn't have been late."

Maybe she hadn't completely changed. Paul almost laughed, but he still felt anxious flutters he could not ignore.

"Daddy," Danielle started. "We weren't sure how to tell you, but we knew we had to tell you. And it's a good thing. So try not to be mad or spin out, okay? *Okay?*"

She had walked next to him and taken his other hand.

"I would really just like to know what is going on," he said evenly.

"Mama sold some land," Julie said flatly. Robin winced.

"She sold the land that was left to you," Katy said, with the earnestness of a twelve-year-old. "And she started a trust for us."

Paul widened his eyes. He didn't feel *anger* necessarily, but *what the hell, Leah?*

"How?" he asked. "How did she do that without me knowing?"

He immediately regretted asking. Leah had secrets; she was smart, and she knew a ton of people. He should have known she'd never let that bequest go to waste. Their girls would have something of value to redeem his awful childhood.

"We can talk about that later," Julie said. Jessie squeezed his hand as Julie handed him a single piece of paper.

"She started a trust for you three?" he whispered.

Julie nodded, eyes shining. "Years ago. Added to it little by little."

Paul stared at the paper without really seeing them.

All those years he had believed Leah, in solidarity with him, had rejected every part of his father, every part of that past., every ugly thing tied to his family name.

But Leah had done what Leah always did, taken something painful and turned it toward the people she loved instead.

Jessie squeezed his arm with her other hand. He swallowed hard.

"She never told me."

"I don't think she wanted credit," Julie said.

Of course she didn't.

"But somehow," Julie continued, "We will see that she gets it. Because so many things in this store are possible now. And Danielle and Matt have some wiggle room. And Katy can . . . well, Katy can keep living like a nineteen-year-old stay-at-home daughter for a little while longer. Because Mama saved us a windfall, Daddy, and — She gestured to the filebox — "she gives *you* the credit for it. She wrote letters to each of us, told us that you didn't want to sell the land, but you didn't tell her no, and that was your green light. She called you our hero, Daddy. And you are!"

Across the store, customers continued browsing quietly, unaware that the shape of a family had shifted near the register counter. Thank goodness Meagan and Lori were there to wait on people. Thank goodness the ribbon cutting wasn't until noon.

Katy wiped under her eyes quickly. "Mama was *sneaky*," she whispered with a laugh.

Julie laughed too then cried a little after. Robin wrapped an arm around her and Ayden.

For one aching second, Leah felt so present that Paul could almost hear her moving through the room with that determined stride of hers, fixing things nobody else noticed were broken yet.

That's when Harrison stepped closer and carefully handed his infant son to Paul.

"Here," he said softly.

What was with everyone passing babies around to mitigate hurt, like they were Advil? Paul took baby Stone on instinct. He was warm, alive, and just heavy enough in his arms.

The conversations around him slowly resumed. Robin finally fixed the printer. Jessie started directing traffic toward the food table. Dakota knocked over a display of sunglasses and immediately blamed Ruthie. It was all normal, human chaos and even though it was a momentous day, it was also a typical day for the Oakley-Jameson clan, too.

Paul looked down at the baby settled against him and then slowly lifted his eyes toward the room. He saw Julie laughing beside Robin, Brittney standing behind Harrison with her arms around his waist, Jessie carrying too many things at once because she refused to let anyone help her, and — *well I'll be John Damn Brown* — that was Maggie walking in the door, escorted by her favorite person and that of so many Myrtle Beach area residents, their celebrity meteorologist Ed Piotrowski. Maggie had been his banker for years before she moved, and it was still her claim to almost-fame.

For so long, Paul had believed survival was the best he could hope for. Not to screw anything up. Not to relapse. Not to be anywhere near the man his father had been. The past year had started to unravel the belief he'd held closely and silently, that he couldn't ask for much better.

But this? This felt different. Not quite healed. Far from perfect. But plenty alive enough to keep going. And maybe that was what Leah had known all along. The best parts of people stayed — in money tucked away quietly for daughters, in shared music, in memories, in babies with familiar eyes, in the way a family kept gathering again and again after every reason not to.

Paul gently tightened his hold on the baby as laughter rose around him once more. Jessie tugged on his arm, her eyes shiny, her other hand now holding up her phone.

"What is it?" he asked, not sure he could take much more of anything that day.

"David just texted me," she said. "*Texted me!* He's moving home, Paul. My baby is moving home!"

THE END

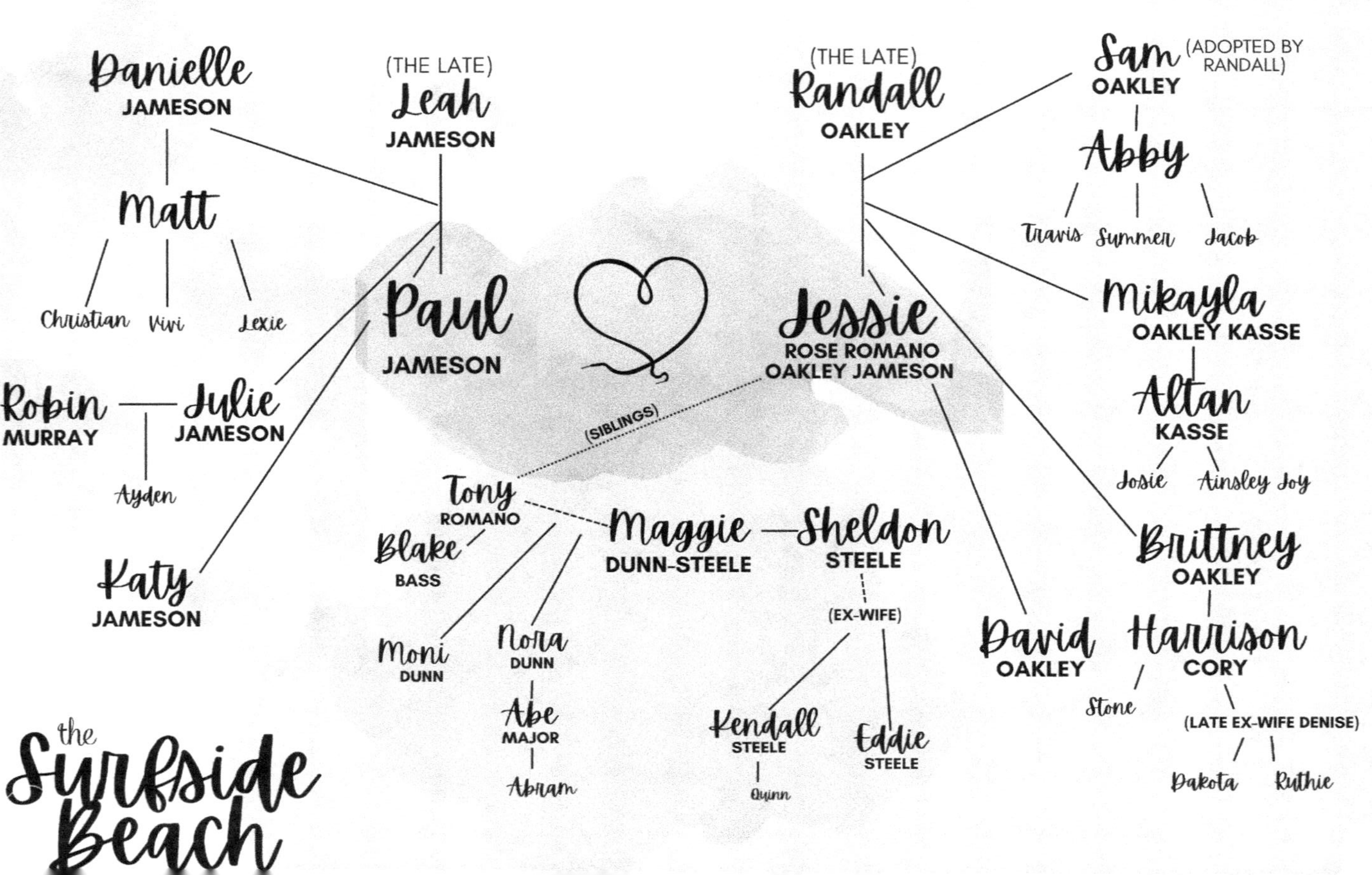
Danielle JAMESON
(THE LATE) Leah JAMESON
(THE LATE) Randall OAKLEY
Sam OAKLEY (ADOPTED BY RANDALL)
Matt
Christian
Vivi
Lexie
Paul JAMESON
Jessie ROSE ROMANO OAKLEY JAMESON
Abby
Travis
Summer
Jacob
Mikayla OAKLEY KASSE
Robin MURRAY
Julie JAMESON
Ayden
Altan KASSE
Josie
Ainsley Joy
(SIBLINGS)
Katy JAMESON
Tony ROMANO
Blake BASS
Maggie DUNN-STEELE
Sheldon STEELE
Brittney OAKLEY
Moni DUNN
Nora DUNN
Abe MAJOR
Abram
(EX-WIFE)
Kendall STEELE
Quinn
Eddie STEELE
David OAKLEY
Stone
Harrison CORY
(LATE EX-WIFE DENISE)
Dakota
Ruthie
the Surfside Beach

LOCAL LOVE

The Grumpy Mustache

3140 US-17 BUS Suite A, Murrells Inlet, SC

grumpymustache.com

Listen, my husband and I ate a couple dinners here and suddenly had new best friends. Holidays together. Business collabs whenever possible. Every dang Saturday night. You don't have to make lifelong buds here, but you'll want to. Tell them you read the book, and they will give you a happy little discount on your bill! I have mostly eaten everything on the menu, so I will suggest street tacos, cheese curds, balls of meat, anything with queso, and any drink you love. The (spicy) margarita, classic daiquiri, smoked old fashioned, espresso martini, whiskey sour, and one-two punch are among my favorites. Sssshhhh. It's been a LOT of Saturday nights!

Benjamin's Bakery & Coffee Roasters

810 3rd Avenue South , Surfside Beach, SC

benjaminsbakery.com

I love having meetings here and getting some writing done. Get the toasted marshmallow latte, the cinnamon rolls, an asiago bagel with veggie cream cheese, anything blueberry, holiday cookies, the dog treats, the roasted beans for home, a baguette...

Tidal Creek Brewhouse

3421 Knoles Street, Myrtle Beach, SC

tidalcreekbrewhouse.com

This is a community hub. So many meetings, runs, coffees, happy hours, events take place right here. Owned by lovely people and made for good times! Order a coconut latte in the morning and a Creekside Cider...whenever!

Los Gordibuenos

357 US Hwy 17 Bus, Surfside Beach, SC

gordibuenos.com

Best chips/salsa/queso in town!

Neal & Pam's

20 South Ocean Boulevard, Surfside Beach, SC

nealandpamsbarandgrill.com

They do everything here, but I love having breakfast, looking at the ocean, sippin' a mimosa, and not feeling guilty 'bout dem potato cakes!

Fratelli's Pizza

1600 Farrow Parkway, Myrtle Beach, SC

fratellispizzasc.com

This pizzeria is a neighbor to my store, and when people ask me if the food is good, I simply say: It is owned by FABIO FRATELLI! Of course, it's great! He is great. Get pizza by the slice in amazing combinations, huge salads, and great wings.

Drippy's Homemade Ice Cream

11 Ocean Blvd S Surfside Beach, SC

drippysicecream.com

A family-owned local chain that serves the most delicious frozen goodness! Peanut butter Oreo is absolutely MY favorite!

Tu Taco

2520 US-17 BUS, Murrells Inlet, SC (Other locations as well)

tutacoshops.com

Trivia: This is basically the only place from which my husband agrees to get take-out. Perfectly yummy street tacos, tostadas, and quesadillas, and inexplicably yummy orange-cheese nachos. Sip a house marg with a Tajin rim while you wait for your order.

The Quay Seafood Grille

1508 S Waccamaw Dr, Murrells Inlet, SC

thequaygrille.com

Most beautiful sunsets you can imagine, surrounded by the ocean and the inlet. Favorites include the seared tuna nachos and she crab soup!

Neal's Creekhouse

3797 US 17 Bus, Murrells Inlet, SC

nealscreekhouse.com

A little bit of everything... date nights, family gatherings, love music, inlet view. Order The Hat Trick for soup/salad/sandwich du jour any day of the week!

Atmosphera

3620 Walton Dr C-1, Myrtle Beach, SC

atmosphera.cafe

We love to order workday lunches from here... pierogis are a favorite!

Conch Café

1870 North Waccamaw Drive, Garden City, SC

conchcafe.net

This place is practically my backyard. It is oceanfront and boasts a huge patio and outdoor bar. Get some fried seafood and a fruity drink and embrace the life!

THE MADE-UP REAL PLACES

Ed's Fishwalk Tavern is fictional, but in my mind, it is located at *Fire to Table* (3415 Highway 17 Business, Murrells Inlet, SC | firetotablesc.com. You have to experience this location to appreciate it, with a huge oak tree, outdoor stage and bar, cozy seating, and a great menu of fun appetizers and smoked meats.

Run This Way, Robin and Julie's store, is based on **Black Dog Running Company**. When I first wrote about Run this Way, I was an employee. Now I am the co-owner. We would love for you to visit when you're in town. Find us at 1600 Farrow Parkway, Myrtle Beach, SC and blackdogr unning.com . Yes . . . we sell shoes AND books there!

BOOK PLAYLIST

Music in & inspiring the story

"The Boxer"   Simon & Garfunkel
"Colder Weather"   Zac Brown Band
"Raise a Hallelujah"   Bethel Music
"Graves Into Gardens"   Elevation Worship
"Ordinary World"   Duran Duran
"Sun to Me"   Zach Bryan
"Three Little Birds"   Bob Marley
"Best I Ever Had"   Vertical Horizon
"Baby Blue"   George Strait
"Holocene"   Bon Iver
"Annie's Song"   John Denver
"Eighteen Wheels and a Dozen Roses"   Kathy Mattea
"Soulshine"   The Allman Brothers Band
"Where Do You Hide Your Heart"   Amy Grant
"A Symptom of Being Human"   Shinedown
"I'll Follow You"   Shinedown
"The Blower's Daughter"   Damien Rice
"Stay"   Black Stone Cherry
"Santeria"   Sublime
"The Only Exception"   Paramore
"Oceans"   Pearl Jam
"Kryptonite" 3 Doors Down
"You're Still Here" Faith Hill
"Best of You" Foo Fighters

LISTEN:

Amazon   Spotify

SET LIST - GRUMPY MUSTACHE - BIKE WEEK!!!

Stars (Sixx AM)	Symptom of Being Human
Kryptonite	Santeria
Mr. Brightside	This is Gonna Hurt
Midwest Kid	Calling Me Back
Proof	Nearly Lost You
Never Tear Us Apart	Dead & Bloated
Zombie	Unglued
Nirvana Medley	Slither
After All	All the Small Things
Breakfast at Tiffany's	The Middle
Hey Jealousy	No Rain
Name	Can't Stop Loving You
Wonderwall	Better Man
Sugar We're Going Down	Corduroy
Dog Days Are Over	Creep
Lightning Crashes	Just Like Heaven
Got You Where I Want You	Hazy
Give It Away	All the Words That Echo
Best of You	I'll Follow You

-break-

LISTEN:

Amazon Spotify

ACKNOWLEDGMENTS

It took me a good long while to write this book for a multitude of reasons, mostly because I can't say no to awesome things, like buying a running store, starting a publishing company with some author friends, and a few writing side quests. Meanwhile, two of my kids graduated from high school, we lost my little bestie, our dog Max, and I entered the stage of life that starts with an M and brings about hot flashes. Life sure is different than it was when I started writing about Jessie, Paul, and the clan back in 2016.

One thing that has not changed is how grateful I am for the people who make the solitary effort of writing a book feel like a team sport and sometimes, a party.

Maegwen Salley-Massie and Lisa Borne Graves, my Dahlia and Zinnia, co-writers, cheerleaders, coordinators of many random things related to books and life. Maegwen, you are the ultimate think tank and hype girl. Your creativity and brilliance know no bounds. Lisa, thank you for spontaneously editing this book in the midst of the deepest life things, for the good cheese, and for the all hours texting. We got this.

Caleb Wygal, bookish brother and festival buddy: I love how we are just getting started! And to Mike Dame, thank you for the levity and crazy you inject into every conversation. Let's make a podcast, boys!

Susan Boyer and Tonya Lowe, both who write books I love to read and have careers I emulate, and whom I am blessed to call friends.

Mike Hopkins, thank you for once again pausing to edit my story in the most witty and sarcastic and helpful way possible.

Nora Smith, you have no idea how you saved the day!

Anna Williams and 963&Co: thank you for helping me elevate the look of the Surfside Beach series with your beautiful images.

Mylena Yee & Nicole Steen: this is what you get for floating me ideas at book signings. I hope I did you proud.

Kelsey Simmons: Of course I thank you for the lovely Back Again Bookshop and for giving the Surfside Beach series a home in Surfside Beach, but mostly I thank you for the camaraderie and our friendship!

To the book clubs, book stores, libraries, and festival friends who take a chance on my stories, my gratitude is immeasurable.

Tana Saturley, thank you for giving Jessie (& Julie, & Brittney) a voice! I can't wait to hear and see and share what you do next!

Diane Whitman, thank you for being my sister and co-Jefe in so much more than a business. I could not do any of this without your support and all the laughs.

To my Black Dog Running Company family – the epic team that runs the store with us (Akemi, Jay, Lori, Kaity, Meagan, & Dayna) and the amazing team and fitness community that runs beside us: You are why. You are how. Keep moving forward!

Whitney Neeves, thank you for being my beta reader and big sister.

Heather Davenport, thank you for sharing a story that truly changed my life. And while we're on the subject, thank you Dr. Crantford and crew for helping me look how I feel!

The Grumpy Mustache gang, including but not limited to Gina and Alice... how I loved attempting to write on Monday afternoons while we shared everything from made up drinks to crazy stories to random snack foods to big dreams. I am so happy this gem of a place is part of these pages.

Betty & Greg, go read the dedication. Make me a drink. Here, try this. Put it on the list. Let's have a staff meeting. May I bring my own food? Barter. Familia.

To my real-life Salty Lips: thank you for playing along with me! And to Southern Comfort Myrtle Beach: I could not be happier that my favorite band is playing again!

Shannon Marie: my ride or die. We ridin'. Forever. (& big love always to Where's Charlie!)

Mom and Dad, for giving me every opportunity possible and following me to the beach!

Josh & Kirsten, thank you for ice cream nights and giving us two amazing granddaughters!

To my bonus kids, including Ayden, Rhea, Alexa, my Montano godchildren, Will & Isaac, and any others who grace my heart or my kitchen or my store or my arms when needed: you got me. I promise!

Jack Burton, thank you for being absolute sunshine every single day of your life.

To my beautiful daughters who grace this cover, you have magically healed and given more than I can ever express. Paige, Miranda, and Kaity, I hope you always feel surrounded by sisterhood and safety and love, because I could not love you more.

Rod, we have a life that has surpassed my dreams. From train rides to bus rides to motorcycle naps to hitching up the trailer . . . from "Let's do the Bahamas every year" to "How many kids do we have?" . . . from you hating on Pearl Jam to you singing Pearl Jam . . . from being the new girl to being your wife of 23 years (and at least 27 more to go), we are truly on a road that has no end, and each day we begin again, and I cannot express my love or gratitude no matter how many words I write.

If you have read this far, thank you. Let's all keep moving forward. Keep trusting in hopefully ever afters. Keep believing God said LIVE.

ABOUT THE AUTHOR

KELLY CAPRIOTTI BURTON finds it easy to write the Surfside Beach series: as a transplant from South Chicago Heights, Illinois, she's truly found her home on the South Carolina coast, drawing inspiration from big, chaotic families like the one she's built with her husband, Rod. Together, they have five children and are always finding ways to create community and gather family. Kelly co-owns a local running store and is, fittingly, always on the run—usually toward the beach, the gym, favorite local cafes and eateries, the sound of '90s rock, or a specific whimsical cabin in the north Georgia mountains.

kellofastory.com
FB & IG: @kellofastory

**THE OAKLEY-JAMESON
FAMILY WILL RETURN:**

ANOTHER
Beachfront
THANKS GIVING

A SURFSIDE BEACH NOVELLA

COMING IN 2027